For Gabrielle
w/love + joy
"Olivia Oatboat"

the

Beejum Book

the

Beejum Book

Eggsies
Exeunt Egi

ALICE O. HOWELL

Copyright © 2002 by Alice O. Howell

Published by Bell Pond Books
Post Office Box 799
Great Barrington, MA 01230
www.bellpondbooks.com

Cover and chapter opening art by Brett Helquist
Additional drawings by Glynis Oliver
Book design by Will Marsh

Library of Congress Cataloging-in-Publication Data

Howell, Alice O., 1922–
  The Beejum book / Alice O. Howell.
     p. cm.
Summary: Teak, a lonely nine-year-old abroad in Europe between the two
World Wars, begins to take magical excursions to a realm known as
Beejumstan.
  ISBN 0-88010-505-4
  [1. Fairy tales.] I. Title.
  PZ8.H838 Be 2003
  [Fic]–dc21

                              2001005706

10 9 8 7 6 5 4 3 2 1

Printed in the United States of America

*This book is dedicated
to Penelope King and Reginald Wilson Orcutt,
my dear parents, who gave me the gift of Beejumstan
—and to all those who find they are Beejums too!*

CONTENTS

The unconscious psyche of the child is truly limitless in extent and of incalculable age.

—C. G. Jung

How It All Began

ONCE UPON A TIME—many yesterdays before yesterday—there was a young girl called Teak. She was almost seven years old, sturdy but small for her age. Her hair was the color of wheat, and always looked as if the wind had tousled it, no matter how hard it was brushed. She had thoughtful brown eyes, and no wonder, since already she had seen so many different places and people. If she seemed a rather unusual girl, it wasn't because she looked different, but because she lived a rather unusual life. And these were the reasons:

First, although Teak had a nice father and a beautiful mother, she saw very little of them, because they were always having to go somewhere else—and this meant having to say a great many good-byes. Second, she had no brothers or sisters. Third, although her family was American, they lived abroad and always stayed in hotels. Teak could not remember ever having lived in a home, a real house, that is, with a kitchen that had a potted geranium in the window and a real stove with a kettle on it, hot and steaming—a house where you could have your very own room, your very own bed, your very own pillow, and books and toys and lots of boy stuff like cars to go *vrrooom*. (She secretly wished she had been born a boy because it was her observation that boys had a lot more freedom and, therefore, more fun.) Lastly, Teak had no friends to play with. Not that she couldn't make friends, but she was always traveling from one place to another all over the world, so she always had to say good-bye to the ones she did meet. Just the sight of an open suitcase on a bed gave her a lumpy feeling in her middle. Another good-bye would be looming.

No, Teak was not a gypsy, though she had met a few.

She didn't travel with a circus, though she often wished that she could. (She was torn between being the lion tamer or a flying-trapeze artist.)

Nor was she the daughter of an army officer or a diplomat. Her father, whose name was Thaddeus King, Junior, was a very important businessman, a Vice-President for Overseas for a big company in the U.S.A. This explained all that traveling. It also explained Teak's name, for her real name was Thaddea King, TK for short.

Her mother's name was Birdie, and she was a writer. Sometimes Teak would see her stories in magazines; there would be pictures and the words "by Birdie King" under the title.

Often the hotels they stayed in were huge and fancy ones with long, long carpets down long quiet halls, and lifts—that's what the elevators were called that were like open brass cages. These were run by elevator boys in brass-buttoned uniforms and pillbox hats. If they were friendly they would let Teak push the buttons for the required floors. Sometimes Teak would not take the lift, but would race it instead, flying up or down the carpeted stairs to arrive red-faced and panting and triumphant when she won, which she usually did. Nanny did not approve.

On other trips, the family might stay in small and quaint inns tucked in the mountains or overlooking the sea, or they might stay in in-between-size hotels called pensions (pronounced funny, like "ponsy-ons"). Wherever they stayed, Mother and Daddy would settle into their room, get out their portable typewriters, and start pecking away at them furiously. A little bell would sound when one of them came to the end of a line. *Ping*, and then another *ping*, never two *pings* at once. Teak would stand quietly and hopefully at the door, but usually her mother would put her finger to her lips and say, "Ssshh!" and Teak would have to trudge back to her room or go to Nanny's.

Which brings us to Nanny. Teak's parents couldn't possibly find baby-sitters everywhere they went, so Nanny had been hired to take care of her. She was a fixture in the family, the one person Teak never had to say good-bye to. She was British, hearty, and roly-poly, with red cheeks and blue eyes—and she had a grip of iron. She was older than Mother and both kind and strict—very strict. But Teak felt safe with her and knew she was fortunate to have her.

There were only a few things wrong with Nanny, but they were not really her fault: She was not another child, and she had no imagination, which meant you couldn't talk to her about ideas or ask her important questions like "Who invented time?" or "What do cows think about?" or "Who decided the first Tuesday?" or even simple ones like "How many grains of sand are there in the world?" or "How many times have you breathed in and out in your life?" Teak's mother was better at those kinds of questions.

Since Nanny was old, she couldn't bend in the middle very well or walk fast in the park or at the zoo, so there were strict rules about not disappearing around corners. Teak would run in circles around her as second best, but she always felt as if she lived with her brakes on. Also, Nanny seemed to be devoted to only two great causes, keeping spotless and good manners, neither of which stood anywhere near the top of Teak's own list. To be sure, she was always squeaky clean herself in blue or white starched uniforms, and she was respectful to Teak's parents, saying "Yes, sir," or "No, madam." She wore her grey hair up with a bun on top, which Teak sometimes thought made her look like a sea lion with a cow patty on her head. She knew this was probably a naughty thought, but she didn't mean it unkindly.

Of course, Teak herself had no idea how hard it was for Nanny—how very hard it was for her to climb up on a camel in Egypt or to rush into the waves at the beach on the Riviera to keep an eye on her charge. Teak had no thought that Nanny might be lonely too, or that she might ever be tired or have a headache or wish that she could wear a red dress with flowers on it. Nor did Teak realize that she was the apple of Nanny's eye, that Nanny secretly loved her to pieces though she felt she had no right to. To Teak, Nanny was just *there*.

So Teak's world was mostly filled with grown-ups. They might look down at her and see only a small girl in short smocked cotton dresses and matching bloomers, with scuffed red knees and a determined look about her, but she saw them as equals, only bigger and more powerful. Well, to be sure, they didn't chew their fingernails.

One of the problems of traveling so much was that everything you owned had to fit into suitcases, so she had hardly any playthings or picture books. Teak had to use her imagination a lot. The first thing she would do in a new hotel room was open the doors of the large mahogany wardrobe, which somehow always had the same varnishy smell but nevertheless had to be checked for monsters. Also under the bed. And under the covers, in case of stray reptiles. Each room had a night table next to the bed with a big china potty in it, and each room had its own washbasin, though the pensions sometimes only had a big china basin and a big pitcher of water. (Teak was always interested in waterworks.) Then, if Nanny was not around, she would climb onto the bed and jump and jump or, if it was a puffy featherbed, she might climb up the headboard and swandive into it. *Kerploof!* It was a delicious feeling, but only to be done at night.

Teak also had a secret family of very small paper cutouts that she had drawn herself. They were a German family, and their names were the Pumpernickels. There were four of them, for Herr and Frau Pumpernickel had been blessed with two children, a girl, Brigitta, and a boy, Hans-Peter. They lived and traveled in an old tortoise-shell cigarette box that had been Teak's father's. Teak would spend long hours lying on her stomach, listening to the imaginary troubles and squabbles of this family. Nanny tolerated and maybe even enjoyed this game, often listening in while she knitted in a corner.

A balloon was a special treat. Teak could lie on her back and throw it, catch it with her feet, and throw it back, over and over. It often was tiresome, though, to be alone. But there certainly was lots of time to think, and thinking was what Teak did best.

On this particular day, Teak and Nanny were alone at the Hotel Galilee in Paris. The previous day, Teak's mother had received a telegram from her father. It came in a folded yellow paper with tickertape pasted on it and said—all in capital letters—

ARRIVING ROME EIGHTEENTH STOP BRING DROMEDARY BOTH TURKEYS LEAVE DRAGON STATION STOP JOIN ME HOTEL FLORA FRIDAY STOP TEAK NANNY TO FOLLOW SOON STOP LOVE REGARDS TKJR

Translated, Teak knew this meant that her mother was to catch the train to Rome, taking her trunk, called Dromedary because it was bought in Egypt and humped when it was full, and Daddy's two suitcases, the Turkeys, but she was to check their trunk, the Dragon, at the Gare du Nord in Paris for Nanny and Teak to pick up when they joined them. Each piece of luggage was given a name. Teak had a small leather case they called the Fiumerol (because it came from Fiume in Italy) and a leather pouch on a strap called the Spy Bag, in which she kept her very special treasures.

So Mother had left once again, kissing Teak in a hurried way, promising a reunion in Rome sometime soon. Teak had fought back her tears of disappointment while Birdie and Nanny consulted over her head. It was always nicer when Mother was around.

The Hotel Galilee was a pension with high ceilings and tall windows now flecked with raindrops, which meant Teak and Nanny were stuck indoors with nothing to do. In those days, there were no radios or televisions. Usually Teak found watching people the most entertaining thing she could think of, but looking at Nanny mending her stockings, squinting in the poor light, did not amuse Teak. She was bored and out of sorts.

She would have enjoyed talking to her very old friend, Mr. Rathbone, who had white whiskers and was very good at answering questions, but he was in Vevey in Switzerland. Mr. Rathbone had once suggested that what Teak needed was an encyclopedia, which Teak wrote down and brought to her parents' attention, but they said no. Encyclopedias came in twenty-six volumes and where would she pack them?

Teak almost wished her redheaded cousins, Jessie and Justin, would turn up. They were twins, just her age, and the children of Uncle Amyas King, her father's older brother and Aunt Bessie MacLean, who was also a red-head and *verry, verry* Scottish. (You weren't ever supposed to say Scotch!) Whenever, Jessie and Justin appeared, Teak's world was turned upside down.

It was still raining when it was time for lunch. Teak wasn't a bit hungry, but she and Nanny went down to the dining room and sat at the table for two. She rolled breadcrumbs, fiddled with the salt and pepper shakers, and kicked her chair rungs and sulked. Nanny was cross and even crosser when Teak made a face at the brussels sprouts. However, by this time the rain seemed to have stopped, and the sun began to shine weakly, so Nanny bargained a trip to the park for three brussels sprouts down the hatch. The deal was made.

Paris was actually one of the places Teak liked. The hotel was close to the Champs Élysées headed by the great Arc de Triomphe, where the eternal flame burned to the French Unknown Soldier. She liked the big toy store with scooters and trucks in the window. She secretly loved the small park with the merry-go-round, and the Guignol, the Punch and Judy puppet show, where husband and wife whacked each other over the head with big sticks. And going to the park meant that Teak could try out the new wooden hoop and stick that the concierge, the nice lady in black at the front desk, had given her to use while they were staying in the hotel. The hoop belonged to the concierge's children, but they had gotten too old to play with it, so it was now kept in a broom closet for use by special young guests. Teak wanted one of her very own, but how could you fit it in a suitcase?

Now Teak could hardly wait. She might even get bread and chocolate for her snack, or *gouter* ("goo-tay," as the French children said). She raced up the stairs, leaving Nanny to struggle up behind her.

"Teak!" Nanny called. "Wait for me. Don't you dare try going down these stairs with that hoop! Do you hear me? You could fall and break your neck."

Teak sighed impatiently. Nanny was always saying things like that. It made her feel like a baby. She knew perfectly well that she could carry a stupid old hoop down the stairs. *Anybody* could carry a stupid old hoop down the stupid old stairs. She would show Nanny, and that would be that.

Well, that was *that* all right. Somehow, in switching the stupid old hoop and stick from hand to hand, the hoop got tangled with Teak's stupid feet, and before she knew it, she was somersaulting down a flight of stairs after the hoop, which had shot away and was bounding down the steps five at a time. Teak wound up on her head on a landing, and by the time the concierge had come flying up from below with cries of alarm and Nanny had come puffing down from above with cries of dismay, she had a huge bump on her forehead—a real goose egg. She tried hard not to cry, but it really *hurt!*

What a fuss and feathers! The concierge clucked and kept exclaiming, "*O, la pauvre petite! Ze poor leetle girl!*" Then she rushed off to get an ice pack. Nanny was not so sympathetic. She dragged Teak back up to her room with a chorus of "I-told-you-so!" and announced decisively, "And no park for naughty, disobedient girls!" Then it was off with her dress and on with her dressing gown and into bed for a *rest,* the final insult for a seven-year-old. Bustling about, Nanny pulled the heavy draperies, closing out the now beautiful sunny afternoon and the smell of chestnut blossoms. Teak was to lie there still and hold that ice pack to her forehead or else. After reminding her several more times how lucky she was not to have broken her neck, Nanny slammed the door shut. *Bam!*

Teak couldn't help it. She could feel the big hot tears streaming down both sides of her face. If only her mother were here! If only, if only!

2

Off on the Train

Precisely at that moment of a May afternoon in 1929, in Paris, it happened. Without any warning whatever, Teak first heard that voice, that furry sort of voice. "Come, come now," it was saying briskly in a very British sort of voice, "it can't be all *that* bad! Besides, if we are to catch the tsax-tsaxty-tseven train in time, you are going to have to pull yourself together. Tch, tch, if I do say so."

Teak opened her eyes, then quickly closed them again, because she was seeing something quite impossible standing on the windowsill. She shook her head in disbelief. The closed curtains made it look as if it were standing on a stage. It was a black and white rabbit with one flop ear and white whiskers. The rabbit was dressed like a diplomat in a cutaway coat and striped grey trousers. He had a wide red sash over his right shoulder with three medals across his front, and in his buttonhole there was a blue carnation. He wore cream-colored spats over his shoes and carried a smart cane with a gold duck on the top.

With a friendly though quite formal bow, he removed his shiny top hat, and continued, "Allow me to present myself. My name is Lonesome, and I am the Ambassador-without-portfolio of Beejumstan. And I have come to extend to you an invitation to visit our great—"

Well, you couldn't say a word like *portfolio* to Teak and not explain it. "What's a portfolio?" she stammered.

The rabbit sighed, and blushed slightly. "I...I'm not really sure myself," he confessed, "since I don't have one. I just wish I had one, that's all. I believe it's something you carry, although in my case I might not have to...I suppose..."

Teak was trying to think about what a portfolio might be. "Maybe it's a beard or a hot-water bottle? Or one of those new cars with horns that go *a-oohga-oohga*," offered Teak, trying to be helpful.

"It could be anything, I imagine," agreed Lonesome. "Then again, perhaps it could be anything I *imagine*. Perhaps if you accompany me, you could help me research the matter."

"Sure," grinned Teak. "Where are you going? I could come for just a bit. I'm supposed to be resting, because—"

"Quite," said Lonesome tactfully, glancing at Teak's goose egg. "That would be splendid, absolutely splendid." He fished a folder out of his inside pocket. "This is our timetable. Can you read?"

"Of course!"

"May I?" asked Lonesome politely. When Teak nodded, the rabbit hopped onto the bed and spread open the timetable. This is what was printed on it:

TRAINS TO BEEJUMSTAN

6:66	7:66
6:67	7:67
6:76	7:76
6:77	7:77

"Why, there are only two numbers in the whole thing!" marveled Teak.

"We find that much more convenient," Lonesome explained. "That way you expect things to be at sixes and sevens, and so they are. The early one, the tsax-tsaxty-tsax," continued Lonesome, lapsing into the way Beejums count, "is a beastly train because the beastliest beasts go on it. The tsax-tsaxty-tseven is the one that your mother suggested."

"Mother? Mother suggested?" Teak's heart leapt. So she was in this somehow!

"Certainly," replied Lonesome. "This is part of my mission as ambassador. Your 'Mother,' as you call her—I always called mine 'Mummy'—has asked me to bring you the message that from now on, no matter how far apart in the world you may be, you and your parents can meet together in our great and beautiful country of Beejumstan. In fact—"

"How, how?" Teak interrupted with a squeal of excitement. She was now hugging her pillow and punching it.

Lonesome flashed a wonderful toothy smile. "Well, not that way, me girl! You have to lie down and relax and breathe very quietly. Now watch the top of my cane."

Teak watched the golden duck trace a big circle in the air. And in it she saw her mother, and she was leaning

toward Teak and singing a most beautiful song, which
went something like this:

When you are lonesome, love,
When we are far away
We can all meet again, my dear,
At the end of every day

for ever since, O ever since, time here began
all Beejums take the little train
the train to Beejumstan.

When you go beebize
When you go to sleep
When you are tired, love,
and you have dreams to keep

ever since, O ever since, time here began
all Beejums take the little train
the train to Beejumstan.

The next thing Teak knew, she and Lonesome were
standing on the platform of a small train station with a
red roof. Teak looked down at herself a bit nervously. She
couldn't remember if she had put her navy blue mackintosh on, and then there was the more serious problem of
Alfred Hampson, her bear.

Alfred always traveled with Teak, but as Teak was
growing older, she was becoming rather self-conscious
about carrying a stuffed bear, so sometimes she stuffed
him under her raincoat and pretended he wasn't there.
Now she had the coat on, but Alfred was missing.

The station was like many others Teak was familiar with, but here among the people waiting were a great number of animals all dressed up. There was a mother pig in blue gingham holding a baby pig in a sailor suit. It was squealing quite loudly. "He's teething," apologized the mother pig.

There was an old zebra gentleman sitting on a bench smoking a pipe and reading a newspaper called *The Beejum Gazette.* Several squirrel boys in overalls were chasing each other and throwing walnuts over the heads of the waiting passengers. Two of them were even playing with a wooden hoop (not as big as Teak's, of course, but plenty big for squirrels), which they were rolling through the legs of the zebra gentleman. They were all being rather rude, and Nanny would have stopped them in no time. A little mouselady was sitting up on the ticket counter buying a ticket. She carried a basket full of lavender sachets tied in colored ribbons. Teak recognized them, because her grandmother had kept some just like them in her hand-kerchief case when she came to stay with them on the Riviera in Bordighera, in Italy, the previous winter.

A giraffe was bent over and listening very carefully to a woodchuck that was wearing a bowler hat and carrying a briefcase and a black umbrella. He was talking about investments and sounded just like Teak's own father except for the high, chattering voice.

Suddenly, around the corner, squeaking and bouncing and chuffing, came the train. Smoke puffed out of its stack in little round and white clouds. It drew up and let out a series of long sighs and hisses: PSSSSSSHHHHH!

PSSSSSSSSSHHHHHH! And out of the long train jumped two funny men who were obviously the conductors. The first was skinny and had a long droopy mustache, and the other was very round and fat. He had lambchop whiskers and a waxed mustache that turned up at the ends. When they saw Teak and Lonesome, they joined arms and began to dance and sing loudly in cockney accents. The skinny conductor sang first and the song went like this:

> My name is Elmer Tucket
> and I'm sure you will agree
> This is the finest little train
> Anyone could see
> upsy-daisy, downsy-violet
> tootly-tootle-too
> clickety-clackety-clickety
> off we go with you!

Then the fat conductor sang:

> My name is Horace Whortle
> A conductor's what I am
> While Tucket takes your ticky-tucks
> I bring you books and jam
> upsy-daisy, downsy-violet
> whittely-whittely-whee
> just think of all the wonders
> when you come with me.

Then they both sang:

Fish and feathers, fur and fluff
Up and down we go
Gathering everybody's stuff
Hiddley-hidey-ho
Punching all your tucky-ticks
Is what we love to do
And Mr. Spilby's at the whistle
Going whooo-whooo-whooo!

When they got on the six-sixty-seven to Beejumstan, Lonesome made Teak sit by the window. The rabbit then carefully placed his top hat and cane in the rack overhead and, giving his striped trousers a little hitch up, sat down opposite Teak.

The train was full of surprises for Teak. Who should she see first but Alfred Hampson, her bear! There sat Alfred, across the aisle, large as life, and next to him a Mrs. Hampson and four little bears. Teak hadn't even known he was married. Alfred seemed a trifle embarrassed at having his private life so suddenly disclosed, but Mrs. Hampson seemed quite at ease and proudly introduced her little ones as Tiny, Teeny, Wee Wee Bear, and Jumbo. Jumbo was the youngest and smallest of all and sat contentedly on his mother's lap sucking his thumb. The little bears were all very well-behaved and quiet, but they stared with wonder at Teak. Eight little round black eyes were wide open studying her. Teak wondered if Alfred had told them anything about her. After a little while, Jumbo took his thumb out of his mouth long enough to give a shy smile, and when Teak smiled back, they all relaxed and began to giggle and whisper.

The train set off with a jerk, then settled into a cheery clatter. Now Teak could study some of the other passengers. She noticed that the baby pig was still squealing and jumping up and down on his mother's lap. She was having a hard time holding him. At the other end of the car, the giraffe was bent over and still listening intently to the woodchuck. Across the aisle the old gentleman zebra was now doing a crossword puzzle in *The Beejum Gazette,* and on the windowsill beside him Teak saw a passenger she hadn't noticed before, a large spider wearing a beret and reading a thick book. By squinting Teak could just make out the title: *The Philosophy of Spinoza.*

The mouselady was sitting in a little rocking chair on another windowsill, apparently lost in pleasant thoughts, because Teak could see she was twitching her whiskers and smiling sweetly. Lonesome leaned over and told Teak that her name was Mrs. Daisymouse and she ran a little pension where Teak could stay sometime, if she wished.

In a corner at the other end of the train car sat old Mr. Rathbone sound asleep. This was the biggest surprise of all, because Mr. Rathbone had been so sickly when Teak had seen him in Bordighera the previous winter. He had sometimes visited her Grandma King, and Teak always liked to talk with him, but it was inconceivable that such an old man would be on his way to Beejumstan. He must have been close to ninety years old. Teak remembered that she had apparently embarrassed her grandmother dreadfully once by asking them both, as they were riding up in the lift, "Are you lovers?" Grandma had blushed and scolded her, but Mr. Rathbone had thought it the funniest thing he had heard in years. He had laughed in the lift, and laughed when he got off, and they could still hear him laughing down the hall. Teak still couldn't see what was so funny about it. It had seemed a perfectly reasonable question to her.

Now Teak leaned over and whispered, "Lonesome, how come Mr. Rathbone is on this train?"

"Why Mr. Rathbone is a Beejum, has been for years. Now, of course, he's getting ready for Aberduffy Day."

"What's Aberduffy Day?" asked Teak.

"Oh that's a special holiday, a very special day you get to celebrate once every lifetime. It has to do with living in more than one Bubble at once."

"Lonesome, I don't understand. How could anyone live in a Bubble?"

"But it's really very simple, you see. We all live in Bubbles. We're in one right now."

"But why do you call it a Bubble?" asked Teak.

"Bubbles are round, aren't they? Well, so is the world. So Bubbles are worlds. How's that for circular reasoning, me girl?"

"You just said Aberduffy Day has to do with living in two Bubbles at once. But people can't live in two *worlds* at once, can they?"

"Certainly they can," said the rabbit, wiggling both ears and his nose while crossing his eyes. "If they get the hang of it. Once they get the hang of it they can go anywhere they want."

"It must be pretty exciting to be in another world," said Teak, squirming in her seat. "Where is that world? Is it far away?"

"Well, now, maybe it is, and maybe it isn't. See, the Bubbles fit inside each other. There's a Bubble around people all the time—only they don't see it. So they go hither and yon, to and fro, back and forth, looking and looking for it. Of course they don't find it—unless they get the hang of it, that is." Lonesome shook his head in wonder.

"Are the ones that get the hang of it the ones that go to Beejumstan?" asked Teak.

"Well, now, I wouldn't say yes and I wouldn't say no. But then on the other hand, I *would* say yes and I *would* say no. It's like this, me girl. Not everybody goes to Beejumstan. Only Beejums do that. But there are other places. There are many, many Bubbles."

"Lonesome, does Mr. Rathbone live in two worlds? Is that why he's on this train?"

"Ah, Mr. Rathbone...yes, he may be getting the hang of it. His life might be taking a more interesting turn, if you know what I mean. You'll see how different he will seem to you when we get to Beejumstan."

Teak suddenly thought of the question she really wanted to ask. "Lonesome, am *I* a Beejum?"

The rabbit turned to her with a toothy smile. "Well, you're here, aren't you?"

By now Teak was thoroughly confused, and a little bit dizzy from watching Lonesome's ears. Anyway she was glad Mr. Rathbone was on the same train.

Lonesome let his ears droop. "I haven't confused you, have I? Maybe you can get Gezeebius to explain more. After all, I'm only a rabbit. Carrots are my specialty, not Bubbles. They always taste like soap to me."

Teak was beginning to like Lonesome's funny way with words. And this Gezeebius sounded like somebody very important. She was just about to ask who he was when, all of a sudden, the train came to a sandy beach and without even hesitating headed straight into the sea. The water rose up the windows and the light turned greenish. Teak was greatly alarmed, but Lonesome and the bears acted as if it were perfectly normal.

"Nothing to worry about, me girl," smiled Lonesome, "we're just picking up the fishfolk."

Indeed, the train was now running underwater, like a submarine, going deeper and deeper. Finally it came to a halt and remained quietly suspended, rocking gently to and fro. Teak's view out the window looked like a giant aquarium. Fish of all sizes were swimming this way and that, and electric eels were lighting the way for them. Some fish swam up and made funny faces, waved their fins at Teak, and she was sure that one fish was blowing kisses at her.

Teak pressed her face against the window and shaded her eyes with her hands and looked into a beautiful deep blue-green world. Three porpoises were obviously getting into a car at the back. One of them carried a picnic basket on his nose. A mother seal was chasing her pup, scolding him. When she caught up with him, she gave him a fond little slap with her flipper and guided him onto the train.

The little seal wore glasses. How things could be so different and yet the same in this world!

"How can they breathe on the train?" Teak wanted to know.

"Oh, they have a tank car full of water. No problem. They all have a lovely time together."

Teak sat back amazed, and the train shot off again and was soon back clattering away on land. Off in the distance, she was now able to see a range of snow-capped mountains.

Lonesome decided to take a short catnap, or rather a rabbitnap, and was actually snoozing when the train suddenly began to accelerate in the most alarming fashion. Faster and faster and faster it went, until everything streaked past the windows in colored ribbons, and before Teak could cry out, the train took off into the air and began to circle through the clouds. When it rose above them, she could look down and see a whole new world. The little bears were now all excited as well. "Look, Mummy, whipped cream! More whipped cream!"

Mother Bear smiled indulgently and said, "Yes, my dears, yes—those are clouds."

They really did look like great puffs of whipped cream or maybe meringues, thought Teak, especially with the sun on them. And the land looked just beautiful down below. It was quite circular. Teak had never flown in an aeroplane before, though she had heard a lot about them; she marveled at all she saw.

All at once, the train stopped and hung in the air, defying even more of the laws of gravity. Again Teak felt scared, but this time Alfred Hampson leaned across and explained, "Now we are taking on the air passengers." And he pointed out the window. Teak almost laughed at what she saw, but stopped in case it would be impolite. There standing in the air was a dignified vulture gentleman, with a watch chain across his front feathers, holding a handsome umbrella and smoking a cigar. Behind him was a lady owl wearing large pearls and carrying a purse. A reticule, Grandma King would have called it. Teak hadn't realized there were lady owls! And behind her were two young seagulls with sailor hats cocked sideways. They looked as if they had just joined the navy, which, in fact, they had. Last of all was a great big, tough-looking bald eagle wearing a huge cowboy hat and big cowboy boots with silver spurs.

Teak was straining to see more, but all she could see were lots of birds hovering in the distance. She quite missed the two parrots who had boarded her car from the other side and now came and sat two rows in front of her. Both were dressed like Arab sheiks and seemed to be quite important characters. Lonesome, who had woken up when the train stopped, said that the green one was Ali Krakatoa and the grey one, who was smaller, was Ibn ben Nibl and that they were high up in the government of Beejumstan, holding positions in the Administration of Crackers. Indeed, no sooner had the train begun to move again than they launched into a loud discussion about the relative merits of round and/or square and/or rectangular crackers. In fact, they screeched and squawked so loudly that they soon had everybody's attention.

Ali Krakatoa intoned, "It's obvious, most honorable colleague, that Beejumstan needs an Official Cracker, the sale of which could provide a source of revenue for the Beejumwealth. Right?"

"Right. Ah yes, right. Crumbs for taxes," Ibn ben Nibl agreed.

"What's revenue?" whispered Teak to Lonesome, who whispered back that it was money the government collected to spend on things.

"Now a square cracker stamped with the Official Seal would be acceptable to all parties. Right?" continued Ali Krakatoa.

"Wrong," said Ibn Nibl firmly. "It would be fine for cocktails and tea but wouldn't do at all for birthdays. Everybody knows that birthdays are round, have always been round, and should remain round. After all, think of the precedent of cakes."

"That's just the point, don't you see? Too much round is too much. The country is round enough as it is. But look, my friend, consider then a compromise—how about rectangular?"

"That requires two bites instead of one. Impractical, impractical."

Now the two parrots began to hop up and down on the seat, one screaming "Practical! Practical!" and the other "Impractical! Impractical!"

In the midst of this, Mr. Tucket appeared to collect the tucky-ticks. "I say," he shouted, "wot's goin' on 'ere?" and everybody calmed down and started fishing for their tickets. When he got to Teak, he smiled kindly at her as a new face, while Lonesome proffered the tickets. So Teak was bold enough to ask, "Where's Mr. Whortle?"

Immediately Tucket's long face changed to a sour look. "And what would you want with that fat old snipper-snapper?"

Teak was shocked. "I'm sorry," she apologized. "I thought you both worked together on the train."

Tucket positively glared. "Wot, me work with the loikes of 'im! I should say not. Never, no, not never ever in a month of Sundays. Not till roosters lay heggs. And," he added at the top of his voice, "if he ever lets that oafish son of 'is near my precious daughter, wot is the loveliest in the land, I'll stick 'is 'ead between 'is two ears! I will that!" At this he glowered up and down the aisle, making quite sure everybody had heard him. Everybody had.

Teak hastily changed the subject. "You must see an awful lot traveling to and fro, Mr. Tucket. That must be such fun."

At this, Tucket stopped looking cross and looked pleased and friendly again. "Bless me, to be sure, to be sure. If I hain't never had no good toime, t'ain't 'cause I hain't never went none." And with that he punched the tickets with a flourish and swept on to the other passengers, leaving Teak to unravel the meaning of his words.

"Why doesn't Tucket like Whortle?" she asked Lonesome in a whisper.

Lonesome whispered back, "Oh, but he really does. They're the best of friends. Have been for years and years. We all know that."

"Then why did he talk that way about Whortle's son?"

"Did you ever hear of Romeo and Juliet?" asked the rabbit.

"No, I never did."

"Too bad. Well, someday you will. And you'll find out that children can be quite persnickety indeed. They simply hate to have their parents pick their friends and tell them what to do or not to do—especially when it comes to getting married."

"I know that!" interrupted Teak.

"Well, you see, Tucket and Whortle would love to have their son and daughter marry each other. So for ages they have been pretending to hate each other. It's very strenuous for them. But now Tucket's daughter and Whortle's son want to be together more than anything in the world, and they've been meeting secretly."

"You mean it's working?"

"Like a charm," grinned Lonesome.

"There should be a wedding, or more likely an elopement, any day now," put in Mother Bear, who had been eavesdropping and just loved romantic tales.

"But how long have Tucket and Whortle been fighting this way?" asked Teak.

"Oh, for about eight years or so, I guess, and it's been hard on them. Very hard."

"That's very loving of them, isn't it," said Teak.

"Indeed, it is," agreed Lonesome. "It's something to remember, in fact. Sometimes it takes a lot of rough stuff to make the way smooth."

Just then the train let out three joyous whistles and whoos and began to slow down until it came to a full stop. All the passengers jumped up at once, and what a happy barking, yapping, growling, squeaking, twittering, neighing, squawking, chattering, and yowling broke out up and down the train. The only thing Teak could do was laugh, and laugh she did.

They had just arrived at Beejumstan. And, sure enough, there was Mr. Rathbone getting up, and he did look quite different, as Lonesome had predicted. He looked somehow younger. When he saw Teak, he smiled and waved and gave her a knowing wink.

Teak was still laboriously winking back at him when she heard Nanny's concerned voice. "Teak, is there something wrong with your eye?"

So she sat up and blinked instead. "No," she told Nanny, "I was just winking back at Mr. Rathbone."

"Well, I never," exclaimed Nanny. "Whatever next!" Then she told Teak to hurry up and get dressed, because it was almost time for supper. The bump on her head was no longer so swollen, Nanny noticed with relief, but Teak did seem a bit dazed. She would have to keep an eye on her. "Come along now, Teak," she said kindly. "Upsy-daisy!"

"Downsy-violet," grinned Teak, and then she jumped out of bed and marched off to the bathroom, the belt to her dressing gown trailing behind her. She felt just fine.

3

Grandma King and the Twins

TEAK WANTED TO TELL the whole world about the train to Beejumstan, but her whole world at that moment was Nanny, and she was pretty sure she would say it was all made-up nonsense or that she had dreamt it. So she bit her lip and said nothing about what had happened.

Nanny, on the other hand, had news of her own. It seemed they were off to Italy in the morning. "And see that you wash behind your ears tonight," she added.

"Why?" asked Teak suspiciously.

"Because your Grandma King is already in Rome. Quite settled in, I imagine. And, can you guess who else might be there?" Nanny did not wait for an answer. "Your cousins—yes, Jessie and Justin, will be there in time for your birthday! Won't that be just lovely!" Nanny turned her back and set about getting down the suitcases again and began packing, and all the time she went on and on about how darling the twins were, how sweetly behaved, and how distinguished they always looked.

28

This, as you can well imagine, was not a viewpoint shared by Teak. She had very mixed feelings about those cousins of hers. But she was really happy about seeing Grandma King again, who was one of Teak's all-time favorite people, so she grabbed her own suitcase, the Fiumerol, and hoisted it onto her bed, ready to pack it herself. She looked first for Alfred Hampson and found him under the bed. When she picked up her bear, she gave him a conspiratorial look, but Alfred just stared into space with his black button eyes and didn't let on a thing. Nevertheless Teak thought she detected just a hint of a twinkle as she tucked him into the middle of her green jersey. However, Nanny discovered him and insisted that he took up too much room. That meant hiding him in the raincoat again, but Alfred didn't seem to mind.

The next day Teak and Nanny climbed aboard a train headed for Rome. The seats in the compartment were dark red plush, and Teak sat by the window and read the signs in four different languages stating that it was forbidden to spit on the floor. This seemed an unnecessary admonition to Teak. It took quite a while figuring out which word was which in German, Italian, and French. Then came the fun of rocking her way to the dining car and sitting properly and trying to eat while looking out the window at the extraordinary landscapes. The train shrieked a warning as it passed farms and roads barred, with people waiting with bicycles, and some would wave and Teak always waved back, wondering what they were thinking. When the train slowed down and came to a station and stopped, people rushed to and fro, hugs were exchanged, blue-smocked porters pushed luggage around, shouting in French and then in Italian. Eventually Teak tired from kneeling on the seat and curled up with her head against Nanny's ample lap. When she awoke, they had arrived.

The Hotel Flora in Rome was a grand, comfy old hotel that was one of Teak's favorites. It was right beside some ruins in the Giardini Borghese, a lovely park where she could play and look at tadpoles in one of the fountains. And maybe Nanny would take her back to what her mother called the *Forum Catorum* to see the hundreds of cats and kittens that roamed wild among the sunken pillars of the ruins of an ancient temple. Maybe they could go back to the zoo and see her friend, the old elephant, who would stand up on his hind legs at Teak's command for a peanut, to the amazement of passers-by.

Teak found that she had been given the same room she had had before. This didn't happen very often, so it almost felt like home. On the way in she waved to Marcantonio, the young valet who polished the shoes they left outside their doors at night. He wore a green uniform with a yellow and black stripey apron that made him look like a wasp. Marcantonio remembered her and waved back and called out, *"Buon giorno, Teakina!"* which was "Good day" in Italian.

Then Nanny was brushing her hair, roughly as usual, and saying, "Now remember to give your grandmother a nice kiss and a hug." Teak felt impatient with Nanny. She didn't have to be told how to behave with Grandma

King—that just happened naturally. She wriggled free, ran out the door, and dashed down the carpeted hall and up a flight of stairs, not waiting for the lift. She knew just where to go because, when Grandma was in Rome, she always had the same suite of rooms overlooking the park. Now Teak knocked at the door eagerly with a great many more raps than was necessary.

"Come in, dear!" It was Grandma's musical voice.

When Teak opened the door, it all looked wonderfully familiar. Grandma had an open drawing room, and already her own pink brocaded curtains were hanging at the long windows. She insisted on carrying some of her favorite things when she traveled so that she would feel at home wherever she was. Through the long windows Teak could see the same tall pine trees waving above a high wall, and she remembered watching a terrible thunderstorm out that window the year before. Grandma had held her hand, and together they had watched the trees being lashed and whipped by the raging wind. It was strange how things can flash through your mind more quickly than a flash of lightning. Where do memories come from? she wondered.

Grandma King was sitting in her biggest armchair. She was dressed in mauve, a color that showed she was still in mourning for Grandpa King, who had died the year before. Teak could still remember her grandfather a little. He used to pick her up in his arms and recite, "A skunk sat on a stump. The stump said the skunk stunk and the skunk said the stump stunk!" Grandma would protest that this was unsuitable language, but Teak loved it, and

she would hug and squeeze her grandfather around the
neck and laugh and say that she was taller now than anyone. Last year Grandma King had showed Teak her sta-
tionery all bordered in black. That, too, was a custom in
those days. Grandma was now a widow, but, as Teak
looked at her fondly, she was a very lovely one. Her white
hair was fluffed up and pinned at the top with a tortoise-
shell comb. She always wore a choker of little seed pearls
around her neck, and her pointed button boots were
peeping out from under her long gown. She always
looked regal, and, in fact, once a lady in the dining room
in Nice had risen to curtsey to her, convinced that she
was the queen on holiday. Today as usual she was looking
"swell elegant," as Teak's father would say to tease. Now,
as she saw her grandchild, she frowned ferociously and
growled, "No kiss!" But her eyes were sparkling. This was
their game.

Teak threw back her head and laughed, then rushed at
her shouting, "Yes, kiss! Yes, kiss!" and she threw her
arms about her and gave her a great big hug. Grandma
King didn't even mind getting mussed up a little. Nanny
would have had a fit.

"But I said NO kiss!" she gasped, and the more she
protested, the more profusely Teak hugged her. And her
nice fragrance of lavender reminded Teak of the mouselady buying her ticket to Beejumstan.

Then she sat down close to Grandma, and they talked
and talked about all kinds of things. She asked Teak how
her parents seemed, and Teak thought she looked a little
sad when she asked. Grandma reminded her that she had

a birthday coming, and that Uncle Amyas and Aunt Bessie would be arriving all the way from Boston, bringing the twins.

Now it was time for tea. Grandma rang a little brass bell which stood on a small table by her chair, right next to her spectacles in a blue velvet case. Teak always laughed at the bell because it was shaped like a lady in a hoopskirt. Everything about Grandma was perfect and just so.

A thickset, dark-haired woman answered the bell, bringing in a tea tray. "Hanka," said Grandma, "this is my granddaughter Teak." Hanka sized her up with a glance, grunted, and tromped out of the room. The teacups rattled in their saucers and the flower vases vibrated when she walked. "I do wish Hanka was a little more *gentle,*" she sighed. "The hotel found her for me, but I'm not sure how long she will last."

On the tea tray were the oblong crackers Teak liked and her favorite cookies. Grandma poured the tea from her very own ancestral silver teapot, which she brought with her everywhere she went. When Teak's father once assured her that they had adequate teapots in Europe, she shook her head firmly and replied, "I think it's most important for that child [meaning Teak] to know where she comes from." Now Teak again looked in wonder, marveling that she might have been poured out of that teapot. Then she looked at the cookies and secretly hoped that no one else would come in, because there weren't that many on the plate. She felt guilty because she knew well enough from Nanny that she was being greedy and selfish. But nobody interrupted them, so she had her fill of them, and even remembered to pass the dish to her grandmother. She really did want to share with her because she was truly her closest friend and ally. Grandma always understood how she felt on the inside even when she didn't say things on the outside.

And all the while the sky outside the window was turning a deeper and deeper purple, and a pink sash of late afternoon light fell on the oriental rug in the middle of the room. Grandma King turned and smiled at Teak with her eyes, and she wriggled back on her chair and let the moment soak in. "I love you, dear," said Grandma quietly.

"I love you, too," replied Teak simply. And she did, with her whole heart.

Then Hanka clomped back in and pulled the curtains, and the mood of the room changed. Grandma was just asking what the most exciting thing was in Teak's life at the moment when a firm knock came at the door. It was Nanny and time to leave. Teak didn't want to go, but there didn't seem to be much of a choice.

A visit from Jessie and Justin (you could hardly think of one without the other) was always an event in Teak's life. It felt a bit like jumping into icy water—exciting, but you dreaded it, too, and were grateful and relieved when it was all over. Uncle Amyas was taller than Teak's father and had a deeper voice. Aunt Bessie proudly belonged to the Clan MacLean of Duart. She was lots of fun to listen to because of her Scots burr, which meant she pronounced words quite differently from anyone else in the family.

She loved the poet RRRRobbie Burrrrns (Robert Burns) and she knew a lot about her family history. She was descended, so she had been told, from one of the famous seven heroic brothers who had all died in a battle, each crying, "Another for Hector!" Justin loved jumping off beds and crying out the family yell: "ANOTHER FOR HECTOR!"

Aunt Bessie was younger than Teak's mother, but they were good friends. Bessie had reddish golden hair and deep blue eyes, but the twins had bright carroty red hair and freckles. Practically all the twins' clothes came from Scotland and somehow matched.

They had already spent two summers with their Scottish relatives on the Isle of Skye, and one of Teak's dreams was to go there some day and have the exciting adventures they talked of.

Jessie and Justin were always getting Teak into trouble. The previous year, the two families had spent Christmas in Gstaad, in Switzerland. They had all gone to the little Anglican church in the late afternoon, driving there in a sleigh. Jessie and Justin had been dressed, both of them, in red kilts of the tartan of MacLean of Duart (you never said plaid!) and black velvet jackets. Justin wore a sporran, a little pouch of seal fur with silver trim that hung on a chain around his waist, and in his right wool kneesock he had a small real dagger, which he called his *skian dhu*. Teak had been jealous. Everybody had fussed over the twins and exclaimed how "adorable" they looked, and nobody had noticed Teak at all. She had felt like a sparrow between two cardinals.

After church, they had gone back to the big hotel, and while the grown-ups were having cocktails, the children had gone to the twins' room, where the twins stood on their heads, showing off their bright red underpants. They had tried to teach Teak how to stand on her head, but she hadn't been too good at it. Her dress fell over her face and she had toppled over and crashed into a small table with a vase on it, which belonged to the hotel—a major crime. When Nanny had arrived, there stood Jessie and Justin, every pleat in place, and every copper curl shining. Teak's dress was now tucked into her bloomers and her hair looked like a rat's nest. The twins had stood there smirking with their feet neatly together, while Teak was hauled off and punished for being rowdy, uncivilized, and showing off. You could hear Nanny's voice rising and falling all the way down the corridor.

Now Teak was a bit sorry that she hadn't had time to tell Grandma King about Beejumstan. She thought that she might be able to trust her. Of course, she could tell her mother, since she knew about it, but as usual she wasn't around.

4

Beejumſtan

THE TRAIN HAD JUST HUFFED to a stop. A sign on the station read "Beejumstan." Everyone got off noisily, with much barking, squeaking, and trumpeting. Teak saw that Mrs. Daisymouse and the spider in the beret went out a special door that connected to a small elevated walkway so they would not get trampled underfoot. She looked wistfully at all the families joyfully reuniting.

Lonesome told Teak to wait a second and disappeared into the station. When he came out he was dressed in what Teak would come to think of as the national costume of Beejumstan. She was beginning to see that she could always count on Lonesome to dress appropriately for every occasion. The national costume was handsome. There was a navy blue jacket with a Russian-style collar, two rows of twelve silver buttons, each bordered by red ribbing. Four silver buttons led down each sleeve to red cuffs. The bottom half of Lonesome was encased in yellow knee britches, white kneesocks with red flashes, and black buckle shoes. There was a cutaway at the back for Lonesome's handsome puff of a tail. His hat sported three shining green cockfeathers, and somehow his ears came through openings in the hat in a jaunty way. And he still carried his cane with the golden duck. Teak was lost in admiration at her friend's appearance.

"Welcome to Beejumstan, Teak," he said with a formal bow. "You are just in time to catch the omnibustle. We're going to see some of the country, so that you can find your way about in the future. I see that you like the Beejum national dress. Would you care for an outfit?" Teak nodded. Lonesome waved his stick and presto! There she stood dressed as a Beejum, in a navy skirt with a white top and across her chest a wide bright red V-shaped suspender on which yellow ducks were embroidered, alternating with white eggs.

As she and Lonesome stood on the platform, the two parrots flapped off the train. They were still screaming at each other.

"Practical!"

"Impractical!"

Now Teak had an idea. "Excuse me," she said, nervously going up to them, because she was afraid of getting bitten by mistake by their huge beaks. "Excuse me," she interrupted as politely as she could.

"What do you know about it?" snapped Ali Krakatoa crossly.

"Oh, let her speak. She must've eaten crackers, after all," retorted Ibn ben Nibl, rolling his eyes upward with an exasperated expression.

"Well," thought Teak out loud, "maybe the taste is more important than the shape. They do just turn to crumbs inside you after they are eaten, don't they?"

Both parrots fell silent, profoundly impressed by this astonishing insight from a mere girl.

"My word!" exclaimed Ali Krakatoa, "she's quite right. We should put her on our committee immediately. *Vox populi! Vox populi!*" They jumped up and down screaming, while Lonesome whispered a translation from the Latin. It meant "the voice of the people."

"We can call them Populi Crackers!"

"You could have them in several shapes," suggested Teak, "so that people and/or animals could pick what was easiest for them to bite."

"So you could, so you could!" cried Ibn ben Nibl, giving a huge hop of delight. He almost flew off the platform. Encouraged, Teak then took out paper and pencil that a pocket seemed to have miraculously provided and, leaning against the station wall, drew four shapes:

This she handed carefully to Ali Krakatoa, who took it in his beak and laid it on the ground to study. "I wonder if you had thought of oblong?" Teak asked modestly. She was thinking of Grandma King's favorite crackers.

"Who is Ob Long? Chinese, I suppose," said Nibl.

Teak pointed to the diagram. "No," she explained, "oblong is sort of rectangular rounded or rounded rectangular. And there are no corners to break off."

The parrots both whistled shrilly with delight. "Brilliant! Absolutely, positively brilliant! The girl's a genius. We must have you on our staff as a consultant!" Then the two turned their backs to Teak and muttered to each other not to forget. "All shapes at once and oblong. Populi Crackers, Populi Crackers. And our slogan can be QUALITY FOR EQUALITY or EQUALITY FOR QUALITY." When Teak heard that, she had another bright idea. They could arrange the letters in a circle and read it around and around. The parrots almost fainted with admiration. They took wing and flew up and down rousing those passengers who had paused to watch to give three impromptu cheers for Teak. There was an excited uproar, and even Mr. Rathbone gave a wave.

Lonesome, who had watched Teak with approval, told her that she would make an admirable diplomat, a person who could help people agree about things. Alfred Hampson and Mrs. Bear were beaming, and Teak began to feel warm and happy inside.

"Well, me girl," grinned Lonesome. "Wasn't that nice. Promising, most promising." With that he took Teak's hand in his furry paw, and led her to a blue bus marked THE BEEJUM OMNIBUSTLE. It was decorated with fringes and baubles and garlanded designs of flowers. The driver had to turn a crank in the front to start it. After a series of hiccups and burps and other strange noises, the motor started and the passengers got on.

Not too far away in every direction Teak could see high-peaked mountains, many with snow on their tops. The encircling mountains were deep blue and purple, the shadows of clouds swept across their shapes. Soon the road took them by a great river called the Wendward. It was fed by innumerable sparkling streams, brooks, and freshets, along which lived the wee folk of Beejumstan. "There are the Elbedridges and the Bunnywidgets. They make up the majority of the population," Lonesome explained. "The Elbedridges often live in those mushroom apartments that grow on trees, while the Bunnywidgets like living close to the ground under things like ferns. But you will find both living in town or sometimes even in small houses. The Elbedridges tend to have beards and wear green clothes and red caps. The Bunnywidgets, on the other hand—see, there's one fetching water from that well!"

Teak looked out and saw a small fellow with brown ballooning trousers, a white belted tunic, green cap, and red pointy shoes. He had no beard. The womenfolk, Lonesome continued, wore whatever took their fancy, and there was much intermarriage. All weddings took place on top of Criss-Cross Hill, a special spot in the Mumbledumpkin Downs.

Since Beejumstan was not very big, it didn't take long before Poppalopolis, the capital, came in sight. By most standards it was not a city at all, more like a small medieval town. The Omnibustle began to bump and bounce a little more because the streets were all cobbled. The houses were joined together, and each had a peaked overhanging roof; all of the windows had window boxes filled with flowers—red and white geraniums, petunias, and bright blue little flowers Teak didn't know the name of.

In the streets, a mixture of wee folk, animals, and people with baskets on their arms were going about their business, walking in and out of the shops, and stopping to chat with one another. Teak thought she recognized several from her ride on the train.

One of the Omnibustle stops was in front of what was apparently a barbershop, for there was a striped barber's pole out front, except this one was curved at the top like a candy cane and there was a big mustache near the top. Through the big front window Teak could see an ostrich barber carefully giving a porcupine a trim. Behind the ostrich was a smaller barber's chair in which a bald Bunny-widget was sound asleep. The ostrich spotted Lonesome on the Omnibustle and waved his scissors, which the rabbit acknowledged with a tip of his hat.

"Is that where you get a haircut?" asked Teak.

Lonesome chuckled at the pun, then answered, "Oscar and I were partners in that shop for a while. A barbershop is a wonderful place to hone your diplomatic skills, you know. I shaved the raspberries."

As the Omnibustle continued down the street, Teak tried to imagine how you would shave a raspberry. And what kind of barber's chair would you need? Soon they passed a small cathedral with twin spires. "Would you like to go in?" asked Lonesome. Teak nodded, so they got off the Omnibustle and walked into the Cathedral of St. Ninnius. Ninnius was so far Beejumstan's only saint, famous from the olden days, it seemed, for having written the ABC Scrolls before moving on to another Bubble. The ABC Scrolls were full of wisdom, Lonesome added.

Teak had visited many cathedrals already in her young life, because her parents were always being taken to them by business acquaintances anxious to display the culture of whatever city they were visiting. She even knew that every cathedral had a special chair or *cathedra* for the presiding bishop to sit in. So did St. Ninnius, only this one was a rocking chair. The statue of the saint depicted a monk with a rope around his middle holding a scroll. He didn't look solemn or sad, but had a lovesome smile that spread out all over the church. There were little chapels, too, and the animals were welcome everywhere. There seemed to be shrines to all of the great souls Teak had ever heard of, and there was a lovely special lady with her hand out. Lonesome looked at her reverently and said she depicted "The Mother of Us All." Teak wondered if Gezeebius were here, and Lonesome explained that Gezeebius was still living and teaching in Beejumstan. Only those that had gone on to other Bubbles could be represented here. An order of nuns came in demurely, and when Teak looked closely, she saw that they really were ermines, all white except for the tips of their tails. They sang most sweetly in a choir until the bell tolled, a rich, deep bonging that spread out into the cool air as they walked out.

Just then Teak saw the squirrel boys with schoolbags on their backs, and she asked about schools in Beejumstan. Lonesome explained that the squirrels attended Miss Tnurk's school. Miss Tnurk was a very patient and capable goat. It seemed she was one of the few that could control those squirrels.

"As for higher education," Lonesome went on, waving his paw, "there is a slight problem. You see, we have an absolutely splendid university here called Apesnose. It has the very finest campus and the most learned faculty in the world. But—" and Lonesome shook his head sadly, "no student has ever been discovered who is sufficiently qualified or brilliant enough to attend. Such a pity, such a pity. But who knows, maybe the day will come when you might apply and join our most distinguished Beejums, and then we could call you Dr. Thaddea King." And here Lonesome made a formal bow to the girl. Teak was quite pleased. She didn't know women could go to universities.

"You would be joining Dr. Syzygy, who's famous for putting two and two together, and Figg Newton, our alchemist, who recently discovered pithium. Then there's Dr. Dimplehatcher, who heads the Gooseflesh Institute. He's a great doctor and helps many Beejums who come to him in fear or distress. And only a month ago we acquired our first lady professor, Virgo Prunefiddle herself. She knows so many facts she has to carry them round in a patchwork bag. To tell you the truth," said Lonesome, "I get a bit nervous whenever I see her."

"Why?" asked Teak.

"Well, she's much bigger than I am, for a start. She's a gnu and smarter than any I ever knew." Lonesome made a long droopy rabbit face. But no matter how hard he tried, he really could not look like a gnu.

"What do they do, then, if they have no students?"

"Oh, they carry on important research, and, in fact, many of the inventions and discoveries in your world were thought out in Beejumstan because this is that kind of Bubble. You know," continued the rabbit, "it's quite funny how you people get all excited thinking you have made up something yourselves. How can that possibly be when you haven't invented yourselves in the first place!" Lonesome stopped on the sidewalk to let that simple thought sink in. Teak wondered if she had made herself up, but decided perhaps she hadn't. She wouldn't have known how. Not in a million trillion years.

They crossed over into a little park and sat down on a bench. There was a pretty fountain splashing, and in front of it some baby spiders were playing hopscotch with a young grasshopper. The spiders were winning, because the grasshopper gave such big jumps, he skipped boxes. Lonesome picked up three small stones and began juggling them while his eyes went whizzing to and fro.

"Your mind, you see, can be like a lovely garden or a jungle—I like gardens best because of carrots and such. But if you keep it peaceful, lovely thoughts will wander into it like shy animals. Such thoughts come and go; you don't really make them up. You notice them. Sometimes they even run away."

Teak asked what he meant, and Lonesome continued. "Well, you can't just think *up* something new, can you? It has to *come* to you. It has to be invited and feel welcome."

"But what about bad thoughts, Lonesome?" asked Teak eagerly. She had never had anyone to talk to this way before.

Lonesome dropped the stones and stopped juggling; then he poked his nose close to Teak's face. "Oh, that's entirely different. Those thoughts burst in the door without knocking. They behave like the old witch Rudintruda. No manners at all."

Teak's ears perked up at the mention of a witch, but she wanted to hear more about bad thoughts. "Why do they do that?"

"They do that because they want something, but they don't know exactly what they want. So they stamp their feet and won't behave at all until you sit down and listen to them and let them have their say, even if they don't make sense. Most of the problems in your world come from people insisting that what they think makes sense and that therefore they are right. But if they were really sensible, then they would understand the importance of nonsense."

"The importance of nonsense?" cried Teak, hardly believing her ears.

"Yup," said Lonesome, flapping his ears left and right for emphasis. "Look, you can study apples or you can eat them. I myself of course prefer carrots, but that's beside the point. When you study about apples that makes sense, but when you bite into one and the sweet juice dribbles down your chin, and the crunch feels crunchy, and the bites make a 'chock' noise—ah, that's beyond sense!"

"Is 'beyond' sense nonsense?"

"That depends on who you are," answered Lonesome.

"How can you tell the difference?"

"Simple. If you can explain something, it's sense."

"So, if you can't, it's nonsense?"

"If you had never eaten an apple, Teak, would what I just described to you make sense?"

"I suppose not."

"Precisely. If I told people about Beejumstan, what would they say?"

Teak grinned. "They'd say it was nonsense."

"Aha! There you have it. And that's perfectly all right with us. In fact, we Beejums much prefer it that way. But just remember that nonsense is every bit as important as sense, because sometimes it's the last resort to help people come to their senses!"

"Please stop, Lonesome, you're making my head ache!" cried Teak.

"That's because you're trying to make sense out of what I'm saying. That's all right now and then, but I shouldn't let it become a habit if I were you."

"Why?"

"Because sense is only the other side of nonsense, Teak, like two sides of a coin. And you don't know what you've got until you've seen both sides." At that Lonesome took out a Beejum coin and flipped it and caught it again in his paw. "Ducks or eggs?"

"Eggs," said Teak.

"Can you have an egg without a duck?" Lonesome didn't wait for the answer. "Gotcha!" And he laughed and laughed at his own joke. Teak shook her head and scratched it.

The baby spiders playing hopscotch decided to change the rules so the little grasshopper could have a chance to win. They said it was all right for him to skip boxes.

In the distance a lion appeared pushing an ice-cream cart. Lonesome hailed him, "Halloo there, Cosmo! You have a customer."

Cosmo, who sported a white paper hat, pushed the cart over. "We have chocolate, vanilla, raspberry, tutti-frutti, maple walnut, cherry, pistachio, lime, and orange and..." He had to stop and think, because he knew there were about ten more flavors. To spare him, Teak quickly asked for a pistachio cone. Lonesome asked for carrot ice cream, one of the ones Cosmo had forgotten. Skillfully he scooped out two enormous helpings and smiled as he handed them over.

Teak was still smiling when she woke up. She could still taste the pistachio on her tongue. Nonsense tasted delicious. She wondered if she could possibly remember all that Lonesome had said. And she could almost hear Lonesome assuring her that now and then, sooner or later, she probably would.

5

The Surprising Birthday Gift

WHEN TEAK WOKE UP on the morning of her birthday, she wondered a bit anxiously what the day would bring. It began with a real surprise. Teak's mother opened the door and whispered, "Happy Birthday!" No one had told her that her parents would be back! Birdie King came in and sat on her bed and hugged her daughter who burrowed into her gratefully. But the next thing Teak knew, her mother was crying. She had never seen her cry before.

"What's the matter, Mother?" Teak asked anxiously.

"It's nothing, really," she sniffed, wiping her nose with a hanky. "I guess I'm just happy to see you again."

"But people don't cry when they're happy, do they?"

"Sometimes they do," she said, trying to look cheerful. But Teak certainly didn't think her mother looked all that happy.

"Where's Daddy?" she asked.

"I don't really know. I think he said he had to go to the bank. But I'm sure you'll see him this afternoon at your birthday party." And Birdie King held Teak close again so that she wouldn't see more tears brimming in her eyes.

Nanny brought Teak to the birthday party, which was held in Grandma King's drawing room. Teak's father wasn't there, but Uncle Amyas and Aunt Bessie arrived with the twins. Teak thought Jessie and Justin seemed to have grown a lot more than she had. Nanny made the usual fuss over them, of course.

"My, my, happy birthday, Teak!" boomed Uncle Amyas in his deep voice, as he embraced her rather clumsily. She noticed that her eye was now level with Uncle Amyas' fourth vest button up from the bottom, which was a sign that she, too, must have grown a bit.

"Happy Birthday!" chimed Jessie and Justin in unison, and they handed her the big flat package that was her present. Teak noticed immediately that Jessie was also carrying a beautiful new Italian doll, most likely a present from Grandma King. Well, after all, she was also Jessie's grandmother. Before she had too much time to wonder what Grandma had given to Justin, Hanka thumped in carrying a cake with white icing and candles. Everybody sang "Happy Birthday to You." Teak's mother had a lovely singing voice, but it sounded a little sad and wobbly today and Teak noticed that her mother's eyes were red-rimmed and that Uncle Amyas had his arm around her shoulder, as if to comfort her. Grandma King presided from her chair, but her eyes turned from tender to a look of concern as they fell on Birdie King.

Soon it was time to open the presents. Teak's mother first handed her the gift from her father. It was a silver automatic pencil with "T.K. III" engraved on it. The III was a joke between them, she knew, because only a son could be a *real* TK the Third. The pencil lay in a fancy box lined with blue velvet. Her mother's gift was a red leather-bound five-year diary with a lock on it. Birdie told Teak it was time for her to begin to be a writer. After all, there were four generations of writers on her side of the family. Grandma King gave her a copy of *Tanglewood Tales* by Nathaniel Hawthorne. It had beautiful illustrations. When Teak opened the twins' present, it turned out to be a kind of fishing game that they could all play together. Nanny gave her a new wool sweater she had knit herself, and said it was made of Shetland wool. It was a nice heathery rust color, and Teak liked it. Finally she was down to the last gift, which came from Uncle Amyas and Aunt Bessie. It was in a long box, and they asked her to guess what was in it. Try as she would, she could not guess what it was. So she opened the package, and that's when all the trouble began.

It was a small black silk umbrella with a satinwood handle, a miniature version of the huge one her father carried. "You will need one when you go to school in the fall," said Aunt Bessie. Teak was just taking it out of the box when Hanka came in to clear away the cake plates. Suddenly she let out a torrent of broken English.

"Not to open in the house! No! No! No! Is bad fortune, very bad luck! It is much worser than shoes on the bed. Never, never, is to open umbrella in the house!"

Teak hastily put the umbrella back in the tissue paper and the box, even though the family scoffed and said

things like, "What superstitious nonsense! Utter rub-
bish!" and to her grandmother, "How do you put up
with that woman?"

Uncle Amyas said, "You must pay her no mind, Teak,
no mind at all."

The twins chorused, "How dumb!" Nevertheless Teak
firmly put the lid on the box, picked up all her presents
without stopping to say thank you to anyone, and ran out
of the room to her own. The party was over.

Three days passed, and it did not rain. Certainly Teak
was scolded by all the grown-ups, especially Nanny, for
the bad manners she had displayed. But the incident of
the umbrella was forgotten by all but Teak. The umbrella
itself stayed in its box at the bottom of the wardrobe.
Each day Teak would take it out secretly and shudder a
little at its sinister powers. She hoped for rain and an
excuse to take it out and open it.

Since the weather was so glorious, Nanny took her and
the twins out to play in the Giardini Borghese every afternoon. Jessie had acquired a doll carriage for the new doll,
who had been named Jaundice because of her yellow-
tinted felt skin. It was a very fancy glossy black carriage
with a hood that went up and down, and Jessie loved rolling it to and fro while Nanny kept exclaiming what a perfect picture she made in her green dress from Liberty's in
London, where the royal family also shopped. Surely, she
insisted, pretty copper curls like that came straight from
heaven. Nanny went on and on, and Teak supposed she
liked Jessie more than herself, and she was hurt by that.
Even more so when Nanny declared that she could see

the noble MacLean blood running in Justin's veins, and what a credit he was to his parents standing up so straight and firm; Teak thought this was a reference to her habit of slouching at table. As far as Teak could see—and she did check—her own veins were every bit as blue as Justin's.

On this particular day, Justin had brought a toy airplane to the park. Its light body was covered with yellow oilskin, and it had a propeller that was wound up by a long rubber band. It could fly twenty feet or more. Teak wished that she had been given a plane instead of a black umbrella or a fish game, which Justin cheated at anyway. Foolishly, she said so.

"What!" exclaimed Justin, and then he looked cannily at Teak. "I just bet you still haven't opened that stupid umbrella. Have you? Have you?"

"Well, stupid, it hasn't even rained yet. You don't need a stupid umbrella when it isn't raining," retorted Teak.

"You haven't opened it because you're too scared, that's why. You sure are dumb. Really dumb and a scaredy-cat. That stupid Hanka doesn't know her top from her bottom. Even my father says so." Then he called Jessie, who came rolling the carriage. She stopped to tuck Jaundice in tenderly.

Justin told Jessie, whose eyes widened with surprise. "I know what. We can help you, Teak. We'll sneak down to your room tonight and open it. Okay?"

"No, don't do that!" cried Teak. "We'll get in trouble."

"Not if we don't get caught," grinned Justin, swaggering a bit. "We're coming tonight, and you are going to open that umbrella." Both red heads nodded decisively.

Dinner that night was a grand family affair and took hours in the hotel dining room. Teak's father, who had reappeared, was the host, and he had several waiters flying this way and that with napkins over their arms. Teak, in a blue silk dress which she felt was too fancy, and the twins, also dressed to the nines, joined the grown-ups. Jessie had on a pretty smocked salmon-colored silk dress and wore patent leather Mary Janes. Justin wore the kilt, which caused the Italian waiters' eyebrows to go up, but he wore it proudly, as all Scots do. Teak had to give him credit for that. As for the grown-ups, they all wore evening clothes—-the men in tuxedos and black ties, the women in long gowns. Grandma had a small bejeweled tiara set on her white hair, and she looked very much the dowager queen.

The family sat at a big round table covered with a snow-white tablecloth. The cutlery shone, and a bouquet of flowers served as the centerpiece. All the grown-ups had three crystal glasses each. A man with a heavy chain around his neck appeared with a bottle of wine cradled in a basket and began to pour a wine to go with the first part of the meal. Teak asked to see the menu to pass the time. She counted at least eight courses, starting with antipasto, followed by soup, pasta, fish, meat, salad, dessert, fruit, and cheese. Teak was allowed to have a tablespoon of wine added to her water glass, but the twins didn't get any because Aunt Bessie thought that they were too young. That gave Teak a good feeling. Also, as the meal progressed, with the family all talking over their heads, it became evident that her table manners were infinitely superior to those of the twins! Both of them kicked their chairs, interrupted their elders several times, spoke with their mouths full, and reached for bread without asking for it. Teak was sorry that Nanny wasn't there to witness this.

Nanny did not sit with the family on these occasions. She generally ate earlier in the dining room with Teak, but sometimes she would have their dinner served in her bedroom. Then Teak would keep her company, sitting on the bed with her legs dangling, watching her iron Grandma King's dainty little pillowcases or what-have-yous until the dinner arrived. While she ironed, she would whistle little songs between her teeth. She had a little alcohol lamp on which she heated a curling iron, but sometimes, if Teak was especially good, she would take out a little pot and melt sugar and butter in it. When it was very hot, she would pour it onto a plate and let it harden into butterscotch fudge.

Eventually, come suppertime, there would be a knock at the door, and Marcantonio would roll in a cart covered with a huge silvery dome. Presto! He would lift the dome and there would be their dinner, piping hot. They would sit at the table near the window opposite each other, and Teak could hear the traffic swishing down in the street below and occasionally the clip-clop, clip-clop of the *carrozza*, the horse carriage, coming back to its position outside the hotel door. Then she would look out the window to see if the horse was having his supper, too. The driver would pull a heavy nosebag over the horse's nose and he would munch on oats. It was a nice horse called Giacomo. Teak actually enjoyed these meals with Nanny more than those with her parents, which went on for hours on end.

And this dinner was going on forever. Teak spent time counting the huge crystal chandeliers and looking at the other guests. The only amusing incident occurred when a waiter didn't pass the spinach to Jessie the second time around. So Jessie complained to her mother, and Aunt Bessie ordered the waiter to come back with more especially for Jessie. And when he bent over her shoulder and offered it to her with profuse apologies, Jessie gave him a dimpled smile and said, "No, thank you."

Most everyone seemed amused by this, but Teak thought she had been unkind and was glad when Grandma King reproached her. Teak watched the faces of her mother and father. They were not sitting beside each other, and she thought her father had a wary look.

Though the meal was taking a long time, Teak did not mind it this night. The later it was over, the less chance there was that the twins would come to her room. Maybe they would even forget all about the umbrella.

Finally, after about five courses, the children finished their pudding and were excused so that the grown-ups could, as Grandma King expressed it, "have their post-prandial coffee in peace." This would be served in little cups called *demitasses* in the lounge.

Teak bolted for the lift, but the twins caught up with her and forced the elevator boy to open the cage door for them. They made signals to Teak but she shook her head violently in denial. She got off at her floor and went straight to her room, where Nanny was waiting for her to take her bath. She dawdled in the huge bathtub, floating on her back, and Nanny kept hurrying her up, saying that it was way past her bedtime already. But she didn't want to be alone when the twins came. She couldn't lock the door. Nanny always kept the key with her because she had once locked herself in and then been unable to let herself out.

At last Nanny tucked her in and switched off the light. Teak lay listening nervously in the dark. Before long she heard the twins coming down the corridor, then pressing down the handle to the door. They pushed her out of bed and made her put her bedlamp behind the bed to keep the room dark. Then they demanded to see the umbrella. Teak wouldn't tell them where it was, but they ransacked the room and soon found it.

Justin poked it at her, and commanded, "Now you have to open it!"

"No, I don't want to and I don't have to," resisted Teak stubbornly.

"Are you dumb! What a scaredy-cat!"

"Shhh!" warned Jessie.

"I am not," said Teak.

"You are so," insisted Justin.

"Then you open it."

"It's your umbrella," whispered Jessie. "If you're not scared, prove it. It's only a black bumbershoot. I don't think it can do anything by itself, do you? How else can we find out?" So Teak took the umbrella, and Hanka's beastly brow seemed to glow in its darkness as she solemnly opened it wide and heard it click into place. The three children sat under it as if under the wings of a black bat, and their faces looked spooky in the hidden light. Jessie by now looked as scared as Teak felt.

"See," said Justin bravely, "nothing happened. I told you nothing would happen." Then he fished three sour-balls out of his dressing gown pocket and handed them out. But Teak didn't feel like candy just then, and besides hers was sticky and covered with lint. The umbrella cast an ominous shadow that she felt deep inside. She was glad to fold it up again after the twins left.

That night Teak found it hard to fall asleep, and she tossed and turned all night. She felt unworthy to go to Beejumstan. How could she look Lonesome in the eye? She had been afraid, but worse she had been a coward.

The next day was, it so happened, a day of disasters. Mother and Daddy had a terrible row, and Daddy left suddenly for Paris. Her mother was openly in tears now. Grandma tripped in her room and fell and sprained her ankle. A waiter dropped a tray full of glasses and dishes in the dining room. It made a terrible crash, and the guests screamed with fright, and the maitre d'hotel, his boss, fired him on the spot in a torrent of Italian words that sounded as if they had better not be translated.

Worst, worst of all, was a cable for Nanny from England, saying that her old mother had taken for the worse, and she should return home immediately. Nanny's eyes, too, were red, and Teak knew that she did not want her to notice that she had cried. To compensate, as she packed her bags, she kept admonishing Teak, reminding her to be a good and helpful child, to remember all the things that she had tried her best to teach her, and she rattled off the whole list without even thinking what she was saying.

Nanny left before supper, after giving Teak a hug and a pat. In the midst of all the confusions of the day, Teak was almost forgotten after that. She had no supper at all that night, and put herself to bed. She found the diary in the drawer of the table and the silver pencil from her father. She opened the diary sadly, found the date, and made her first entry:

THIS WAS A DREDFUL DAY.

As she wrote the last word, she realized that all of it must have been her fault. Hanka was right. An umbrella should never be opened in a house.

However, nothing, mind you, happened to Jessie or Justin. Nothing at all.

The next day, with a good bit of grumbling, Hanka moved into Nanny's room, taking her place. Every time she looked at Teak, she seemed to be reading her mind. And when she found the black umbrella standing beside the wardrobe, she picked it up and shook it at her. "Ha-ha!" she exulted, "now Hanka knows. Hanka knows all. Hanka knows the umbrella opened was!"

Teak decided, then and there, that she hated Hanka, she hated her cousins, and most of all she hated herself.

That night it rained. In fact it poured for the next three days.

6

Figg Newton the Alchemist

NEVERTHELESS AND NOTWITHSTANDING, in a few days, or rather nights, Teak found herself on the 7:66 to Beejumstan. Whortle was the conductor this time and, of course, did his best to insult the likes of Tucket, who couldn't even speak the King's English. But Teak knew now that he was only pretending, so she sat back to enjoy the show along with the other passengers. On this occasion, Whortle was puffing up and down the aisle. He had quite a time squeezing sideways around two young elephants, because all three of them were so big, but that didn't stop his ranting. He insisted that he himself was descended from royalty and could prove that he was sixteenth cousin twice removed of Timaeus of Taunton and therefore the girl hadn't been born worthy of his only son! No indeedy. He certainly sounded convincing.

When the train drew into the station, Lonesome was waiting for Teak. He looked sharply at the child, but all he said was, "We're looking a mite peckish, aren't we?"

Teak looked at her feet. She was still ashamed. "The best thing to do, me girl, when things go wrong is to do something right."

"But—"

"I know about the umbrella," said Lonesome quietly, "and there's something I'd like to say about it, but only if you want me to."

"Please."

Together they walked over to a bench on the station platform and sat down. The crowd dispersed, leaving the two, the girl and the rabbit, together. Lonesome began to open and shut an imaginary umbrella and started prancing about like a lady with a parasol. Teak had to giggle. "Teak," asked Lonesome, "what is an umbrella made of?"

"Mmmm...wood and wires and stuff."

"Right. Now, tell me, how can those bring bad luck?"

"I don't know," said Teak. "But they did, didn't they?"

"I...don't think so. No, Teak, they didn't. You just thought they did. That's not the same. You believed what that woman Hanka said. That, me girl, was a superstition. Not a real cause and effect. There are lots of superstitions in your world, some even involving—um," and Lonesome looked at his paws, "the feet of my relatives. The important thing for you to remember is that *you* create *your* own reality. Everyone does. You created the powers of the umbrella in your own mind. Those other things that happened would have happened anyway, most likely, but that woman, for some reasons of her own, was set on making you feel guilty, and she succeeded." Now Lonesome pointed the imaginary umbrella straight at Teak.

"But—"

"If she had told you that if you touch a hot stove, you would get burned, that would have been true cause and effect. Or that if you hate people, you will lose the gifts they may reveal to you—things about yourself that you might need to know. *That* would have been true. But to blame that poor umbrella for all those other things is just plain—"

"Dumb," finished Teak.

Lonesome grinned his approval. "Sometimes it's very smart to know when you are dumb. And sometimes it can be dumb to try to be too smart. I know someone who could tell you a lot about that."

"Who?" asked Teak, still trying to unscramble Lonesome's love of opposites.

"A wonderful fellow called Figg Newton."

"Isn't he one of those scientists you mentioned?"

"Yup," smiled Lonesome, "only in your world they would probably call him an alchemist."

"What's the difference?"

"Well, that's hard to answer, but you might say a scientist studies to find out more about the world outside of him, while the alchemist studies the outer world to find out more about the world inside."

They set off on a walk into the country. Teak tried valiantly to fall in step with Lonesome, but it was exceedingly difficult because of the hops. "Figg Newton," Lonesome continued, "began as a scientist, and he discovered pithium."

"What is pithium?"

"Well, now, I don't rightly know myself, being a rabbit and all, but it has to do with putting atoms together rather than splitting them apart. It's something your world hasn't even started worrying about yet, but they will. They will, indeed."

"But what's an atom?"

"I haven't a clue. I never saw one and I wouldn't know what to do with one if I did. The only thing that I really consider myself an expert on is carrots. Are you interested in carrots?"

"Oh, yes," replied Teak, "carrots are pretty good, but I think I might be more interested in atoms. I really think that I'm interested in lots and lots of things. In fact, when I grow up, I expect to know all about the whole wide world! I know a lot already for a person my age—I think." Teak was puffing herself up a little as they turned in the gate of a charming little garden filled with hollyhocks, blue delphiniums, and red and white roses. The roses trimmed a tiny little cottage with a red door.

"I wouldn't say that if I were you!" warned a voice that came from a bed of tall lilies.

Teak looked hard but she couldn't see anybody. And then she saw the bright green backside of an Elbedridge, who was bent over and digging with a small spade. It was Figg Newton himself.

When he stood up, he was still so short that Teak had to bend over to shake his hand, and as she did so, she noticed one peculiar feature she had seen on no other Elbedridge. Figg Newton had an extraordinarily long nose. Not like Pinocchio's, for this one was fully six inches long and turned up at the end. It soared over his trim white beard like a pink cannon. Teak had never seen a nose like it before, and she tried hard not to stare at it because Nanny had taught her that staring was a most impolite thing to do. But Figg Newton tapped it sagely and twinkled at Teak and repeated, "I wouldn't say that if I were you, or you might end up having a nose as long as mine! Come in, lass, and I'll put the kettle on the hob, and we'll have a nice cup of muddleberry tea. Then I can explain to you why I say that."

"Please yes, sir," said Teak, and she followed Figg Newton into the wee house. She had to stoop to enter the door. Lonesome stopped to nibble a little fresh clover growing by the garden fence and said he would join them later. As Figg Newton led the way, Teak noticed that his green suit was worn and frayed and he walked somewhat stooped over and with a gimp. There was a wispy look about him.

Once inside the house, they passed a hat rack made of antlers with several small red caps hanging on it. "Let me show you my library first," said Newton, opening a door on the left. "We have to pass through here."

The room they first entered was a room of marvels. There were bottles galore and retorts, scales big and little, canisters large and small, and rows and rows of apothecary jars with dusty labels and mysterious symbols on them. A large circle with twelve divisions, sort of a pie ornamented by animals, was painted on the ceiling. "That? Oh, that's a zodiac," he said. There were dusty charts with triangles and circles and squares hanging on the walls, and one, Teak, having been in Greece, recognized was written in Greek. "That? That's the Emerald Tablet of Hermes." It sounded wonderful, but Teak couldn't read a word of it. Old leathery tomes with what Teak thought were Arabic letters on them were piled on top of Latin and Greek ones. A cabinet on the wall bulged with rolled scrolls or parchment. There was a tile oven in the corner and beside it a table with calipers, tongs, and compasses. The windows were of bottle glass and let in a wavering green light. Various insect cocoons hung in the corners, eyed by a stuffed lizard on top of a cupboard. The smells were most exotic: part garlic, part turpentine, mixed with beeswax, rose oil, and rotten egg. Quite a lot of rotten egg. "Everything proven was once just imagined," whispered Figg Newton to Teak. The girl just stood there noticing and noticing, but the Elbedridge was trying to hurry her along. "Come, come, lass," he laughed. "This is my laboratory, not my library. Alchemy, which is my profession, means doing things, not just reading about them. It's not enough to know something. You have to be able to understand what what you know means, and then you have to do something with it after that. But, of course, it helps if half of what you know is based on facts." Here Figg Newton spoke with a good deal of emphasis.

"Your Nanny, for instance, is practicing a kind of alchemy."

"Nanny?" exclaimed Teak.

"Oh yes. She takes butter?" Teak nodded.

"Sugar: and then what?"

"She mixes 'em in a pot."

"That's all?"

"No, she does it over a little burner."

"Is it hot?"

"Very."

"And do the butter and sugar look different then?"

"Yes, and when she pours it onto the plate it's gooey and sticky, but then it gets hard and cold and yummy."

"Exactly," said Figg Newton. "You have proved my point. Your Nanny is an alchemist but she just doesn't know that."

"Should I tell her?" asked Teak, hoping she would get the chance.

"Not necessary, really." The old Elbedridge began to count on his fingers, muttering: "Mixing, heating, cooling, that's *dissolutio, oxidatio,* hmm, *congelatio*... That's three separate processes. She turns *theoria* into *praxis.*"

"No," interrupted Teak. "It's fudge. Butterscotch fudge, and it's yummy."

"Don't know what to do with yummy. Hasn't come up in my experiments," said Figg Newton. He fished among his parchments and wrote down the word—YUMMY. "Perhaps its origin is Tibetan?"

Teak stood silent. Suddenly she felt sorry for Figg Newton. "Didn't you ever have any fudge when you were a child?" she asked.

Figg Newton looked at Teak over his glasses, confused, and answered sadly, "I never was a child."

They now came to a thick wooden door with heavy bolts on it. Figg Newton heaved a heavy sigh. "I don't go in here much anymore, but given your inclinations you will profit from seeing the library." With that he opened the door.

The house had seemed small on the outside, but Teak was beginning to notice that the rooms were bigger than the house. It was as if the inner space were flexible and stretched according to need. In any case, they now walked into a very large and long room, and she could see other rooms opening off this room in the distance. Figg Newton lit several candle sconces to the left and to the right. Now Teak could see that all the walls were covered from top to bottom with books, and there were stacks and stacks of them on the tables and floor as well. "Here in Beejumstan, I have access to all the books ever written in the world."

For Teak, owner of three books, standing there was like standing in a kind of heaven. All those books! Then, as she looked at the shelves, she saw armies of spiders crawling up and down the books. And there was the spider with the beret putting back *The Philosophy of Spinoza!* Teak assumed this was a book on spinning. Despite herself, she gave a little shudder at so many creepy crawly creatures wandering all over the books. But the alchemist waved an arm cheerfully and explained. "These are my librarians. They just love the work that they do, spinning webs and making connections. Always respect a spider. She knows exactly what she is doing when she does it, which is a lot more than either you or I can say."

With that, he closed the door and propelled Teak back through the laboratory and across the little hall to the right-hand side of the house. Here everything was in contrast. They entered a perfectly lovely room for living in. It had beautiful pictures on the walls, a spinet to play music on, flowers on the table. There were inevitably just a few more books, but each was bound beautifully in fine leather and tooled with gold. Lonesome was already curled up having a rabbitnap in an armchair.

"Only poetry books allowed in here," smiled Figg Newton, limping through the cozy kitchen, which was filled with sunlight and potted herbs. He filled a kettle and put it on the small iron stove, which needed only a fagot or two to heat up again, then reached up for a canister labeled MUDDLEBERRY TEA.

As soon as the tea had "muddled," and they were sipping away at it, Teak asked, "What's a fact?"

"Well, a fact," answered Figg Newton, well pleased by the question and slurping quite loudly because the tea was so hot, "a fact is a little piece of knowledge or evidence that is absolutely useless until you connect it to something else. Then it acquires a meaning. For instance:

"15,010 barbarians wore bedsocks last Tuesday.

"It was precisely 7:06 A.M.

"The president has a pimple on his nose.

"By themselves these may be true statistics or facts, but they are quite useless. The world is full of them, and when you go to school you will learn a lot of them, and they will pile up like buttons in your head and rattle around for years until you need a particular button. It's what they *mean* that counts."

"You mean because the barbarians had cold feet?"

"Oh, you could go in any direction with that fact," said Figg Newton, who was now well launched and off, happy to have such an attentive audience. Strangely, the soft sound of music came flooding into the cozy parlor. Figg Newton leaned back in his chair, folded his hands over his tummy, and closed his eyes as if he were debating something. Then he opened them, looked sharply at Teak, and said, "Maybe I should tell you a story. A true story."

And as Teak listened to the story the alchemist was beginning, she noticed that from time to time the pictures on the walls would fade away in their frames and others would take their place. One of the rosebuds slowly opened and shook its lovely head, and through it all Lonesome lay curled up, one ear aflop, snoring ever so gently and smiling in his sleep.

7

Figg Newton's Tale

"YES, LASS, LET ME TELL YOU the story of how I got such a long nose," Figg Newton continued, clearing his throat as he thoughtfully filled and lit his old meerschaum pipe. "It all began many, many years ago when I was but a bit older than yourself. I decided then that I wanted to be the smartest Elbedridge in all the world, to be the scholar of scholars. I knew that to accomplish this, I would have to learn everything about anything and anything about everything.

"I began by studying all the classical languages: Latin, Greek, Arabic, Sanskrit, and Hippobeejum, of course, the presumed ancient tongue of our own Hippopotaymus the Semi-mythical. For me this was the easiest part, because I had always loved different alphabets and etymology (that's the study of where words come from). Then I was ready to study the sciences systematically, subject by subject. I read book after book on mathematics, algebra, geometry, trigonometry, physics, chemistry, geography, geology, zoology, ichthyology (that's fish), peskitology (what makes people so pesky), engineering, medicine, and on and on. Pretty soon I ran into a problem. I noticed it as I was studying botany. It seemed that the more I studied flowers, the fewer flowers could I see. So I had to get a pair of spectacles in order to read more books. I read on and on in the natural sciences, and by the time I came to entomology (that's bugs), I found I couldn't see the beetles in my own garden, so I had to go out and get a second pair of spectacles, which I placed in front of the first pair. By the time I had tackled all the history, economics, and political science books, to say nothing of the biographies of famous men and women and Beejums, my nose had to grow long enough to support five or six pairs of spectacles, which, for some reason, I had to wear all at the same time, since one seemed to give me more insight through the other.

"By then I was a young man, but I was so old and laden down with information, I didn't even *know* I was a young man. Naturally, I didn't go to the fairy ring dances, because I was too busy studying sociology and anthropology, and I couldn't see the stars at night, because I was far too busy studying astronomy! And all the time that the other Elbedridges my age were out spooning under the moon, hugging and kissing, getting married and having baby Elbedridges, I was home studying the reproductive cycles of frogs and sycamore trees. I was rapidly becoming an expert at everything, Teak, but I *knew* absolutely nothing."

"How come?" Teak asked sympathetically.

"That's a good question and I'll give you the answer. It was because I experienced nothing. It was all up in my noggin," and he tapped his head, "and nothing had happened to me here." Figg Newton laid a gnarled hand over his heart.

"Well, by that time I had ten spectacles on my poor nose. It had grown long enough to support them and had big calluses where they sat. I had read most of the books, would you believe, in that library. But needless to say, I was still greedy for more books and proud of my learning. Finally I started on philosophy and stumbled onto the importance of the *meaning* of things. I was very excited, so I read on and on through all the schools and branches of philosophy, only to discover that there were many different kinds of meaning, which meant different things to different people. Up until then I was happy at having so many answers, and now I discovered that there were a hundred times more questions than there were answers—questions that no one has ever really been able to answer. I started to lose sleep. The biggest question, of course, was what is the *meaning* of life. Why do we exist? What are good and evil?"

Teak nodded thoughtfully. She knew just a little about questions herself.

"Well," continued Figg Newton, "that led me to the study of religions and my twelfth pair of spectacles. By then it took more than a quarter of an hour just to polish them all and place them on my poor patient nose. And if I got them in the wrong order or couldn't find a pair, everything looked cockeyed. I am sure that the people of

Beejumstan must have been shaking their heads over what an eccentric fellow I was. But I was oblivious of anyone but myself.

"Oh, Teak, Teak, Teak...," and here he heaved a tremendous sigh. "In the books on religions I read all about the different ways people in your world had tried to find and serve the Great One. There seemed to be so many different ways, and more often than not each one thought his way was the only right one. And then people would get into fights because all of their Teachers, their wisest individuals, had said there was only One Way. I was very confused by all this because at that time I had had no experience of how I could best serve the Great One. Then a terrible thing happened. I discovered that I was going blind."

"Oh, no!" protested Teak.

"Yes, it was so. Instead of seeing more, I had lost the sight I had been given. At the stroke of midnight I thought that my last candle was sputtering out; I could barely see it but I could still feel the flame with my hand. I had come to the end of my books. And what do you think happened next, my dear?"

He paused. "I burst into tears, and all my spectacles fogged up at once! One last flash of fog and the light went out entirely. I was all alone in the dark, sobbing my heart out. Without a doubt I knew more *about* things than any other Beejum, but I did not really understand. I had done it all by myself for myself. I had wasted the better part of my life for nothing, or so I thought, and I suppose I felt I had driven myself into this darkness so far that even the Great One would be unable to find me. I was truly lost."

Here the elderly Elbedridge shook his head at the dreadful memory, and he had to pause to light his pipe again and take a few puffs to steady himself. Teak thought she detected a tear glistening in his right eye. "What happened then?" she asked, afraid that Figg Newton would stop.

"Well, there came a knock on my door, and even though I was too miserable to answer, the door opened, and I heard Noodlenip, Gezeebius's attendant, calling my name—"

"Excuse me," interrupted Teak, "but who exactly is Gezeebius?"

"Gezeebius, my dear, is the Wise Old Man of Beejum-stan. You will surely meet him soon. Lonesome will take you to him, I'm certain. He usually lives beyond the Gates of Mystery, on top of Mount Pook, east of the Klorox Mountains. Gezeebius had and has what I had been looking for all along, only I was just too foolish to realize it."

"What was that?"

"Wisdom, my girl. But wisdom only comes when you turn facts into information and information into knowledge and knowledge"—here he tapped his head and then laid his hand on his heart—"into experience. And that means *living*. Not just everyday living, mind you, but living and paying attention, and noticing at the same time! Connecting what goes on outside you with what goes on inside you, and what goes on inside you with what goes on outside you. It sounds as simple as breathing, but you have a choice even in breathing. You can breathe without thinking, unconsciously, or you can breathe and be aware of breathing. Try it."

Teak tried it. It was true. She had never thought about breathing before. Then she thought about the outside and inside bit. She scratched her head.

The old alchemist smiled. "Do you remember your cousin Jessie asking the waiter for more spinach?"

"Yes, I do."

"Where was it?"

"In the dining room the night of my birthday."

"Well, here is a BIG question. How do you suppose Jessie, the waiter, and the dining room all got inside you, along with all your other memories?"

Teak was totally stumped. "I really haven't the faintest idea." Which is what Grandma King always said in perplexing circumstances.

"And am I right in supposing that you thought Jessie was a bit unkind to the waiter?"

Teak nodded her head. "Then you noticed and learned a tiny lesson about thoughtfulness. You made a connection between an outside event and an inside experience."

"Oh," said Teak. It was something for her to think about when she had time.

Then Figg Newton resumed his story. "Well, as I was saying, there I was, helpless, when I heard Noodlenip come in, and then I heard him call his master to come as quickly as possible. The next thing I knew, I felt Gezeebius's strong arms lifting me, and together they carried

me to the small pallet that was my bed. And there Gezeebius stood over me and took off my twelve pairs of spectacles, one by one, and smashed them to bits with his
foot. When I cried out in protest, he simply said, 'You
won't ever need those again.' And then I knew for certain
that I was blind for good!

"He had Noodlenip sweep up the bits of glass and
bathe my face and body, and Gezeebius himself made me
some hot chicken noodle soup and spooned it into me,
mouthful by mouthful. Then he told me to sleep a little
and not to speak a word until he was through. I believe I
slept for three days and nights.

"Occasionally I could feel him bathing my eyes again,
and I smelled roses. Gezeebius said it was a special oint-
ment for healing. And he stayed with me, and I knew that
he was praying. I could feel strength slowly flowing back
into me.

"I still do not understand how I deserved this, but
when another dawn approached, the light seemed to fall
gently onto my eyelids, and when the sun rose—miracle
of miracles!—I was able to sit up and *see* things for the
first time. I could really see the *Cerastium tomentosum* and
the *Gypsophilia paniculata,* and I heard Gezeebius chiding me
gently, because he read my mind. 'Why not call them
snow-in-summer and Bristol fairy flowers like the other
folk do?' So I was quick not to think that I could see a
Turdus beejuminius, and instead was thrilled to see a Beejum
robin. And when the ladybug flew in the window I waved
to her as a personal friend. Teak, that precious morning I
felt reborn to a fresh new world!

"Oh, I wanted to speak so very badly, to thank Gezeebius for the return of my sight, to ask him how he had known to come to my rescue, but he only put his finger to his lips and told me that there is a saying that when the pupil is ready, the master appears. Then he said, shaking his head with that long, white beard, 'Figg, my friend, you will have to remain silent for six full days and nights. During that time you are not to touch another book. On the seventh day, if you are strong enough, meet me on the top of Criss-Cross Hill and we can talk further.'"

"And were you well enough?" asked Teak.

"Yes, I was, though still quite shaky about the knees, and my head felt light without those twelve pairs of specs. For one thing, some of my neighbors, whom I hadn't noticed in years, came trooping into my house carrying good things to eat like my dear neighbors made for me when I was a boy, such things as raisin flummocks and Whipadiddle Pie. Oh, how good that Whipadiddle Pie was! I had forgotten, I had forgotten!" At this point the old alchemist had to wipe his eyes in earnest on a large hanky he pulled out of his pocket. "All this helped to repumpitate me. Speaking of repumpitation, let me pour you another cup of muddleberry tea, and here—do have an Ob Long with it. These are now the official crackers of Beejumstan. Just out. And I hear that you had something to do with them!"

And to Teak's amazement, he opened a tin box on the table by his chair and produced some oblong biscuits, each clearly stamped with the Official Seal. Teak tried one. It was delicious.

"As I was saying, kind folk came to help me. Some Bunnywidgets cleaned out the house and put away all those books, and the spiders volunteered to catalog them so others could use them. Neighbors brought me flowers and fruits, and best of all some of them came singing and playing beautiful music. I had studied musicology, but I hadn't heard any music in twenty years!

"It was very hard to receive so much and not be able to speak my thanks, but I did keep my promise. On the seventh day, a most beautiful young lady Elbedridge, Lissabelle Ann, appeared with her donkey, Mimosa. She came to be a very special friend to me."

"Who? Lissabelle Ann or the donkey?" asked Teak.

Figg Newton blushed. "I came to marry Lissabelle Ann, bless her, and we kept Mimosa until Gezeebius needed her. But that happened much later. That morning Lissabelle Ann insisted that I ride Mimosa while she walked lightly at our side.

"We traveled across the emerald green countryside that I had forgotten all about because I hadn't seen it since I had begun my study of topography. But now I could see it all, and the beauty of the trees and the flashing waters of the Wendward River. We stopped on the bridge and looked down and waved at the fishfolk. And, strange as it may seem, I saw everything in a deeper way because I did know a little something about what I was seeing. My eyes began to fill with tears again and I apologized to Lissabelle Ann, and I'll always remember her response. 'Figgy'—she still calls me Figgy—'tears wash the eyes so that they can see better.'

"The greatest book ever written was slowly opening itself to me—the book of nature. Truly, it was as if the Great One had said to me, 'Your reward for seeking the truth that hard is that I can reveal to you how beautiful the world is.' I had had eyes, of course, but I couldn't really see. The truth and mystery are never hidden, my dear, it is we who are too blind to see them. It's that simple. It is a great privilege to know this when you are blind. Suddenly those things I had always considered obvious began to glow almost from within.

"Everything was opening its secrets to me in silence, without a word. Everything shone in my heart now instead of my head. The more I appreciated, the more I could see. It was a whole new way of learning, by listening to silence. What an extraordinary long journey it took for me to get from my first book to this new lesson! You see, Teak, it's not that it was wrong to study. My mistake was that I had gobbled and gobbled up all that knowledge without ever using it for the good of someone else. It's really only when you can explain something to someone else that you know that you know it. So you keep what you give away! And I was still a long way from my life's work, alchemy and the discovery of pithium.

"Finally we reached the top of Criss-Cross Hill, where all Beejums go to get married. And we sat down there and ate some egg sandwiches Lissabelle Ann had made, while Mimosa croppled some grass. The sky was bright blue and everything sparkled, especially the eyes of Lissabelle Ann. I had never noticed a young lady Elbedridge before, but she was the prettiest one in all the land. I still swear it to this day. Of course, today her hair is as white as mine, but she's still my lovely Lissabelle Ann. You will have to meet her, Teak. Right now, she's off on a visit to her Aunt Minnie."

Figg Newton continued his tale. "Pretty soon, Lissabelle pointed to a small cloud headed our way. The minute I saw it, I realized it had to be Gezeebius on his *Cloud of Unknowing*. This is the way Gezeebius gets around Beejumstan. Sure enough, there he was sitting in the middle of it, and we could see Noodlenip in his bright red pixie suit waving.

"The cloud floated over the meadow, Noodlenip dropped anchor, let down the ladder, scrambled down it, and pulled the cloud down like a big balloon so Gezeebius could climb out.

"Lissabelle Ann and Noodlenip decided to go for a stroll together, and Gezeebius came over and sat down on a rock beside me. He had washed his white beard and it glistened and flowed majestically all the way down to his big toe.

"'Hello, friend Figg,' he greeted me. 'How are you feeling today? You look much, much better.' And I spoke and told him I was. Then I noticed that he carried a small metal box in his hand. It was cube-shaped and looked as if it were made of lead."

"And was it?" asked Teak.

"Aye, indeed, so it was. And then Gezeebius told me in quite a simple and straightforward manner that all I had been searching for was in this box."

"What was in it?" begged Teak.

"Why, a most surprising thing, dearie, a most surprising thing. Wrapped up in cotton wool it was, too."

"Was it alive?"

Figg Newton laughed. "In a way no, and in a way yes. Perhaps you should decide for yourself. Would you like to have a look at it?"

"Oh yes, please!" cried Teak, most excitedly.

"Well, come along then," said the Elbedridge. He rose from his chair with a bit of a creak and slowly led the girl down the center hall to a door at the end. There he carefully removed his red shoes and suggested that Teak do the same. They put the shoes side by side. Teak was quite surprised at how much bigger her own shoes were than Figg Newton's.

"This is my special place," he explained. "I come here daily to be quiet and listen."

The room was nearly empty of furnishings. There were two small cushions on the straw matting that covered the floor. There was a low round white table in the middle of the room, on which was a deep blue glass bowl with a candle in it. Against the wall facing the door hung a square of deep blue velvet, in the middle of which hung a small round mirror. Figg Newton went over and took the little mirror down very carefully and showed it to Teak. She looked at it curiously. There was a mirror on both sides. In one side you could see all of yourself, and in the other just a portion of yourself greatly magnified.

"What a strange thing!" exclaimed Teak.

"Gezeebius called it the Looking Glass of Circumstance. Tell me, what do you see in it?"

"I see myself!" cried Teak.

"AHA!" Figg Newton burst out. "That's the whole point of the gift, but I was as puzzled then as you are now. Look a little closer now, lass. Tell me, what else can you see?"

Teak turned the mirror over and over. Then she noticed some words were engraved around the rim like a big coin. It read like this or this or this as you turned it.

"Can you read it?" asked Figg Newton.

"Yes, I think so. It says: IS ALL THERE IS THE GREAT ONE THIS."

"Are you sure?" Teak turned it a little.

"IS THE GREAT ONE THIS IS ALL THERE."

"Are you sure that's all?"

"No, I'm not sure," Teak said very quietly. Then she looked harder. "I think it also says: THERE IS THE GREAT ONE THIS IS ALL."

Figg Newton put his hand on Teak's arm. "If you can remember those words, maybe you will not make the same mistake I did and you won't waste so many years. After contemplating the mystery of this mirror for many years I have come to see that all those Teachers were right, in that there *is* only one way. But the key is that they had found it *within themselves!* Teak, all human beings are alike in what they are given inside. The 'way' the different religions talked about answers the question 'How?' not 'Where?' or 'What?' and the 'hows' are all the same. This is what the Teachers meant. They meant there was only one way how. It's the 'wheres' and 'whats' that are all different. Which makes life far more interesting. People in your world have been killing each other thinking there are different 'hows,' when there is only one, instead of respecting the different 'wheres' and 'whats,' which are only forms the Great One plays hide-and-seek in."

"But what does the mirror mean?" persisted Teak.

"That is a question no one else can answer for you, my dear. When I look in the mirror, I see myself, not you. It tells me that what I am looking for is already in me. All I can do or anyone can do is what Gezeebius did for me: give you back to yourself. Look again in the mirror, turn it about."

Teak held the mirror and as she moved it here and there, it reflected everything around her.

"Tell me, can the mirror see or get upset at what it sees?" asked Figg Newton.

"No, I don't think so. It shows things."

"Things as they are? Or things as they seem to you? Do you suppose we both see the same things?"

"Oh dear, that's hard." Teak thought about it, then sighed. "I guess not. You know so much more about what you are seeing."

Figg Newton cocked his head and looked at Teak. "It's a little like being one and many at the same time, isn't it! As if everything in the world reflects everything else. There really are no limits, only obstacles...Well, enough of that—take one last look and tell me what you see."

So Teak looked in the mirror once more and saw her face caught in the act of wondering.

"Remember this, do not forget," whispered the old alchemist.

They walked back to the little parlor, where they found Lonesome awake and amazed at the length of his nap. He coughed a bit apologetically and said it was way past his carrot-time and time to leave. So the girl and the rabbit said good-bye. But as they were going out the door, Figg Newton rushed into his laboratory and came out with a little white stone.

"This is a *calculus alba*, Teak. I would like you to have it as a memento of this day."

When Teak got up the next morning in the hotel and was dressing for breakfast, with Hanka growling around the room, she saw a little white pebble lying by her bed. It was surely the one Figg Newton had given her—or was it one she had picked up in the Giardini Borghese? Was she really learning to live in two worlds at once? Thoughtfully, she took up the little stone, carried it over to her spy bag, and dropped it in. She tried to remember what Figg Newton had called it, but she couldn't.

But many, many years later, like so many things she learned in Beejumstan, it came back to her. The wee white stone seemed to be showing that the two worlds were really One.

8

Teak's Experiment

HANKA WAS UNLIKE ANY WOMAN Teak had ever met. Compared to her, Nanny had been like a nice warm loaf of bread. Hanka seemed to live in a dark and sour interior world full of bitterness, fears, witches, and old wives' tales. A hardy peasant woman, she had come from the Balkans with a British diplomatic family, where she had picked up the rudiments of English, but then had lost her job, yet had been fortunate enough to find employment as a maid at the Hotel Flora. Now Teak's parents had temporarily employed her to fill in for Nanny.

Jessie and Justin called her the gorilla because of her dark hairy arms and legs and the fact that her black eyebrows met thickly over her nose—none of which, of course, was her fault. Wherever she walked, she marched with a heavy step—tromp, tromp, tromp—and everything would rattle around her. Justin loved to imitate her behind her back. She also muttered to herself a good deal in her native tongue.

Her one distraction in life was embroidery, and Teak marveled to see the delicate stitches and exquisite designs that those coarse, heavy hands could produce on the sheerest of linens and lawn handkerchiefs. Hanka was also truly devoted to her grandmother, so she knew that she couldn't be all bad.

Jessie and Justin loved to get her to tell stories of witches and vampires, of spooky forests, and the terrible events she swore had taken place in the village in the mountains where she had grown up. Even in her broken English, she managed to describe werewolves with flashing eyes, kidnapped babies, changelings, devils and demons, curses carried out by venomous serpents. The twins laughed at it all, but there were two of them to dispel each other's fears at night. Teak was all alone, and Hanka filled her with guilt and foreboding. If Beejumstan seemed to be a happy place, this everyday world in Rome made her feel anxious and insecure.

Mother looked pale and drawn, and Teak only saw her once a day. She seemed so sad. Teak wondered what her father could have done to upset her so. Maybe he wasn't as nice as Teak thought he was. Or maybe it was Teak's fault, so she worried about that.

Grandma King carried a cane now and, despite her ankle, was actively sponsoring a project involving other American ladies in Rome. It was a ball to be held at the Embassy, which Teak knew was a dance with music where everyone dressed up in fancy clothes. Ambassadors, ministers of state, consuls, and all their wives were invited, and there would be several princes, counts, and famous actresses. So Grandma King was very busy and had little time for Teak. Both her father and Uncle Amyas were away, and Aunt Bessie divided her time between the twins and helping Grandma King. And no one had heard anything further from Nanny—not even a word.

Teak ate all her meals now with Hanka. They ate in a special section of the dining room, ahead of the other guests, with a few other children and their nurses or governesses. Sometimes she was grateful for this, because Hanka's table manners were atrocious. She put her elbows on the table, chewed with her mouth open, and spooned her soup the wrong way and slurped. Once she even licked her knife clean of butter. Nanny would have had a fit! The other children were either babies or tiny, whining tots, and Teak felt humiliated being lumped in with them. In addition, she had entirely lost her appetite and felt revolted by even the sight of food. Hanka would then tell her in agonizing detail of poor children starving in India, of how their little ribs stuck out before they died for lack of food. And look at all that she had! If shame didn't do the trick, Hanka would try bribery, smiling a gap-toothed smile. She would even try feeding Teak herself, picking up the fork and saying, "Here's vun for the Mama!" as if she were a baby. At this Teak would run from the table.

Hanka had also hinted, little knowing the havoc she was creating in Teak's digestive system, that where she came from snakes were known to bite children who didn't go to the bathroom properly. Now Teak was afraid to go. She began to look sickly and even to lose weight. Her own ribs were beginning to stick out. But Jessie and Justin looked stronger and healthier all the time. How they would have laughed at Teak for believing a stupid old snake story!

So Teak was unhappy. She was all tangled up in the nets of guilt and hate. They sat like two black witches on her heart. Of course she knew that, as Lonesome had said, she didn't *have* to believe the things Hanka said. Nobody else did. But—

A few days later Teak's mother was smiling radiantly as she returned from shopping carrying a bouquet of tulips and white carnations she had bought on the steps of the Piazza d'Espagna. She gave Teak a quick kiss and told her that her father would soon return and would be taking her to the Embassy ball. And he had given her the most beautiful new gown to wear that he had bought in Paris. Still smiling, she peered into Teak's face and noticed a single freckle on her nose. "Well, what do you know, Phineas really is back!" That was the name of the freckle which disappeared in the winter and returned in the late spring. Teak was glad that her mother looked happier.

Hanka was given the task of taking the three children on an outing. She dressed in black and wore a triangular kerchief on her head because they were going to visit St. Peter's Basilica. The girls were sent to their rooms for berets, but Justin, being a boy, didn't need to worry about covering his head.

The cathedral was immense. Its inner cavernous space was filled with soaring twisting columns. Sunbeams slanted down, and you could see holy dust shimmering in the air. The children walked around craning their necks and looking upward; even the twins were impressed. Hanka taught them to genuflect and to cross themselves, and she dabbed a bit of holy water on their foreheads. They walked from one statue to another and inspected the stands of little flickering votive candles. The air smelled faintly of incense. There were many, many people, worshipers and tourists. Teak had hoped that the Pope would be there, but he wasn't. For once, the children were all good and quiet. The wide-eyed twins talked in whispers and almost walked tiptoe across the massive marble floor. When it was time to leave, Hanka held each of them up to kiss the toe of St. Peter's statue. It was a tradition for good luck and guaranteed your safe return. Teak noticed the toe was almost worn away.

They had lunch at a *trattoria* and even had lemon ices sitting outside on metal chairs. Then they went back to the Hotel Flora for "quiet hour." After that, Hanka took them out to the park again. Hanka enjoyed the park, because there she could sit on the bench in the sunshine with some of the other nannies and nursemaids. Here she would try to talk with them and here, too, was a ready-made audience for her tales of the macabre.

Jessie went off with Jaundice, the doll, in the new doll carriage. Justin had brought a new red scooter and a pair of roller skates his parents had brought over from Boston. The children were to share these. No one in Rome, it seemed, had ever seen roller skates before. They were the heavy metal ones with clamps you tightened onto your shoe soles with a special key.

Justin rode the scooter first, while Teak started with the skates, wobbling a bit. Pretty soon Justin wanted to trade. "No," said Teak, who was just beginning to get the hang of skating.

"Oh, come *on*, Teak," wheedled Justin.

Teak continued to refuse until it looked as if Justin would start to fight for the skates, and then she gave in. Justin probably thought this was due to his powers of persuasion, but Teak knew that if she gave in at just the right moment it would guarantee her a longer time with the scooter.

"Thanks," said Justin gruffly before sitting down to fasten the skates to his feet with little pants of satisfaction. Soon he sped off noisily past an amazed and admiring group of nannies and passers-by.

Teak now had the scooter all to herself and was able to pump up and down in peace. Soon she was off in her own world of thought again. She wondered if anything ever happened twice exactly the same way. For instance, could it happen that the fat man in the black suit over there who was blowing his nose would put his handkerchief back in his pocket and do it all over again, and at the same time that the Italian woman watching the pigeons would scratch her leg again? Could one ask the horses and carriages, and cars and birds, and the clouds and the waves in the sea, all to repeat themselves simultaneously?

Teak thought not. It was not in her power or anybody's power. Maybe not even God's. God never seemed to do anything the same twice. So what happened to a moment in time when it was gone? Where did it go? Teak was stunned by this insight. Mercy! as her grandmother was fond of exclaiming. She wished she had thought of asking Figg Newton.

She now took the scooter to a spot where one path crossed another between two hedges. Then she looked left and right at everyone and everything, noticing, and missing nothing. Then she took a deep breath and pushed the scooter across that path. There! That moment had passed. Gone forever and ever! So what was time? You couldn't catch it or hold it—whatever it was.

She shook her head in wonder. Then she pumped the scooter past the place where Hanka was sitting and regaling her colleagues. "Absolutely true! I svear!" Teak heard her saying. "It happened in my own village. The hair, you see, it grows on the dead. They cut the hair and shave the beard of old uncle to bury. No? Two veeks," and she made appropriate gestures with her hands, "digs up again the box. Hair grow and also beard! Even nails of fingers."

There were gasps of astonishment and disbelief from the other nurses. One was frantically rocking a pram, paying no attention at all to the baby inside. Teak thought it looked seasick.

"True! Absolute true!"

That evening, up in their room, Teak told the twins what she had heard Hanka saying. "Do you believe it?" she asked them.

"No!" laughed Justin. "That's just more gorilla talk."

"How could you find out?" pondered Jessie.

"Simple," he said to his sister. "Just find something dead and cut off its hair!"

"But how do you know if something's dead?" persisted Jessie.

"Well, it's just not alive, stupid."

There seemed to be a kind of logic to that, thought Teak. Maybe some sort of experiment was called for to prove once and for all that Hanka was lying all the time. In a way she hoped that she was.

Just then Teak noticed Jaundice lying on Jessie's bed. Jaundice, being a doll, was certainly not alive, so, perhaps she was sort of dead, or at least the nearest thing to dead that was available with hair on its head. Teak decided to try the experiment on her. While the twins were out of their bedroom saying goodnight to their mother, Teak found a pair of scissors. It took her only a few seconds to cut off all of Jaundice's yellow hair. The doll now looked yellower than ever. In fact, she looked an absolute fright. Teak almost hoped that her hair would grow back for Jessie's sake. She did seem fond of the ugly thing.

Satisfied now, Teak threw the doll's hair in the waste-paper basket, but then she thought it might be wiser to keep it in case it could be stuck back on again. So she retrieved it and ran down the stairs to her own room, where she hid the hair in one of her handkerchiefs and stuffed it at the back of one of the drawers of the night table. She sure wondered how long it would take Jaundice to grow another head of hair.

Teak was almost asleep when she heard the uproar coming down the corridor. Hanka threw open the door and blazed on the light. Jessie stood behind her in her nightgown screaming at the top of her lungs, with tears

pouring down her cheeks. Justin stood there in his pajamas with a triumphant grin on his face pointing his finger at Teak.

"She did it, all right. She did it, Hanka! Tell 'em about
it, Teak!"

Teak was speechless. She sat up in bed wide-eyed.
Doors down the hall were opening, and the hotel guests
were wondering what all the unearthly commotion was
about. Even Marcantonio came running on the double
and appeared at the doorway, sent by the hotel manager
to insist upon quiet.

Jessie, suddenly in the limelight, shook her red curls
and yowled even more dramatically. "You've ruined my
baybeee!" she sobbed, and her voice trailed off piteously.

Finally Teak found her voice and spoke up. "Don't cry
like that, Jessie! It will grow back again. You know it will.
Ask Hanka!"

"*Vat?*" screamed Hanka.

Teak got out of bed and tried to comfort Jessie. "You
said so yourself, Hanka. This afternoon in the Giardini.
You did, you did! Tell Jessie the truth!"

"Vat I say?"

"You said that hair grows on dead people! I heard you,
I know I heard you!"

"Is true," admitted Hanka, to the consternation of
several guests who had gathered there. "Is true on dead—
but not on *dollies!*" She looked anxiously this way and that
fearing Teak's mother might be on her way, but she was
out to dinner that night. "Teak," shouted Hanka, "you
are crazy girl. You vait! Hanka spank sense into you!"

The twins were ordered roughly back to their room, while the guests shook their heads at the spectacle of the poor trembling girl and this barbarian of a nurse.

Hanka spanked her as promised, but somehow that wasn't as bad as the memory of Jessie's grief-stricken face. The whole experiment had been a failure.

9

Kidnapped!

TEAK'S LIFE HAD BEEN in such a chaos that she could hardly wait for her next visit to Beejumstan, which for her had now become a place of refuge, of green pastures, wisdom, beauty, and peace. Therefore it came as a big shock when she jumped lightly off the 6:67 and found everything in an uproar.

Precisely half of the Beejums Teak saw had fallen sound asleep. Whortle, the plump conductor, had just blown his whistle, but as soon as the train stopped he slowly sank to his knees and curled up right there on the platform, snoring happily. Every other Bunnywidget was sleeping, and so was every other Elbedridge. They had all slumped down wherever they happened to be; most were cheerfully snoring, whistling, twitching, making little sleepy noises, and dreaming away. Those who were awake, however, were in a dither and a clamor and a squawking.

Some husbands it seemed wouldn't or couldn't get out of bed, while in other households it was the wives. The

95

Omnibustle driver was awake, fortunately, but in Poppal-opolis storekeepers slept on their counters, and half the customers, depending on their size, were curled up in potato bins, behind brooms, or even in sinks. A mouse baby in a bonnet was fast asleep in a jar of peppermint jellies. Every other hen, duck, and swan had its head tucked under its wing, as did Oscar the ostrich barber, in his chair by the big window, and some freshly hatched little chickabiddees were peeping away and crying, "Mummy, mummy, please wake up! I'm hungry!"

Miss Penelope Tnurk, the lady goat schoolteacher, had dropped her pince-nez down her long nose and had her head on a stack of copybooks right on her desk, and half the students were napping on their slates, while the others were having a high old time shooting rubber bands and jumping from desk to desk with glee. Some little rac-coons, dressed in their cub scout uniforms, were playing catch with Miss Tnurk's globe, and half of those naughty squirrels were playing trapeze from the rafters of the schoolhouse or throwing the wet blackboard sponge at the ceiling and making what they thought very pretty pat-terns. And one of them had taken advantage of the opportunity to stick the braid of a sleeping Bunnywidget girl in her inkwell. In town, a mischievous and musical young girl orangutan was playing "Pop Goes the Weasel" on the church bells of St. Ninnius Cathedral.

It was rumored that Rhubarb the Terrible, the current Pompompity (or leader) of Beejumstan, successor to the twin lobsters, Humidor and Thermidor, was so sound asleep in his bathtub that even tickling had been of no use. Worst calamity of all, it was hinted that Gezeebius had floated off on his *Cloud of Unknowing* and Noodlenip could not locate him. "He must be off visiting another Bubble," explained a passerby, a shivering zebra. "And I never thought to bring my bumbershoot today."

Teak could understand nothing that was going on nor anything that those who were awake were shouting and screaming at each other, because in Beejumstan, to use one of Grandma King's favorite expressions, pandemonium reigned. No sooner had this phrase entered her mind than the heavens opened and a cloudburst fell. Only instead of the rain coming down decently in drops, it all came down at once, about five inches of it, in a tremendous SPLAT!

"That'll teach 'em! Whoooey!" screeched a high eldritch voice up in the whirling sky. This was answered by a long thin sirenlike wail that ended in a torrent of cackling. Teak looked anxiously and in vain for her friend Lonesome. The girl was soon soaked to the skin. A flood was already swirling madly through all the streets and roads of Beejumstan carrying along bug and beast and Bunnywidget alike. Yet even this failed to waken any of the sleepers, who more than likely were simply dreaming they had wet their beds.

Up on a rooftop stood General Principles trying to restore order. He was shouting orders and waving his sword. "Every Beejum to his post! This is a national emergency! Do or die! EXCELSIOR!" But not a soul was paying him any attention. Even his dear ladylove, the ballerina Popova, was sound asleep in his other arm. She was still wearing her toe shoes with the scarlet ribbons, and her tutu was soaked and dripping like a fountain.

At last Teak spotted a familiar rabbit. Lonesome was standing under a green awning putting on a bright red slicker and a fireman's hat. He was obviously hurrying to dress appropriately for the occasion. "Lonesome!" Teak shouted. "Over here! Over here! Hurry!"

Lonesome reached her in several astounding leaps. "This *is* a to-do," he sputtered. "Those two must be at it again."

"WHO?" shouted Teak, trying to make herself heard over a fierce wind that had suddenly come up. "WHAT is going on? WHERE is Gezeebius?"

Lonesome had lost control of his ears, which were blowing in circles over his head, his hat notwithstanding. "They say he's off in another Bubble," he shouted. "It's not usually this bad, though." Now it was beginning to thunder, and lightning forked fiercely over the dark sky, but all sleepers merely turned over and slept some more. "No," continued Lonesome, lowering his voice, "this looks like the work of Rudintruda and Idy Fix."

Teak desperately wanted to know what was happening to Beejumstan and how Gezeebius could go to another Bubble, but there was too much confusion and chaos for any hope of getting an explanation from Lonesome now.

Lonesome produced a pair of Waterloos, rubber boots that were just his size, one out of each pocket of his slicker. He tried to balance himself on one foot sufficiently to pull on a Waterloo. This was exceedingly difficult in the wind, and he had to take little hops to keep from falling. Then a big gust of wind forced him to take a big hop into the middle of the street to avoid plopping into the water streaming in the gutter. Somehow he managed to pull on the first Waterloo while he was in the air. The rain was pelting down again, though now, mercifully, it came in drops. Lonesome hopped back onto the sidewalk and pushed Teak ahead of him until they were standing under the awning of the Beejum Bakery. Through the shop window they could see the baker sound asleep with his head on the counter and his cat curled up asleep in a bowl full of dough. A very much awake young mouse was scampering around, making tracks in the flour on the counter, stopping occasionally to blow muddleberries in the cat's direction.

"But will Gezeebius come back?" Teak finally managed to ask. "I haven't even met him yet."

Lonesome was now quickly pulling on his other Waterloo. "He always has so far, but no one ever knows for sure. And that's what Rudintruda and Idy Fix are always counting on."

"Who are they?"

"*Shhhh!*" warned Lonesome, looking left and right. Then he cupped his paws around Teak's ear and whispered, "They are two of the nastiest, meanest witches anywhere ever. Rudintruda's the one who is doing all these weatherworks. Idy Fix's specialty is spells. That's why half the population is beebize, sound asleep. Poof! Gone! Sometimes, like today, the two work together. They team up and then it's a major catastrophe. When Gezeebius is around, they don't dare show their ugly faces. They stay hidden in the Worry Woods in the Klorox Mountains and carry on with their knitting. Their specialty is hair socks. Look like normal knitted socks on the outside but the inside is full of prickly, itchy goat hair. They sometimes go in disguise to the gnat market and sell them to unsuspecting people looking for a bargain. They live with their old hag of a mother called Smelly Stinka. She never goes anywhere anymore, but I've heard she's a whiz at potions and poisons and goo. Cooks 'em up in a huge black cauldron. Imagine rotten eggs and tomatoes bottled with—"

In spite of her confusion, Teak started to giggle as she thought of quite a few suggestions to add to the list. She couldn't help thinking how Hanka would fit into that family. But a sudden loud thunderbolt brought her back to the seriousness of the plight of Beejumstan. "What can we do? Can we help at all, Lonesome?"

"Shhh!" warned Lonesome again. "First we'll have to get you outfitted. Come on, let's nip in here and borrow a few things." So saying, Lonesome took Teak's hand in his paw and led her into the bakery. On a coatrack he found a yellow slicker and fisherman's hat. Magically, in the pockets there was also a pair of handsome Waterloos just Teak's size. She put them on gratefully. The baker never moved; the cat opened and closed her eyes and purred, which temporarily halted the mouse's mischief.

Now dressed for any weather, the girl and the rabbit warily went out the shop door and walked out onto the street. "Shhh! They might hear us," whispered Lonesome.

"The witches?" whispered Teak in turn.

But it was too late. Suddenly from above, out of no-where, a large net dropped over the two of them, and with a burst of fiendish laughter the two witches zoomed down on their brooms. With horrible screeches and cacklings, they picked up the net containing the trapped Teak and Lonesome. Then, carrying the net between their brooms, they flew off at top speed, dodging bolts of lightning.

10

Teak in Hot Water

Teak woke up. Momentarily disoriented, she shook her head, not knowing which nightmare was worse as she began to remember the awful problem of Jessie and Jaundice. The experiment wasn't supposed to turn out that way. She got out of bed and shivered as she stepped barefoot onto the cold bathroom floor. Somehow she had to make amends.

The solution was suddenly obvious. All she needed was to find a piece of pretty material to make a head scarf to cover Jaundice's indignity. One of those triangles like Hanka's that you tied under the chin. Mother would be sure to have something.

After breakfast, Teak hurried to her mother's room, knocked on the door, and opened it, but she was not there. In desperation, Teak began opening her drawers one after the other. On the third try, she found exactly what she was looking for wrapped up in tissue paper in an open glossy box with *La Mouette* in fancy letters on the side. In fact, it was perfect. Jessie would love it! It was some pretty soft material, black with pink roses on it. It would make Jaundice look better than new.

She found her mother's nail scissors in the top drawer. They were curved, which made cutting a little difficult, but with determination, she was able to cut out a fairly large rough triangle of the material. When she held it up, it looked almost scalloped. Maybe Jessie would think that was even prettier. Teak then replaced everything and refolded the material carefully in the tissue paper. She hadn't taken much. Her mother would probably never miss it. Then she ran quickly to the twins' room.

They must have been having breakfast with their mother because they were not there either. It was a simple matter to tie the material around Jaundice's shorn head. Teak looked at her with satisfaction, greatly relieved. The doll looked just like some of the girls she had seen entering St. Peter's. Jessie would surely be pleased.

Jessie was indeed mollified, and the doll was seated back in her carriage, ready for the next outing in the park. Nobody knew where the scarf had really come from. The children thought it was from Hanka, and Hanka thought Aunt Bessie had provided it.

It rained all day, and Hanka was instructed to take the children to a museum. Teak didn't take the umbrella. At the museum they looked at a lot of statues of strong men and ladies without any clothes on. Many of them lacked an arm or half a leg or even had the face bashed in. Teak wondered why they didn't have more whole ones. Some of the men statues, however, had a leaf stuck on them where their legs began. Why on earth, wondered Teak, would a man wear a leaf *there?* It would drop off the minute he took a step! She decided the ancient Greeks and Romans couldn't have had a whit of sense.

They came back to a fine surprise for Teak. Her father had returned, and both he and her mother were smiling a lot. She even overheard her father say to her mother, "Birdie, you are going to be the belle of the ball tonight in your new gown!" How her mother was going to ring like a bell at the ball, Teak wasn't sure, but it sounded just lovely to her.

Teak felt cheered up for the first time in a long while. Her parents, in a fit of parental indulgence, promised to say goodnight to her before they left for the Embassy. And indeed they kept their promise.

Teak was sitting on the bed in Hanka's room, eating fried filet of sole with lemon butter on it, which Marcantonio had brought up to the room on the rolling table with the silver dome over it. Hanka was ironing the baby pillow cover she had embroidered for Grandma King, and the damp linen steaming smelled clean and nice. It reminded Teak of Nanny.

All of a sudden, the door opened and there stood Thaddeus King Jr., all decked out in his best evening clothes, the ones that made him look like a swallow. In his hand was Jaundice's cut hair. And there behind him stood her mother, dressed in the most beautiful ball gown, black crepe de chine with pink roses—only right in the middle of her lap was a huge triangular hole—spang in the middle where those fig leaves go! The expression on her parents' faces beggared description. Her mother's eyes were so full of hurt and anger that you could see the white all around their icy blue. She said not a word. But her husband roared.

"My dear, your daughter is SICK! Sick in the head! You must find a doctor for her tomorrow. Only a sick mind could conceive of such behavior. Can you imagine Jessie doing anything like this?" And with that he threw Jaundice's curls at Teak's feet, turned his back, and slammed the door.

Hanka was left to do the punishing. As she herself felt responsible that her charge had entered her mother's room and perpetrated such a crime right under her nose, so to speak, she let loose a violent multilingual tirade of rage and abuse, most of which mercifully Teak could not understand. She covered her ears with her hands. But some words burnt through like hot sparks; the words "VICKED! VICKED! VICKED!" erupted and fell over her head. Teak could feel herself condensing into a small black knot of despair. She felt unworthy of living.

Hanka grabbed her by the scruff of her neck. At first Teak thought she was going to strangle her, but instead she propelled her down the corridor, still shouting imprecations. When they got to Teak's room, Hanka almost tore the clothes off the child, yanked her into the bathroom, turned the water on in the tub, and flung her into it. Then she turned her back and stalked out, slamming the door.

It was while she was in the filling tub that Teak decided that perhaps the kindest thing she could do for everyone concerned would be to drown herself. That way, perhaps, the soul of one of those poor starving little Indian girls could come into her and have a fresh start. And maybe *she* would actually enjoy eating brussels sprouts and eggplant and all that awful stuff, and maybe *she* would be understood and appreciated by her family.

The more Teak thought about it, the more interesting the idea became to her. She wasn't too sure about the drowning part, but she knew it involved staying under water and not breathing. So without further ado, she took a deep, solemn, and dramatic last breath, and pinching her nose tightly with the fingers of her right hand, she bid the world farewell and sank beneath the waters.

Beneath the surface, Teak could hear the thundering roar of the water pouring from the tap. It sounded appropriately majestic, like the very voice of judgment. And so, as far as Teak's imagination went, she took leave and invited the soul of a good little Indian child to take over and enter her body. It was all quite simple.

With a gasp for air, the new Teak surfaced and was reborn into a new life and a new world. She looked around, amazed by what she saw! (This was the fun part.) Look at those beautiful glossy tiles on the wall! Look at the beautiful mosaic of little black and white squares inlaid on the floor! And all those fluffy clean white towels with "Hotel Flora" embroidered on them! Here Teak hastily corrected herself, because probably the Indian child would not be able to read. She now turned off the water tap and contemplated her skinny pink legs and wondered what her real name was. All of a sudden, it was wonderful to be alive again, and she thought of rediscovering Alfred Hampson, her bear, and the hidden treasures in her spy bag, all of which would be like new presents for the new girl she now was. Teak smelled the fragrant soap gratefully and began to wash her arms. And the girl could go to Beejumstan!

In all the excitement of her "rebirth," however, she had forgotten all about Hanka. The next minute, the woman thundered back into the bathroom and ordered Teak out of the tub and into a towel. "Vat take the devil's child so long?" she snorted.

"Why am I a devil's child?" asked the new Teak, truly amazed.

"Because you are evil child and vicked girl. You ruin Mama's dresses and little girl's dolls. You are such bad girl, BAD!"

Teak turned a sweet face of angelic innocence up to Hanka's baleful countenance and said, "*I never* did any such *thing!*" (The poor little Indian child would never have done anything like that. She most likely had never even laid eyes on a stupid doll way over in India.)

Hanka was taken aback by the sheer effrontery of such a statement. Hastily, she crossed herself. "You lie. Ah, you are now in the power of the Serpent, son of the Evil One!" And she hastily backed away from Teak in fear, making the sign against the Evil Eye for extra security, pressing down the two middle fingers of her right hand and pointing her index and pinkie straight at Teak.

"I am *not* lying!" Teak screamed, bursting into tears and thoroughly frightened. "I'm not, I'm not, I'm not! I never did any of those things!" And hanging on to the towel at her midriff, she tore out the door and fled screaming up the corridor on her way to Grandma King's room, again leaving a trail of opened doors and the heads of puzzled guests behind her.

Hanka had to run this gamut herself, puffing after Teak with her dressing gown, shouting, "You go to your grandmother, you just go, and see if you can lie to her! How such a saint of a woman has such vickedness in family, Hanka no know!" The various guests shook their heads in perplexity and withdrew.

Teak could run a lot faster, and when she got to Grandma King's room, she did not wait for an answer to her hurried knock, but now, naked as a jaybird, she flew through the door into the safe haven of Grandma's arms. There she huddled shivering with both cold and fright.

Hanka was so agitated that she forgot her position. She, too, burst through the door, without even a knock, and commanded Mrs. King to spank this evil and insufferable child who had just topped everything by telling an impossible lie. Grandma King drew herself up calmly and firmly, stretched out her hand for Teak's bathrobe and ordered the hysterical woman out of the room. Then she turned to her granddaughter and helped her put on her dressing gown.

"Well, it seems it's a good thing I wasn't able to go to the ball tonight," she exclaimed. "Now, Teak, you tell me why I, of all people, should spank you. You know that I am not very strong or able to spank such a big child as you are. I really don't believe in it anyway, so I am sure it would hurt me more than it would hurt you." She looked so sad and worried about her that Teak regained her composure and said politely that it was perfectly all right if Grandma King wanted to spank her, and if she couldn't do it very hard, that was all right too, because she knew it was good for the circulation.

Despite herself, Grandma King smiled, but then she began to ask Teak about the doll's hair and Mother's pretty dress, and especially she asked Teak how she could logically deny that she had done anything wrong, as she continued wide-eyed and tearfully again to insist.

So, nestling close to her and still sniffling, Teak told her all about her "drowning" and the poor little Indian child, who honest and truly had done none of the awful things Teak had! And, really, she hadn't meant to do anything more than a scientific experiment.

And, wonder of wonders, Grandma understood!

She took out a hanky from her reticule and dried Teak's eyes, and told her that her Grandpa King, who had been a clergyman, had even done this kind of "drowning" for grown-ups. It was called baptism. In Grandpa King's church they dropped water over the brow of the one being christened, but in some churches people ducked right under the water the way Teak did. She said that it was a ritual to make you feel reborn and like a new person, but you still—unless you were a little baby—had to make amends for your mistakes, whether they were deliberate and on purpose or made through ignorance or not knowing. She explained that everybody makes mistakes, and that, unfortunately, was the way people learned best.

But it was the hardest way of learning, the very hardest. And Grandma looked off into space so thoughtfully that Teak knew in her heart that even Grandma King had probably made some mistakes. Then Grandma reached up and touched her cheek, and she began to cry again, but this time it was not in fright or anger. It was in the sheer relief of being loved and understood.

So instead of spanking her, Grandma held her close without saying anything more. Then she got up and, using the telephone, called down to the concierge and ordered up hot cocoa for two. Afterward she sought out Hanka and had a talk with her in her room. Grandma King herself put Teak to bed, and after the light was out Teak stared into the darkness trying to decide who she really was. Perhaps she was not truly the poor little Indian child after all but a renewable Teak.

And for years and years after, whenever Teak needed an inner refreshment, she continued to dunk herself in the tub, to listen to the tapwater roaring, and to burst up out of the water feeling cleansed and ready to learn something new.

II

Teak Does a Brave Deed!

"*Idy, dear, what have we here?*" croaked Rudintruda over a terrible rumblebumpling of thunder.

"*Wheeee, wheeeee! We'll see, we'll see!*" screeched Idy Fix back. It seemed an awkward time for poetry, thought Teak as she desperately clung to one of Lonesome's ears.

The net was swinging and swaying perilously. Poor Lonesome was crunched up in a ball of wet fur and red slicker. Teak's Waterloos had fallen off and she could see them falling through a grey cloud. She was now thoroughly terrified and she hung on for dear life. They streaked at high speed through boiling mists, shot up on air drafts, and dropped as suddenly into vacuums. When the lightning flashed, Teak could see one of the witches leaning forward into the storm like a bicycle racer. She had hooked black eyebrows, and her nose and chin seemed to meet over a mean streak of a mouth, and naturally she had bristly warts. The only reassuring thing was that the brooms seemed to have red taillights.

Both witches were apparently partial to swift nosedives that made the prisoners in the net as miserable, frightened, and sick to their stomachs as possible.

"*Fun, fun, fun!*" whooped the witches. "*Let's do it, till they're done!*"

Teak kept her eyes closed most of the time and held on to Lonesome with one hand and the net with the other. After what seemed an endless journey, she managed to open her eyes. She saw that they had flown over the top peaks of the Klorox Mountains and were spiraling down to a murky black lake that seemed to lie in the hollow crater of an extinct volcano—at least she hoped it was extinct.

"*Not much longer, deary. Even we are getting weary!*" sang the witches, and they cackled ecstatically, pleased at their own genius for making rhymes. At last they dropped the net. Teak and Lonesome landed with a big bump on the gritty shore of the lake, which seemed to consist of black cinders and lumps of coal.

The witches skillfully dismounted from their brooms, which remained standing on their own where they were left. Then Teak noticed with a start that shapeless monsters with gleaming and luminous red eyes were appearing from the crevices in the crater walls. They seemed unable to speak, communicating only in snarls, mutterings, grunts, and whimpers, but they hastened to follow the witches' orders.

"Those are the Cantankerous Beejypusses," whispered Lonesome, rolling up his eyes. "They are beastly beasts, always cross and in a foul mood." And in truth they all kept pushing and shoving each other rudely, slapping each other's hands out of the way. They growled in the most irritable way, and it was obvious they were being thoroughly disagreeable on principle. They had to be the ones who took the early train, the tsax-tsaxty-tsax one, thought Teak and she shuddered.

Soon Lonesome was more or less able to stand upright, but he weaved about unsteadily. He still had on his slicker, but the fireman's hat was gone and he was down to one Waterloo. His expression could only be described as Resigned Rabbit.

Teak, too, was a miserable mess. Her kneesocks had dribbled down her legs, her shoes were gone, her wet hair was plastered to her head, and her clothes were soaked through under her slicker. For a moment, she almost missed Hanka. Rough and scary though she was, the witches were even worse, and Hanka would have had a towel and some dry clothes for her, and probably something hot to drink. Now Teak stood there shivering and shuddering, wondering what would happen next. She had never felt so alone.

Rudintruda began to inspect the front of her while Idy Fix examined the back. Slowly the two circled her. "A poor specimen of a child, if you ask me! Spindly, too small for my taste," whined Rudintruda. "And just a mite cowardly, wouldn't you say?"

"Looks like a card-carrying member of the Poor-Little-Me Club, that's what!" declared Idy Fix with a piercing look and a poke of the nose. "I say, girl, do you know Sobkin the Supersensitive?"

"No," said Teak hoarsely.

"Well, you will, you will. She'd just *love* you! Rudie, dearie, maybe we can arrange an introduction. Have a little party?" Then she poked Teak sharply in the stomach with her scrawny forefinger. It hurt.

Next, she turned her attention to Lonesome and decided to put a spell on him. "Oh, *do* put a spell on him, Idy, dear!" cried Rudintruda, clapping her bony hands. "That would fix him fine. Then we could have rabbit stew for supper, and tomorrow we could have rabbit croquettes. I have the best recipe, Idy, from Mother. It's up in my horned toadery box. Just let me fly up and get it. Won't take a minute! And just think, we'll have four rabbit's feet for good luck, too."

"Rudintruda, shut up!" snapped Idy Fix crossly. "Can't you see this takes concentration?"

Rudintruda's feelings were hurt. After all, she was only trying to be helpful. She was so upset that she took it out on Teak by causing a personal cloudburst just for her. A small black cloud appeared just over the top of Teak's head, and she was drenched all over again. Rudintruda at last calmed down, which let Idy Fix get down to work. Now the witch began to croon and to rock to and fro, waving her long fingers in slow circles and spirals in front of Lonesome's head. His eyes began to cross and uncross and roll around in circles.

> *Flix, flax, flox*
> *Pix, pax, pox*
> *What a stupid little habit*

What a stupid little rabbit
Within the hour, within the hour
I shall have you in my power!

sang the witch through rotten teeth that clearly she never brushed.

Teak was very scared as the witch began her spell. Lonesome was slowly turning into a huge barley-sugar lollipop. It started with his two feet and crept up to his head, finally reaching his ears and whiskers. Teak could see right through him.

"Isn't he sweet!" remarked Idy with a wicked grin. She walked around him, stuck the stick he was on into the ground and broke off part of a whisker and sucked on it. "Mmmm, delicious. Have some, Rudy?"

"No, I'm too busy. Putting a spell on children is much harder than rabbits. I may have to look up a specially horrible one. I fancy transmogrifying her into something smaller, fatter, and juicier for supper tonight. We could have rotten oysters to start, then the girl on putrid potatoes, with a salad of slugs, and the rabbit for dessert."

"Sounds good, although I thought that stew..." And here she trailed off.

Teak listened to the two witches cackling away. Her fears mounted. She had never felt so abandoned or so powerless. Terror was sending its icy fingers up and down her spine. But then she looked at poor Lonesome—and she got very, very upset as she saw what Idy Fix had done to her dear friend. Teak felt a hot, glowing, burning, bursting indignation in her chest. She got angry! Red hot mad! Finally she was so livid that she stood up straight and roared at Idy Fix at the top of her lungs, "YOU LEAVE LONESOME ALONE! DON'T YOU DARE DO THAT TO MY FRIEND! DON'T YOU DARE!"

"Well now," sneered Idy Fix, "aren't we being uppity! But it will do neither of you a bit of good. You are utterly in our power, dearies, and we have just the place to store each of you for future use. Yes indeedy, the perfect place."

The witch turned and, clapping her hands, chanted:

> Open, open, open, ope
> Reveal all those without a hope!
> Quickly lost and cheaply caught
> Is one who thinks but other's thought.
> Cheaply caught and quickly lost
> Are those who won't pay freedom's cost!

As she sang and waved her black sleeves, the ground slowly slid open, revealing an enormous glowing red cavern below. Teak looked down and saw hundreds of boys and girls sitting on ledges as if they were paralyzed and unable to move. They looked like rows and rows of dolls. And what was strangest of all was that all those with blue clothes sat together on one ledge encircling the cave, and all those with red or yellow or green or checks or dots were each in a row of their own. They obviously were under a horrible spell, frozen still, and powerless to act. It was a dreadful sight.

As soon as Teak saw them, she was afraid again, but then she began to see what she had to do. Not only must she escape somehow herself, but she also had to save

Lonesome and all those poor children, as well as the Beejums asleep in Beejumstan! But how? How? How could she break the witches' spells all by herself?

Just about then, the two witches decided that they needed to wash up before dinner and that maybe a little shower of brimstone would be refreshing. After all, their prisoners had no way to escape, so why not let all the dimensions of horror dawn on them slowly? But they did one final thing before they left. Stepping to the edge of the chasm, they screeched in one voice, "King Ching! Ting Ling!!" Then off they waltzed, arm in arm, cheerfully cackling at the high humor of it all. Teak and Lonesome Lollipop were left beside the gaping wound in the mountain.

As soon as the witches were out of sight, Teak tiptoed bravely to the big open hole and looked down. Imagine her surprise and then fright as she did so, when slowly, very slowly, up rose the head of a gigantically enormous, or enormously gigantic, Chinese dragondog. As he came into view, Teak could see that his immense body was covered with dark blue and red scales. He had a ruff of living golden flames of fire, and when he opened his mouth, he disclosed long sharp fangs that were encrusted with jewels—emeralds, diamonds, and rubies. Teak could have fit into that maw like a gumdrop, that's how big he was.

"AAAAAAAARGGGGRRRRRRRRRRRRRRR!!!" was what came out of him.

Teak sprang back in terror. The creature was huge and menacing.

"AAAAAAAARGGGGRRRRRRRRRRRRRRR!!!"
repeated the monster.

"Oh, no!" Teak gasped. "Who are you?"

The monster dog cocked his head and scratched it
with one of his bejeweled claws. To Teak's amazement,
printed on the bottom of his paw were the words
"MADE IN JAPAN." Seeing that, Teak was puzzled.

"Who am I? Don't you *know* who I am? I thought
everybody had heard of me. I'm supposed to be famous.
At least, that's what they tell me. I am King Ching the
Watchdog. Nobody, absolutely *nobody* gets by me!" And
he gave another terrible growl. "GGGGGGGGGGGGR-
RRRRRRRRRRR!" Now it sounded as if he had bells
and chimes in his middle.

"Do that again!" Teak requested, intrigued.

"Do what?"

"Growl like that. It sounds funny."

"It's not supposed to sound funny," snapped King
Ching like a great steam shovel. "It's supposed to sound
scary." But Teak thought he began to look a little bit
scared himself. "It's got to be scary or I'll lose my job." At
this he gave a great big sigh and a huge blue flame leapt
out of his throat. Teak had to jump nimbly to one side.
"Oh dear, oh dear," he moaned, "and I have such heart-
burn, such a terrible tummyache! It's all this gas! And
nobody ever thinks to bring me a pail of water."

Teak was beginning to feel braver every minute. "What
you need," she said, "is some bicarbonate of soda. That's
what Nanny would give you. You must have acid indiges-
tion. But would some water do for now?"

"Oh, yes," smiled King Ching gratefully. "I'd do anything for a drink." And he gave a green-flamed burp. "Sorry. Excuse me," he apologized politely.

Teak felt sorry now for King Ching. She soon realized, however, that she had nothing to carry water in.

"Can't you come out?"

"No," sighed King Ching. The sighs came out purple. "They've got me chained."

"If I try to undo you, will you promise not to hurt me?" asked Teak bravely.

"I promise, oh, I promise," replied King Ching.

"Well, you'll have to hold your breath."

"Okay, I'll do my best." And the dragondog sucked in a whirlwind of a breath. He almost vacuumed the child into his innards but turned aside just in time.

Teak picked herself up and tried to find a way to release King Ching from the heavy chain leash that held him. She discovered that the end of the leash had been snapped onto a metal ring set in a boulder, and after a struggle she was able to release the heavy snap and set King Ching free.

Teak took up the chain of the colossal dragondog and led him down to the lake, where he could drink his fill. There was a lot of hissing and steam to start with as the water went down. Then King Ching sat down and gave a huge greenish-blue sigh of relief. Then he lifted his heavy paw and tried to shake hands with Teak, as he wagged his immense purple and red shiny tail. "Thank you so much," he said gratefully and gave the brave girl a huge jewely smile. "Now tell me what I can do for you."

Teak took charge. "Tell me who all those children are down there."

"They are prisoners of their own opinions," answered King Ching sadly. "They believed anything that Idy Fix told them, and so they fell asleep and could not move or grow or think for themselves."

"Are they all Beejums?"

"Mercy, no! They come from where you come from. They are the children in grown-ups who became lost when they stopped learning to ask questions and to wonder at the beauty of life. When you grow up too much, you end up thinking you know everything, and believe in your own opinions so strongly that you can't listen to other people's. It's really so sad!" A tear trickled down King Ching's cheek and fell into the flames of his ruff and turned to steam.

"But why are the ones together dressed in all the same colors?"

"That's the way Idy Fix controls them. If any of them wake up by accident, they see that everybody else is just like they are, and so they fall back to sleep again. They all believe every word Idy Fix says. That's part of the spell. In fact, you are the first person not to believe me when I growled at you. Why didn't you?"

"It was your paw," Teak grinned. "You are supposed to be a Chinese dragondog, aren't you?"

King Ching drew himself up proudly and flared out the flames of his golden ruff. "Indeed, I *am* a Chinese dragondog! My lineage is impeccable. Idy Fix told me that I came as a puppy with handmade papers tracing me back to the Imperial Kennels of Shih Huang Ti. My ancestors were the first to guard the Great Wall of China."

"Well," interrupted Teak hesitantly, "perhaps I should not mention it, but on the bottom of your paw are the words MADE IN JAPAN. So I knew you weren't really what you thought you were."

"I'm not?" yelped King Ching.

"I guess Idy Fix tricked you as well!" said Teak, laughing at King Ching's surprised expression. She laughed so hard that King Ching couldn't help but join in. And his laughter was something to behold because it came out in flames all colors of the rainbow. "To think she put a spell on me!" he roared.

At this point the sight of Lonesome Lollipop stopped Teak's laughter. They were still in peril, and she had to do something fast. The witches might be back any moment.

Teak remembered what Figg Newton had told her about the importance of doing, so she stopped to think for a moment. "Aha!" she cried, "I have it. I know what we must do. Let's mix up the colors of the children first. Then, King Ching, you wake them up with fire and water. And when they wake up, they'll have to stay awake because they'll have to hear different opinions."

Immediately she jumped back into the cavern and set to work mixing up as many children as possible. She put a blue girl with the green boys and a green boy in with the reds and mixed the yellows with the checkered ones. When some of the Cantankerous Beejypusses appeared to see what was going on, Teak was much too busy to be frightened, so she shouted commands at them to help, which they obeyed, having no good ideas of their own. Of course, they muttered and complained but they grudgingly did what she said anyway.

Just when all the children had been jumbled successfully, the monster dragondog began barking and flaming all the wildest colors at them. Teak and King Ching shouted and roared, "WAKE UP BEFORE IT'S TOO LATE! WAKE UP!"

All the children began to awaken, and at the same time Lonesome's eyes opened and blinked, and he began to turn back into himself from the top down, ears waving and whirling. At that moment, Teak saw the witches in the distance skipping down the mountain pass. Clouds of black dust puffed out of them as they skipped. They had used their best powder of coal dust called *Poupoufe Noire.*

"Hurry! Hurry! Quick! The witches are coming back," shouted Teak.

"I'm melting as fast as I can!" Lonesome gasped.

The children had already awakened and had begun getting up off their seats, wiping their eyes in wonder, and running around in colorful confusion, talking together, asking questions, laughing and hearing new ideas for the first time. The cave buzzed with excitement.

As the witches got closer, they noticed something was dreadfully amiss. They looked around first for the girl and the rabbit. Not finding them, they assumed that King Ching had swallowed them down. That wretched dragondog must have eaten their supper before it was even made!

So they poked their long noses into the cave to give King Ching a scolding and were they surprised! For there, perched on the back of King Ching, sat Teak and Lonesome. Rudintruda and Idy Fix began to curse and scream.

Then with a great roar, King Ching charged out of the hole in the mountain, knocking over the two witches, who fell into the cavern, where they would have to face all those children they had mistreated.

We are reasonably sure that the children were able to escape the terrible spell and return to where they belonged. So when you see a grown-up with a gleam in the eye, who can play and have fun and rejoice at the beauty of life, you can be sure that one is safe from the terrible spells of Idy Fix. Happy children don't care what colors you are wearing, and they are interested in each other's opinions. Above all they still know how to play and to see the sense in nonsense such as this.

Aha!

As for Teak and Lonesome, they flew back to Poppalopolis, the capital of Beejumstan, safe on the broad back of their new friend King Ching. This time there were no storm clouds or bolts of lightning, just a beautiful and radiant evening sky with the twin spires of St. Ninnius Cathedral catching the golden rays of the setting sun.

The minute they landed, all those sleeping Beejums woke up at once as if nothing had ever happened. Only here it was time to go to bed again! But before they did, they decided that a celebration was in order—a celebration in honor of Teak and Lonesome and the Breaking of the Spell. Such was decreed by Rhubarb the Terrible from the palace, as he gratefully got out of his cold bath, and a parade was led by General Principles and Popova, who twirled a spangled wand, frequently throwing it high in the air and gracefully catching it without missing a step. Before you could say "Jack Robinson," paper lanterns were lit, the grasshopper orchestra hastily assembled, and a great festival of general rejoicing began. Cosmo sold every single one of his ice cream cones. The Elbedridges trooped in from the countryside to dance, and even Figg Newton appeared with Lissabelle Ann on his arm. King Ching was hailed and given a permanent new job as a living monument in Puddleston Park. The Bunnywidget children had already discovered the fun of climbing up and sliding down his great red and blue back. Teak and Lonesome were the heroes of the hour.

All that remained to remind the Beejums of the day's deluge were some large puddles here and there, which baby ducks were using for wading pools. And not long after dawn the next morning, each of those pools quietly reflected the same single white cloud sailing high overhead. Gezeebius was returning to Beejumstan!

12

Insides and Outsides

The summer had passed peaceably in Skagen in the north of Denmark. Birdie King rented a very small cottage with the idea of writing a novel. Teak's father was away, as usual, but various friends of her mother came to visit. Hanka had mercifully been dismissed, leaving Teak for the first time to fare for herself. Now she had learned how to ride a small rented bicycle, which freed her to venture alone through the dunes to the wide stretches of empty white beach. There she would play by herself, gathering shells and watching the wheeling gulls and sandpipers wading in the tides. She enjoyed her solitude immensely. No grown-ups talking over her head or telling her what to do! She could think and feel the warm sun on her arms and the cool salty breeze. She drew pictures at the water's edge and sent messages to Lonesome and watched the waves come up and bear them away with a whomp and flat, long whoosh. She heard the waves withdraw with sucking sighs and saw them whoosh back again, spreading little white smiles of foam at the edges of wave and sand. She was happy. Maybe the secret of happiness is to know *when* you are happy.

One day she was interrupted by another child, a Danish boy, a bit older. He had a bright beach ball and before long, despite the language problem, they began to play together. The weather had changed to stormy grey and the wind had been blowing from another direction for several days; the shore's edge was now covered with brown seaweed. The boy threw Teak the ball, but the wind blew it over her head and into the water. Without thinking, she ran through the seaweed to fetch it. Only it wasn't seaweed! The beach was lined with brown jellyfish with long red streamers and they stung her legs so badly, she screamed with pain. The boy ran away scared, the ball bobbed way out to sea, leaving Teak to limp home in tears, pushing the bike. Her legs were swollen and covered with a red rash. The kind Danish cook, who came in daily, washed her legs with vinegar and gave her a treat of cool milk clabber. The bowl came covered by a fine net weighted down all around by tiny winkleshells. This was to keep any flies away while the milk was turning to clabber. Teak never told her mother about her mishap, afraid that solitary trips to the beach would be forbidden. She wore what she called her Farmer Browns (bib overalls) and no one else noticed.

Grandma King joined them the last week. She stayed at a hotel but came to visit. She had learned to knit. Teak watched her pushing the two needles together and a blue scarf lengthening, but she never caught her turning the work around. So the mystery remained. It had to be magic. Most everything about Grandma King seemed magical.

Grandma hired a car for an expedition. They drove to a place where a whole village had sunk beneath the sea. They were able to look down and see the rooftops, even the church steeple, silent and dim under the water. Teak wondered if the fish could hear the church bell. Later she would even wonder if it had really happened or whether she had dreamt it. Memories were so strange. It was hard when you looked back, thought Teak, to tell the difference between a story read, a dream remembered, and a real experience. She had wept tears over the story of the heroic death of Roland as he tried to warn his king, Charlemagne. That had hurt just as much as the jellyfish stings. Life sure was full of puzzles.

Then it was decided that now the summer was over they would all return to Italy, and that Teak would have to go to school in Rome. It was hard for Teak to leave Skagen. The idea of school sounded scary.

The school chosen was an Italian one on the Via Savoia, and Teak was enrolled even though she didn't yet speak the language. This made it very difficult for her. Although she was bright and eager, she had great difficulty understanding or keeping up with the lessons. She heard the name Mussolini a lot and learned how to sing *Giovanezza, primavera di bellezza,* which was supposed to be about the joys of youth. She was teased by the boys and greatly admired by the girls, but none of this helped. Before long her parents agreed that the idea had proved to be a failure, so they talked of hiring a tutor.

Then Teak fell sick with a terrible earache. For days she lay in bed with a fever while the doctor came and went, shaking his head. Teak's mother had to give up her writing to nurse Teak, and her father even canceled one of his trips and stood at her bedside looking anxious. For once Teak had what she wanted most of all—her parents' presence and attention—but she was too sick to enjoy it.

Teak improved a little before Christmas, but she was not herself yet. To the family she seemed listless and pale, and she had lost her appetite and was downright skinny. The doctor recommended mountain air and a change of scenery. Thus it was that the family decided to meet in the Austrian Alps for the holidays. The altitude and crisp snow and sunlight, they thought, would surely benefit both Teak and her grandmother. Teak would get some fresh air and exercise, and perhaps Uncle Amyas and Aunt Bessie and the twins might join them. In the meantime, they began plying Teak with large gooey horrible spoonsful of cod liver oil.

Teak's father felt strongly that part of Teak's problem was that she needed to play more with other children her own age. "The fact that Teak is an only child only makes her more introverted than necessary," he said to Birdie more than once. On the morning they were to leave for Austria, Teak overheard this. It troubled her because she didn't understand it, and whatever it was sounded bad.

So she went to Grandma King. "What does 'introverted' mean, Grandma?"

"It means 'turned inward,' I believe," she replied before realizing what Teak was really asking.

"Is that bad?"

"No, dear, it's not bad. It's just different."

"But what does it *mean*? Why does Daddy say that I'm that word?"

Grandma sighed. "It simply means that you are an Inside person, and he is more an Outside person himself. And Outside people have a hard time understanding Inside people, and Inside people can't imagine what it's like being an Outside person."

"Why? Because they stay out of doors?"

"No, that's not what I meant," she smiled. "Outside people think that Inside or introverted people are too much wrapped up in themselves, always thinking and pondering about things. They think that they are too self-centered. While the Inside people think that the extroverts—that's the Outside people—waste an awful lot of time rushing about with each other and doing un-important things. They think they are too shallow."

"Is Justin an outside-vert or whatever you called it?"

"Well, perhaps he is, but that's a perfectly normal thing for a boy to be."

"Aren't I normal, Grandma?" asked Teak anxiously.

"Of *course* you are, darling!" laughed Grandma King. "For heaven's sake, don't worry your head about things like that, Teak. Just be your own dear self and enjoy life. The world needs people like you every bit as much as it needs people like Justin and people like Jessie. I like you all the way you are turning out."

"What are you, Grandma?"

"Well, I guess I must be a mugwump. When I'm with people, I'm an extrovert, and when I'm alone I'm an introvert."

Teak looked grave and puzzled. "But I can't help being alone. Besides, when I am I'm never *really* alone." She was thinking of the Beejums.

Grandma raised her eyebrows and looked at Teak. Then she put her arm around her. "I wouldn't tell that to anyone just now, if I were you. They might not understand. None of them was an only child."

"Do *you* understand?" Teak whispered miserably.

"I think I do, dear, but perhaps you can explain what you mean."

Before Teak could start, their conversation was interrupted abruptly by Thaddeus King, who came in with Grandma's train ticket and passport. He was in a rush to return to his work. Teak's chance to talk to her grandmother had passed, and she went back to her room quietly. She thought Grandma King was right about the twins. They had to be outside-verts because they would not understand about Beejums, Bubbles, and all. Teak decided they didn't have time to imagine stuff like she did. They had each other.

Later she wondered if she should ask her mother about it. After all, Lonesome had said it was all her idea. But why did she never mention it? And why was it that she had never seen her mother in Beejumstan, or missed her there for that matter? The only person she'd seen so far was old Mr. Rathbone, and she had seen him only once on the train, and now she had heard someone say that he was in the hospital and dying.

When she got to her mother's room, the Turkeys and the Dromedary were on the beds ready to be closed and locked, but her mother was still busy typing. Nevertheless, she invited Teak in, as she looked so forlorn.

"Come in, lovey," she said. "Are you all packed up and ready to go? We're leaving after lunch, you know."

"Yes, I think so." She stood there in the doorway, trying to phrase her question. She didn't want to make things worse. Both mother and daughter looked at each other with the exact same expression. Teak really looked a lot like her mother. Finally she took a deep breath and asked, "Mother, do you go to Beejumstan?"

"To where?"

"You know. Beejumstan."

"Goodness!" exclaimed Birdie King. "Why that's extraordinary! I had no idea you remembered Beejumstan. You were just a little girl when I first mentioned the idea. And you've remembered it all this time!" She was really amazed.

Teak shook her head. "No, I don't remember that. It was Lonesome who told me it was your idea."

"Who is Lonesome, dear?"

"A rabbit," she answered, "and he doesn't have any portfolio. I'd like to get him one, but I don't know what one looks like. He says he's an ambassador without one, like Uncle Amyas's friend."

Teak's mother smiled at her. "It really isn't a thing at all. It simply means an ambassador-at-large, one who can

go to any country. Come here, dear, and look at this."
Teak went up to her, and she put her hand on her type-
writer. "Do you know what I think?"

"What?"

"I believe—no, I'm certain of it. One day, you will
grow up to be a writer. Only you'll be a much cleverer and
better one than I am."

"Do you really think so?" Teak's face lit up.

"Yes, it looks that way to me. You listen to people, you
notice things, and you certainly have a wonderful imagination." She gave Teak a friendly squeeze and a kiss on
the tip of her nose. "Phineas is off to school, I see."

Teak giggled and squirmed as her mother laughed.
"Now run along and get your spy bag and let me finish
this up."

As Teak reached the door, convinced that after all she
did have the best mother in the world, Birdie called after
her. "Teak, Daddy and I will have to leave you in Austria
after New Year's. But we're going to find someone to take
care of you, don't worry." When she saw the smile leave
Teak's face and that pinched look about her mouth, she
quickly added, "But I hope we can meet again in Turkey.
That would mean you would go on the most beautiful
train in the world."

"The Orient Express?" Teak asked, but all of her joy
was gone.

"That's right! How did you know?"

"Oh, Mother, I've been on it before. With Nanny."

"Well, perhaps you are right. But you must have been
very little."

"I was," agreed Teak. She remembered the tiny little bathroom between compartments and Nanny lifting her to wash in the tiny round stainless steel sink. She remembered the swaying and whooshing of the train when it passed other trains. She remembered there was paper around the little piece of soap. And Nanny's voice sounding so different in the roar of the train. She asked Birdie about Nanny.

"Yes, we finally have had a postcard. She's terribly busy taking care of things, her family, the house…" Birdie's voice trailed off.

"Will she ever come back?"

"No, Teak, I don't think she will. After all, you are getting to be a bigger girl now. You'll be off to boarding school before you know it. Or if not, we'll have to get a governess. Now run along, I really must finish this." She gave a helpless little sigh and turned back to her typing. Teak listened to the metallic clatter of the keys and waited to hear the little ping of the bell at the end of a line. Then she turned and left the room, closing the door softly behind her.

Slowly she shuffled back to her own room, the tears pricking the back of her nose. No more Nanny! And nobody even imagined how this felt! It was the worst possible news.

When she opened the door, her room had that naked look again. All her things had been packed by someone, and her two suitcases stood side by side at the door. Her navy blue mackintosh was folded over them, and Alfred Hampson was lying nose down on top of it.

Teak picked up the bear and looked at him. He seemed so different, so still and lifeless. How could he be married and have four little bears? Teak thought about what her grandmother had said, and she thought about what Lonesome had said. It really was muddling to live in an outside world and yet to carry a whole other world inside you. Another Bubble.

"I know all about you," Teak said to Alfred defiantly. "You are an extrovert!" But Alfred remained impervious and totally noncommittal. He didn't blink an eye.

With a long sigh, Teak picked up her spy bag and sat down on the bed to wait for Marcantonio to come for her suitcases. There would be yet another good-bye.

13

A Matter of Time

TEAK WAS FEELING BETTER. The family had rented a wooden chalet in Seefeld, a village up in the mountains above Innsbruck in Austria. The roof had a huge puff of snow on it, and this made the house look like a house in a fairy tale. In fact, it was not unlike some of the houses in Beejumstan.

Uncle Amyas was already there, and since he was older than Teak's father, he took charge of everything the minute they arrived, arranging who was to sleep where. Teak and Jessie, of course, were to share a room, and Justin could sleep in a small room off of Louise's. Louise had come with Uncle Amyas all the way from Boston to be Grandma King's maid again.

Grandma King had once told Teak that Louise was French peasant stock and that she had come to her interview barefoot when she was sixteen, before the Great War. The minute Teak saw her again, she knew somehow that Louise was a fellow introvert. Her flat face always wore a slight frown and she said hardly a word. But she was kind and loved animals.

The twins and their mother had not yet joined the family. They had stopped in Scotland on the way from Boston to visit Aunt Bessie's relatives, and were due to arrive at one o'clock the following day.

When Teak went into the living room, she noticed a cuckoo clock on the wall. She would soon discover that every hour on the hour the cuckoo bird would come out and announce the time, hoarsely crying "Coo-koo...." This was accompanied by a great whirring inside the clock before the little bird came out. The whirring somehow reminded Teak of King Ching. The clock also had a heart-shaped pendulum surrounded by carved edelweiss flowers that swept to and fro going tick-and-tock, tick-and-tock.

Teak was given the privilege of unpacking her own things for a change, and she had the choice of which bed to take in the small wood-paneled room. She chose the one closest to the window. When she stood on her bed, she could look out the window across a deep valley to the towering mountains on the other side. It was a beautiful sight. She really liked the sloping fir trees covered with white capes of snow. They looked like white monks on a pilgrimage.

She opened the Fiumerol and got as far as unpacking her socks, which were on top, when she came across a book Grandma King had given her for Christmas. It was *The Jungle Book* by Rudyard Kipling. It looked pretty interesting, she decided, so she curled up on the bed and began to read about Mowgli and the wolves. Soon Teak was lost to the world. Her clothes, naturally, remained where they were in the suitcase.

Soon she was discovered by her father and roundly scolded for her inability to do "the simplest thing" when asked to do it. After this came a lecture on immaturity, responsibility, and acting like a child. Her father also pointed out this was a house, not a hotel, and that the others would notice what she did and what she did not do. Everything depended on everyone pulling together and doing their share. Teak heartily wished that they lived in a jungle. Wolves wouldn't be this fussy. Teak's father left her with a final admonition to finish the job properly.

Louise was not too happy either. It seemed that she was expected to cook for the entire family as well as take care of three children. She thought that was too much, and it probably was. When she came to Teak's room, not long after her father had left, she found Teak just finishing "the last page" of the chapter. She really was intending to unpack then, but Louise walked off to look for Teak's mother, muttering a torrent of French, and Teak could hear the anger and resentment in her voice.

Now Birdie King came to reproach her daughter. "Teak," she told her firmly, "we will have to take away your book if you keep on this way. I really would hate to do that. We'll simply have to make a rule. No reading during the day. I want you out in the fresh air anyway. You can read for half an hour at bedtime and in the morning before breakfast." Then she looked at the bluish circles under Teak's eyes and added, "But not before seven

o'clock. Will you promise me that?" Teak nodded unhap-
pily. "Otherwise we really will have to take your book
away. Now, unpack those suitcases, hang up your things,
and see if you can help Louise like a good girl. She has so
much to do. You could set the table and fold the napkins
and things like that." Then Birdie went off to fetch Teak
her own traveling alarm clock so that she would know
when seven o'clock came. It was a pretty blue leather and
brass one that folded up into a box.

Teak obeyed very reluctantly but she pouted and
sulked. How come grown-ups did stupid things like give
you a really good book and then tell you not to read it!
She made a big mess of her unpacking, stuffing most of
the contents of the Fiumerol into one drawer so everything got jumbled up and wrinkled. She could hear
Nanny having conniptions but since she wasn't there and
wasn't going to be, who cared? Teak didn't.

She decided that Austria must be a dumb country, and
she spent the rest of the time before supper idly kicking
the furniture and scuffing her shoe. Finally she hurt her
toe and stopped. She was being a spoiled brat and she
knew it, but that only made things worse. She thought
Mowgli, the boy in the book, was lucky. He didn't have
other people around telling him what to do. Teak decided
that she would sleep on the floor that night because beds
were sissy.

That night she tried to carry out this intention. She
even took off her pajamas. She just bet that Mowgli
didn't have to wear pajamas. What Teak hadn't realized
though was that the floor in a house in Austria in late

December is not quite the same as the earth in a hot jungle in India. She braved it out for almost ten minutes until she was shivering so much that she had to change her mind. Defeated, she climbed into her nice warm bed which had a big feather puff on it. In no time at all she was sound asleep. She didn't even hear the voices of the grown-ups or the nine "coo-koos" of the clock in the living room.

The next morning she was wide awake at a quarter to six. That was what the little phosphorescent numbers on her mother's clock said it was. More than an hour before she could read! She stood up and looked out the window. The stars were still out. Suddenly she had a fine idea—why not move the clock hand around and *make* it seven!

No sooner thought than done. Teak turned on the bedlamp, fixed the clock forward, and settled back happily in bed to read the next chapter about Mowgli. But as she was reading, another thought slowly drifted into her mind. It occurred to her that the other clocks in the house would not agree with the one her mother had loaned her. This called for another plan.

She got up again. The hall lights had been left on so people could find their way to the bathroom. As quietly and stealthily as Mowgli, she crept into the rooms of her sleeping parents, her grandmother, Uncle Amyas, and even the snoring Louise. She carefully changed each clock or watch that she could find by moving it forward exactly one hour. It was really exciting trying to be that quiet, but she knew that she could do it as well as any boy, even Mowgli, could.

The ultimate challenge was the cuckoo clock in the living room. For that one she had to stand on a chair. When
she was face to face with this clock, she noticed that it
had pinecones dangling on chains and that pendulum
swinging to and fro. She decided it would be wisest just
to stop the pendulum. Seven cuckooings might wake
everybody up. It was a simple matter to stop it. Teak put
back the chair and triumphantly went back to bed and
Mowgli. She missed one of the most beautiful sunrises in
the world, not seeing how the sun turned the snow on the
Alps to a flaming salmon color. That's how good the
book was.

To be sure, the whole family exclaimed that they all must
have been really tired to sleep until nine o'clock! Perhaps
it was the mountain air. Louise was quite relieved that
they had, for she had somehow overslept too and would
not have had their breakfast ready any earlier. Since it was
a holiday, nobody seemed to mind very much. In fact, for
a change, everyone seemed in good spirits. Uncle Amyas
had hired a sleigh, and the family was to go for a sleigh
ride that very morning. Everyone except Louise, of
course, who had to cook a welcoming lunch for Aunt
Bessie and the twins. They would all have to be back
before one. Louise decided spaghetti for nine would be
the best solution, so she was off to the grocer's on foot.
     The sleigh ride was great. It really was. There sat
Grandma King like an empress all bundled up in furs,
and Mother beside her. Uncle Amyas and her father rode
backwards. Best of all, Teak got to sit up front next to the

driver and she got to hold the long whip. On the straight-
aways, she was even allowed to hold the horse's reins.

The horse was white and called a *Schimmel*. His harness
was red and covered with big shiny bells which jingled
with every step. The day was crisp and sunny, the horse in
high spirits, and the sleigh glided almost soundlessly over
the snow on its metal runners. Everybody's cheeks were
getting rosy, and as they talked puffs of steam came out
of their mouths with every word. Farmers waved to them
with mittened hands and greeted the young driver with
big smiles. Teak changed her mind about Austria right
then and there. It had to be one of the best countries in
the world.

At intervals along the road stood little wooden shrines
to the Virgin Mary intended to protect the traveler or
passers-by. When they came to the little onion-towered
church in the next village, they stopped to look because it
was so pretty and friendly. In it were wonderful carved
wooden statues. Teak wondered how people could be that
skillful with wood and a knife. She had once tried carving
a dog out of a bar of soap. It had been impossible.

Next they stopped at a *Konditorei* to have some hot
chocolate. It was delicious and topped with a cloud of
whipped cream which her mother called *gevippel*. Everybody laughed and got white mustaches as they drank
through it. And they let Teak pick out a pastry from the
glass case that held an incredible display of breads, cakes,
and cookies. Grandma bought her a treat—a twisted
paper cone full of *Gummisalat* (rubber salad). This consisted of little gelatinous animals in different colors.

They were sweet and chewy. And Uncle Amyas bought some little black coils of licorice and told her they were called *Baerendreck,* which meant bear poop. Just wait till the twins heard that!

Then Uncle Amyas announced it was high time to return home. They mustn't be late for the arrival of Aunt Bessie and the twins. Uncle Amyas was always extremely punctual and a great stickler for details, which was probably why, thought Teak, he was such a successful banker and so rich. He probably was also one of those Outside people, because he spent so much time and so many words on practical matters that seemed terribly uninteresting to Teak. On the whole, she admired her tall uncle, but she was glad to have her own father. Not that she had him very often.

The trip back was every bit as pleasant. The nice driver in the green felt hat let Teak hold the reins all the way back, except when they had to pass an oxcart drawn by two swaying oxen whose steaming breath almost made clouds. Teak heard her grandmother praising the views and the air, and saying what a fine straight back young Teak had and how well she handled the horse. Perhaps, given the opportunity, she might turn out to be as good a horseman as Amyas had been as a boy. Thaddeus, you see, was allergic to horses. He suffered from horse fever as well as hay fever. All this floated up to Teak as she sat proudly driving the Schimmel through the snow-sparkled countryside.

The sleigh brought them to the door just in time for lunch. Aunt Bessie and the twins would be arriving any minute in the hired motorcar that Uncle Amyas had arranged to meet them at the station in Innsbruck.

The house smelt of fresh bread, garlic, and tomato sauce. Teak's appetite was returning; she felt hungry again. Louise was setting the bread and butter on the large wooden table in the dining room. Teak noticed that the chairs all had hearts cut out of their backs. The whole house, in fact, resembled the cuckoo clock, only it was a different color.

The grown-ups assembled and sipped some sherry, waiting for the sound of the motorcar. But one o'clock came and went and Aunt Bessie MacLean had not arrived. Excuses and explanations were made, but when yet another half hour had passed both Grandma and Uncle Amyas were getting quite worried, and so Teak worried, too. Words suggesting mishaps, accidents, avalanches, and breakdowns were used with increasing frequency. Birdie King, who took life more or less as it came, was the only cheerful one left.

"There has to be some simple explanation," she said consoling them all. "Maybe they had a flat tire or maybe they got mixed up about the time."

"They couldn't be mixed up about the time!" snapped Uncle Amyas crossly. "They know perfectly well that we don't have lunch at two o'clock. I'm putting through a trunk call on the telephone. This is totally out of character for Bessie. She knows that when I say one o'clock, I mean one."

Louise looked the most put out of all. The spaghetti was done and getting cold.

Just then Uncle Amyas noticed that the cuckoo clock had stopped. He got up and went over to it and swung the hands around from six to two, and the cuckoo went crazy, popping in and out, screeching *coo-koo* sixty-six times. On the sixty-sixth, a large black limousine drew up outside the window. Jessie and Justin piled out in matching MacLean tartan tam-o'-shanters and scarves, closely followed by Aunt Bessie in a new mink coat. She had to walk more slowly on the snowy path in her high-heeled boots. She was smiling placidly, happily anticipating seeing everyone again. It hardly looked as if they had suffered an avalanche or anything out of the ordinary. The chauffeur was following, carrying the bags.

Uncle Amyas shot out the door. "What in the *world* happened to delay you? Are you all right? Do you realize it's already two o'clock? We've been worried half to death!"

Aunt Bessie looked at her wristwatch. "No, dear," she said, "it's exactly three minutes past one. I really don't think that is unreasonable." The chauffeur was next consulted and his watch agreed. Pretty soon everybody was running about checking their clocks and watches saying how strange this all was. Only Teak stood rooted to the ground as a new thought crossed her mind.

Her mother noticed the amazement and guilt wash over her features. "Thaddea King," she said gravely, "do you have something to explain to us?"

She did.

Several weeks were to pass, needless to say, before Teak was able to take up with Mowgli and *The Jungle Book* again.

On the other hand, she learned that time was not to be trifled with.

The arrival of the twins forced Teak into becoming more of an Outside person, whether she liked it or not. The only real problem with this was that she always ended up doing things she hadn't planned on doing herself.

The very next day, the family decided to lunch at a big hotel. It would give Louise a break. This hotel was situated at the top of a snow-covered hill and had a huge sunny overlook with tables and chairs. People were sledding, and the slope was dotted with people of all ages in colorful wool caps. Once there, Uncle Amyas rented a big luge for the twins and a smaller sled for Teak.

The children set off together, but when it came time to go down the steep hill, Jessie got nervous and asked if she could use the smaller sled. Teak was only too happy to swap, so Jessie went off in the direction of a smaller slope.

Justin was eager to show off to his cousin, having had experience already in New Hampshire. So he and Teak headed for the really steep hill that fell directly beneath the hotel. "Nothing to it," he assured her. "you get on, hold tight, and I'll do the steering."

Cheerfully, Justin and Teak brought their sled to the top of the big hill. Halfway down was a man with a black beret. He had a large camera which stood on a tripod and had a large black curtain attached to the back of it. The man was obviously taking a photograph of the hotel. He would squint up at it, holding his hand to shade his eyes, and then he would stick his head under the curtain and hold it there. He would reemerge and move the camera carefully over a few inches to the right and look again. This was all a laborious procedure because of the depth of the snow.

"Hey, he must be taking our picture!" exclaimed Justin happily. "Let's give him some real action. Get on the sled, Teak. You sit in the front." Teak sat down, while Justin gave the sled a running push, planning to jump on behind. But he missed.

Off shot Teak at what seemed sixty miles an hour. She had no idea how to steer. Austrian sleds were luges, the kind you sit on, not the kind you lie down on. Now she was headed straight at the photographer who had his head back under the curtain again.

"*ACHTUNG!*" yelled Teak at the top of her lungs. "*ACHTUNG! ACHTUNG! ACHTUNG!*" Teak's father had told them that you had to cry out "*Achtung!*" if you saw anybody in your way, so they could move before getting knocked over. He had had them repeat "*Achtung!*" several times to be quite sure.

The photographer just managed to save his camera a second before Teak shot right over the spot. On flew the sled, lickety-split, sailing over a three-foot path cut across the snow and careening faster and faster all the way to the bottom of the hill, where it finally crashed into a snowbank. It threw Teak up in the air, knocking the wind right out of her. She landed head down in the snow.

When she finally extricated herself, her nose was bleeding but she could see Justin jumping up and down, wildly waving and clapping at the top of the hill. The man with the camera was patiently setting up the tripod again as Teak panted and puffed back up the hill pulling the sled behind her.

The next trip down, Justin sat in front, saying he knew how to steer with his feet. Skillfully he aimed the sled straight at the photographer a second time.

"ACHTUNG! ACHTUNG!!" yelled the children and the photographer had to jump for his life again, carrying his camera with him. This time he shook his fist at them.

There was not a third time and no more sledding either. Her father had found them out. But the children added *"Achtung!"* to their vocabulary and used it all during the holidays as a warning signal. It came in handy for snowballs too.

Strangely enough, Teak didn't get the scolding that she had expected. In fact Uncle Amyas tousled her hair and whispered, "Worthy of the Kings!" as if he were pleased with her. Grown-ups certainly were a puzzlement!

14

On the Way to Gezeebius

LONESOME WAS WEARING a new costume again. He was dressed in lederhosen, those short grey leather pants with green and red felt suspenders. On his head he wore a green Tyrolese hat with ear openings, of course, and there were little badge pins and feathers attached to it. He looked ready to climb a mountain with a yodel or two.

"Where are we going this time, Lonesome?" asked Teak. "And why are you dressed up like that?"

"Well, in the order of your questions—first, I thought it was high time we paid a visit to Gezeebius. Second, I'm dressed just the way you are, me lass, ready for climbing." This was true. When Teak looked down at herself, she found that she too was dressed in lederhosen. Only she had leather suspenders trimmed with a felt edelweiss flower on the crosspiece. On her feet were thick woolen socks and climbing boots with studs in the soles to keep you from slipping. She stamped her feet a few times, and they made a pleasing clumpy noise. Nothing pleased and excited her so much as being dressed like a boy. She knew that she was as brave and strong as any old boy, so she marched up and down proudly clunking her boots to be sure everyone knew this.

"Does Gezeebius live far from here?" asked Teak, ready now for any adventure.

"It depends on how near you are," answered Lonesome obscurely. "But I dare say we will have to go hither and thither, and hither and yon to get there. He lives on top of Mount Pook and we'll have to step lively if we hope to reach the Clackclocks by lunch time. Are you ready?"

Teak looked in the direction of Mount Pook. It was certainly the highest of all the Klorox Mountains. She thought she could see just the tiniest speck of a cloud resting on top of it. It might be the *Cloud of Unknowing*.

They set off briskly, going up hill and down dale in the lovely green foothills. Here there were clumps of heather, and sheep croppling, and larks singing. It was a fine day. There certainly was a lot of hithering and thithering, but their general course was eastward. Teak had to exert herself to keep up with her companion because of the length of Lonesome's hops. Sometimes the rabbit would get far ahead and have to stop for a nibble of something until Teak caught up.

About midmorning, Beejum Time, they reached Netherkin Woods, where, Lonesome explained, lived Mercy Muchmore. She was a kindly, wise woman and a great friend to all the animals about. She knew lots and lots about herbs and healing balms, and she was an old friend of Gezeebius. Hardly had Lonesome finished his description, when they ran into the good lady herself. She was quite plump and rosy cheeked, and she carried a basket on one arm and held a staff in the other. Her blue dress fell to the ground, and a fresh clean apron embroidered with roses covered it.

"Why, hello, Teak!" she called. And when she saw Teak's surprise at her knowing her name, she added, "I've heard so many nice things about you."

Shyly pleased, Teak peeked over the edge of the basket. It was filled with little blue-violet blossoms. "What are those?" she asked.

"Oh, these are persnippety buds. They're for persnippety tea. It's the best tea in the world to have during a persnippety attack. Sets you to rights immediately."

"What's a persnippity attack?" Teak inquired further.

"Why, Teak," teased Mercy Muchmore, "haven't you ever felt cross and irritable for no particular reason? Not in the mood to do those things you know you should be doing? Or sort of drifting off but you don't know why or wherefore?

"Well, then, that's a persnippety attack. It usually happens when you have lost touch with your true nature and can't see the rhyme and reason of things. Then things feel uneasy and wrong. Now, if you can stop at that moment for a good cup of persnippety tea, it can do wonders. It gives you just enough time to remember your blessings. Why don't you both come in and have some right now?"

"We can't stop for too long," murmured Lonesome.

Mercy Muchmore's hut was quite close by, and when they came to the small clearing in the woods they found a waiting line of patients—two porcupines, a bear cub, and an old squirrel with a sore tail. There was even a young fawn whose antlers were "teething," breaking through their fuzzy covering. Birds were everywhere, chittering and singing, and when Mercy Muchmore opened the door to her house, two doves flew to her shoulders and started cooing into her ears while she infused the tea.

Teak had been allowed to carry her staff and was told that its name was Thumpstick. "Is this a magic wand?" Teak asked.

Mercy Muchmore laughed. "Well, yes and no, dear. Thumpstick helps me get around without falling down. You must remember that nothing is magic all by itself. All magic comes *through* you. You see you have to plug one end into the need of someone and the other end into the Source. That's good magic. Sometimes you pick up a few bits of handy know-how as the magic passes through."

"Is there bad magic?"

"Oh my, yes! But that kind always short-circuits in the end. People who use the energy that way don't plug in both ends. If you plug in only one end or the other, it can be a disaster. If you forget the real need of the other person, you get too much juice yourself, and you end up being a flash in the pan. And if you forget the real Source, you begin to believe that you are the source, and you soon run out of juice and are no good to anybody, not even yourself. Anyone who knows the first thing about healing knows that the patient is healed by the magic within himself or herself connected to the Source of all healing. Now, enough of that! Come drink your tea."

As she talked, Mercy Muchmore waved her arms this way and that as if she were plugging in a curling iron like Nanny used to do. Teak wondered a little about the nature of the Source, but wanted to think about it before she asked more questions.

The inside of Mercy Muchmore's house was as interesting as that of Figg Newton, but it was much more feminine and cozy. The walls were covered with drying bunches of herbs, which gave a wonderful spicy fragrance to the interior, and there were many pictures of baby birds, animals, and humans who must have been dear to her heart. Nanny would have said that the place was a terrible clutter, and so it was, but everything was clean and radiated a sense of comfiness and affection.

They sat down at a round wooden table in front of a large open fireplace. A black pot was suspended on a bar above the fire, and there were leather bellows to puff up the flames. Next to the fireplace was another large basket. This contained a calico cat and about four or five wee kittens, all purring at once but in different keys. Teak was enchanted and stopped to pet them. They were so newborn that only two could open their eyes.

"Look, Lonesome, they still can't see!" exclaimed Teak.

"That's just the way I felt when I got here," sounded a familiar voice, and in walked Mr. Rathbone—or was it really he? He looked so young and well and fit. "Yes, 'tis I all right. Almost ready for Aberduffy Day!" He rubbed his hands cheerfully, leaned over and picked up one of the kittens, a little black and white one. It nestled in his hand, opened a tiny pink mouth and yawned.

Teak wondered about Aberduffy Day, but Lonesome reminded her that tea was ready. It turned out to be delicious with a spoonful of honey in it. Very repumpitating, as Figg Newton would have said. And there was a plate of oatmeal cookies. Mercy Muchmore was now busy wrapping up something in big green leaves. "I'm giving you some Blaskells to take along with you for lunch. I made a specially good batch of them this very morning. I must have known you were coming."

"What are Blaskells?" asked Teak. She certainly was adding a great many new Beejum words to her vocabulary.

"Mercy!" exclaimed Mercy. "Have you never tasted a Blaskell? It's bread prepared in a house touched by a tree, that's what it is, and it's the best there is for keeping body and soul together."

Mercy Muchmore reached from her table for a large garden hat with a pointy top and, placing it on her head at a jaunty angle, she drew Teak to her knee and spoke to her seriously. "Teak," she said, "it would help you and the people in your world to know that all the food you eat carries its experience to the one who eats. When you eat even a piece of bread you are eating the world. The flour carries within it the grace of all the days of sun and rain that the wheat waved in and all the nights of moonlight and starlight, the dew and the birdsong, and even the voices of the farmers and their families living by the fields. But if you forget to be mindful and say thank you in your heart, you do not receive that grace. It is your mindfulness that makes the bread come alive. Then it can feed your soul as well as your body. It takes grace to receive grace. So even the tree touching my house has added something very special to the Blaskells I baked this morning. Every mouthful of food has a story to tell, only most people don't know how to hear it. If only you knew how many voices the Great One sings with! Would you be remembering this henceforth when you eat? It's a way of sharing things and of tasting and savoring life." Teak nodded her head thoughtfully.

With that she leaned over and gave Teak a big warm hug and a kiss, and she blew a fond kiss to Lonesome as well. She got up and put the Blaskells into a rucksack and strapped it onto Teak's shoulders. When she opened the door and they walked out, the animals were still there, patiently awaiting their treatments. Teak ran around the hut and found the great oak that the house was nestled to. It felt very alive. She went up and shook hands with a branch and, strange as it may seem, she knew that the tree was very, very pleased to be thanked for a part in the Blaskells and the cookies. Looking this way and that, Teak stole up to the trunk of the tree and laid her head against the bark. It felt warm and good. Trees would never be just trees anymore.

Then, with a wave goodbye, Teak and Lonesome resumed their journey. After they left Netherkin Woods, the climbing began in earnest. They climbed and climbed and climbed. Teak decided it wasn't always easy to meet a Wise Old Man.

After the first set of craggy peaks, they came to a hidden plateau. It was as if the mountain had a lap hidden behind its bony knees. Here was a lovely stretch of earth covered with heather, bluebells, and the tiny bright flowers that grow on the tundra in high places. Lonesome explained that because it was always colder in high places, the flowers had to work harder and be brighter because their growing season was short. There were butterflies about, and they could hear a distinct humming and murmuring of bees.

In the middle of this hidden area stood a strange sight: a circle of huge stones. They were old and grey and weathered and at least five times as tall as Teak. She counted them and found that there were twelve in the circle and one biggest of all in the middle. Beyond them stretched a well-worn path, bordered by smaller stones, leading upward to two gigantic pillars with a crosspiece. When she looked through the pillars, she could see the highest peak of Mount Pook itself centered between them. It was an awesome sight.

"Well," said Lonesome with considerable satisfaction, "there they are! Those are the Clackclock Stones, and you can see the Gates of Mystery yonder, and way up to the Peak of Pook. And, if I'm not mistaken, right behind that middle stone and working hard is good old Dr. Azibov Sobelow. You're in luck; he probably knows more about the Clackclocks than anyone else. He and Dr. Syzygy have spent years studying them."

Lonesome hopped up on a rock and waved his paws. "Hi there, Azibov! Over here! 'Tis I, Lonesome, and I've brought a friend!"

"Wonderful!" shouted Dr. Sobelow in a very deep voice. "Come along over!"

As they made their way over to the great standing stones, a flock of friendly upstarts flew around them— small black and white birds that flew in a fleet dipping motion.

Dr. Azibov Sobelow, judging by his appearance, was a Bunnywidget. A very big one. He wore a smock adorned with a marvelous array of pockets, and there were more on his ballooning trousers. Each one was embroidered with a letter of the alphabet. When he saw Teak's look of astonishment, he chuckled. "It's wonderfully convenient. Mrs. Sobelow made it for me, because she said that my head was always in the stars, and I was getting too frightfully absentminded."

At that, he looked down his chest and pulled a pipe out of the P pocket and some matches out of the M one. Then he looked for his tobacco in the T pocket, but it wasn't there. After he slapped himself in several places, he located it in the bottom of the B pocket. As the tobacco was called *Bodget's Best for Beejums,* he had filed it there. He lit his pipe with a few puffs, returned the matches to M and the tobacco to T this time. "I'll probably lose it all over again," he said cheerfully. Then he wiped his hands on his trousaloons and shook hands with Teak as Lonesome introduced her. "First trip up here, eh?" he boomed. "You certainly picked a fine day for it. I was just about to have a spot of lunch. Let's all sit down and have a bit of a wig-wag, shall we?"

Teak and Lonesome were only too glad to sit down after that long climb. Teak took off her rucksack and fetched out the package of Blaskells. She was curious to see what they were. And Dr. Sobelow, after looking in the H pocket for ham, found his sandwich quite correctly stashed in the S pocket by his wife. Teak politely passed around the Blaskells, which turned out to be little rolls stuffed with indefinable melt-in-your-mouth goodies. Dr. Sobelow gave a hearty shout of delight when he spied them. "Ah, dear Mercy, dear Mother Muchmore, has been baking again!"

"Is she your mother?" asked Teak, a bit surprised.

"She's the mother of us all, she's everybody's mother in Beejumstan," he laughed, "and if she gave you these Blaskells, then she's your Fairy Godmother for sure. You are the most fortunate young man to happen on her. Not everyone can see her, you know. Most unusual that you did, actually, coming from where you do. In your Bubble, most people don't believe she exists, but as you can see she does. And the lovely thing about her is that she can teach anybody who believes in her how to look and really see, and how to listen and really hear."

"How are we 'sposed to do that?" asked Teak, thrilled that Dr. Sobelow had taken her for a boy.

"Well, as you know, I am always trying to discover the truth about things, like my good friend Figg Newton. I did a heap of studying and looking for the truth and meaning of things. It was all most perplexing. Then one day Mother Muchmore passed me in a meadow where she had been collecting herbs for healing. She looked straight at me and out of the blue said, 'Consider the obvious!' Then she laughed and explained that everybody seems to overlook the obvious because they think that the truth has to be more complicated! Especially you folks, who, unlike Beejums, think the truth of things is hidden. The problem with humans—ahem, with all due respect to you, Teak—is that most of them are blind. It never occurs to them that all they are seeking is really right under their noses in *simple* things. Here in Beejumstan we know that you can learn the biggest things from the littlest ones." Teak now remembered that Figg Newton had said much the same thing, so it had to be very important.

Azibov Sobelow smacked his lips loudly and with the greatest pleasure. "Mmmmm! These *are* delicious! Thank you so kindly for your generosity in sharing them."

Teak took a bite of a Blaskell, careful to think of where they came from, and indeed she could see the oak tree blessing the little hut of Mercy Muchmore with its lovely green and golden leaves. It certainly was the most "deliciousest" Blaskell she had ever tasted.

"What are those big stones here for?" she asked after she had swallowed the last crumb.

"These stones, young fellow-me-lad, are the famous Clackclocks, and we suspect that they were set up here thousands of years ago—or just a tick ago, depending upon which time you live by. We think they may act as a kind of clock or sundial for those above, perhaps in another Bubble. Right now, for instance, it's ten past August, because the shadow of the middle stone fell here at dawn. But if it fell back by that stone, it would be quarter to May. And when it's way over there, we know it's half past November."

"I see—I think," said Teak, frowning.

"It works like a charm, never needs winding, and keeps the seasons right on schedule," beamed Dr. Sobelow.

"But how can months and hours be the same?"

"Good question, that! You see, in a way, a day is a baby year, and an hour is a baby month, or a minute can be a baby day, depending, of course, on what system you're running on. The Clackclocks run on twelves."

"So do watches," said Teak.

At this, Lonesome pointed his nose at the sky and said softly, "Hum-deee-dum-dumm," which was his "This-is-important" hinting noise. "Hum-dee-dum-dumm—aren't there a lot of twelves where you come from? How many folks on a jury?"

"Eggs in a dozen! Inches in a foot!" cried Teak.

"Labors of Hercules? Tribes of Israel? Gods on Olympus?" suggested Azibov Sobelow.

"Apostles!" Teak jumped up and down. "Thingama-bobby signs!"

"*What*, may I ask, are they?" questioned Sobelow.

"She means signs of the zodiac, I believe," interpreted Lonesome.

"Yes, yes, that's it!"

When Azibov heard Lonesome say "She," he peered intently at Teak. There was a definite twinkle in his eyes as he said, "Twelve really is a very special number. It pops up all the time, and when it does, you pay attention."

"You mean it's an AHA!"

"It certainly is an Aha! It's a highly symbolic number."

"What does 'symbolic' mean?" This was another new word for Teak.

"Well," said the scientist, "a symbol points from something you know to another level of understanding. The word itself means 'throwing together' or, as we Beejums like to say, putting two and two together. Every *thing*, especially in your world, has a symbolic meaning to it, or maybe more than one. So the thing is one half and the meaning is the other." Dr. Sobelow fished into his B pocket and pulled out a small cube. In fact, it looked like a baby's block. He placed it in front of Teak. "All right now, Teak, take a look at that block and tell me, how many sides do you see?"

Teak studied the cube carefully. Then she answered, "Three."

"That's right," said Azibov. "Now tell me, how many sides are there really?"

"Six," said Teak.

"How do you know that they are there if you can't see them?"

"I saw them in my mind. I know there are six."

"Aha!" roared Dr. Sobelow. "That's exactly the way a symbol works. You have to match what you see with something that comes from inside you. Then it acquires meaning and another dimension. To see anything as symbolic, you have to match it up with a new insight, a new understanding."

"Does that work with anything?" asked Teak.

"It certainly does. Look, try again," he urged. "Here I will take a pen out of my P pocket." And he did. "What could this be symbolic of?"

Teak thought. "Writing?"

"Very good. Writing, communicating, and on and on...Now, what if you didn't have a pen? How would you communicate?"

"I'd talk," said Teak.

"And if you couldn't talk?" asked Sobelow.

"I'd use my hands and fingers," laughed Teak, thinking of the Italians.

"And if you couldn't do that?"

Teak was stumped. She thought and thought. Then she said, "I guess I'd just think."

"Aha!" said Dr. Sobelow, waving the pen. "All that came from looking at a simple pen."

"It's like a game," said Teak.

"That's true," said the scientist, and he carefully put the pen back in the F pocket for fountain pen. Teak looked at him and he stopped, reconsidered, and put it back in the P pocket.

Just then, Lonesome coughed politely. It really was time to be going. "I think we really should be hopping off," he said. "Thank you so much. We are on our way up to visit Gezeebius, you know."

"Well, that's wonderful. Be sure to give him my love. And, Teak, do ask him to tell you a story. He probably will anyway. And I'll tell you a secret—if he does, be sure to think of it symbolically. There's always more in his stories than you think. Mercy, much more, much more!" And Dr. Azibov Sobelow laughed at his own little joke.

Teak handed him her very last Blaskell and helped him to find the B pocket to store it in. Then she reached up to whisper into his ear. "I'm really a girl," she confessed.

"Well, I never! No!" and he gave her a big wink. Now Teak would never be sure, but nevertheless she was pleased.

Then she and Lonesome said good-bye and turned to set off for the Gates of Mystery. They still had a long way to go that day, year, minute, or whatever it was. They passed through the Clackclocks and paused by the middle stone. "It all depends on your point of view, and that depends on who you are, when you're coming from where you came, so to speak," summarized Lonesome.

Teak woke up, much to her disappointment, just as they reached the Gates of Mystery and were looking up at the Peak of Pook. It took her a while to realize where she was—on a bed in a small bedroom in a small hotel on the Greek island of Poros. Her mother had decided to research background for an article she was writing. Now she seemed to remember that they would sail back to the mainland that morning.

Sure enough, Birdie King came in and told Teak to hurry up and get dressed. They had only an hour to get to the dock.

"Where are we going *now?*" asked Teak peevishly.

"Athens," Birdie told her daughter cheerfully, "and Daddy will be there." They had left him in Istanbul when they came to Poros.

"I don't want to go to Athens. Why can't we just stay here? Why can't I live in a house like Jessie and Justin do?" Teak got out of bed grumbling. Her hair was sticking up in all directions and she just wanted to go back to

Beejumstan. However, she managed to get herself together and they reached the boat in time.

The Mediterranean was stretched out like blue silk, with pink and gold reflections from the sky. The water was almost fragrantly salty and warm. Teak watched the chalk white houses of Poros recede dreamily in the distance as the small boat steamed sturdily away. Somehow the silence of the shore seen from a passing ship was the stillest silence Teak could think of. Just like flat was flattest when you put your palms together and pressed very, very hard.

15

The Gimmie Attack

WHEN TEAK AND HER MOTHER landed at the harbor of Piraeus, they got into a large green taxicab driven by a man with huge black eyebrows and a big black mustache. He drove like a maniac, and waves of smoke from his fat cigar washed over the passengers in the back as they hurtled along narrow roads. Birdie King did not know the Greek word for "slow," so she had to tap the driver on the back and try to communicate in sign language. It didn't work, so they resigned themselves to a hair-raising trip. They drove sometimes on the left side and sometimes on the right, narrowly missing donkeys and cats and geese, to say nothing of people. The driver just squeezed the rubber horn—*ahooogah, ahooogah*—and laughed all the way to Athens.

Teak's father was there to greet them as they tottered from the taxi with relief. Teak had almost thrown up during the ordeal. Now they went upstairs in the well-named Hotel Grande Bretagne, which overlooked a square that contained a small park filled with fragrant orange trees. Teak's room was right next to her parents', and she had a little balcony all to herself with an iron railing. When she stood out on it, she could see off in the distance, high on a rock, the beautiful gleaming white columns of the temples of the Acropolis—temples built by the Athenians over two thousand years ago, as her father explained. Looking to the left, Teak saw something not so beautiful but intriguing in its way. It was a billboard advertising a brand of shoe polish, depicting a huge lion with one paw on a round can of polish. On the cover of the can was a lion holding *his* paw on another can of polish, and on and on. They kept getting smaller and smaller and smaller. In a vague way, she saw this as an explanation of worlds within worlds or Lonesome's idea about Bubbles within Bubbles. In any case, Teak decided this was a good hotel to be in.

At tea time, they went down to a great salon with palm trees growing out of large pots. Her parents had tea, and Teak had an orangeade with a straw. A small orchestra played music, and some couples were dancing on a patch of polished wood. The women wore short frocks with the waist almost down to their knees and weird hats called *"cloches,"* which was French for "bells." They really did look like upside-down bells. Teak thought they were ugly, and she noticed that most of the women put red stuff on their cheeks and their lips. But the music was nice and lively, so Teak sat back in her chair and sipped the orangeade and watched it all with wide eyes. People never failed to interest her.

The next day, Birdie King decided to go shopping, and she took Teak along with her. They walked up and down the streets and went in and out of several fancy clothing stores, which didn't interest Teak in the least. Birdie bought herself some silk stockings and a new argyle cardigan for Teak. Then they passed a leather goods store and looked in the window at the handbags and purses—and there in the right-hand corner of the window Teak's eye fell upon her heart's desire.

It was a small black leather combination wallet and change purse. It was open, and she could see that it sported no fewer than five small compartments and two outside pockets that closed with snaps. It would be perfect to keep in her spy bag. Then and there Teak developed a passion for this wallet. She knew that she wanted it more than anything else in the world! She began to beg and wheedle her mother for it in that special voice she used when she wanted something badly and was afraid she wouldn't get it.

Teak's mother looked at the price and shook her head. "You don't need that any more than a cat needs a flag!" she said, using one of her favorite expressions. "It's much too big for your pocket. You would have no use for it."

"Oh, yes, I would! I could put my centimes in one pocket and my shillings in another—it would be handy for all sorts of things! Please, Mother, please give me that wallet. PLEASE!"

But her mother said no. She didn't want to hear another word about it, and with her hand at her daughter's back she actually pushed her away from the store.

During the next few days, Thaddeus King Jr. actually took some time off to be with his wife and child. They drove out to Marathon, past all the lovely grey shimmering olive trees and small flocks of sheep. They even saw baby lambs frisking, *but—*

And Teak's father took the time to explain to Teak all about the heroic young Pheidippides, who ran all the way from Athens to Marathon and back again bringing the news of the Greek victory over the Persians in a fierce battle. The distance was twenty-six miles each way, and the messenger dropped dead from the effort. Together the three Kings climbed the grass-covered knoll under which the brave dead soldiers had been buried, *but—*

They climbed the Acropolis, and Teak's father told her that Socrates himself had worked to build the Temple of Athena. They stood and looked out over the panorama of the city on a radiant day, and they could see Mount Hymettus, where Teak's favorite breakfast honey came from, *but—*

They even went to Sunion, where there was an exquisite white marble temple on a rock overlooking the blue sea, and they had a real picnic from a wicker basket, and Teak waded in the water, *but—*

Teak was even allowed to keep a real live tadpole in some water in a Hymettus honey jar. She got to keep it right in her room. Her very first pet, *but—*

But what, do you suppose? None of these pleasurable events made her as happy as they should have. She moped through all of them half-heartedly, because all she could think of was that little black wallet, and she continued to beg, cajole, bargain, and whine to have it. She became a pest. A spoiled brat. It was a royal persnippety attack.

After a week of this, Birdie sat Teak down on her bed and said to her savagely, "All *right*, I'll buy you that blasted wallet, which you certainly don't deserve considering your pestering and sulking—but only on one condition!"

Teak brightened up immediately. "Anything! I'll do anything, Mother! Honestly!"

"Well then, you listen to me," Birdie King said, jabbing a forefinger at her. "I want you to promise me, on your honor, never ever to ask me for another thing."

"That's simple!" shouted Teak.

"It's not as simple as you think, ducky. There is never an end to the things one wants. Right now, Thaddea King, you have become a slave to that wallet. It owns you, even though you don't own it. It has become your master. It has driven you all week, and it has spoiled a lot of fun for all of us. I just want you to know this and to remember every word that I am saying."

"I promise. Just let me have it, and I'll never ask for another thing!" Teak looked up at her mother anxiously. "When can we go? Can we go before lunch? Maybe someone else will buy it. Oh, Mother, can we go now?"

"I will take you in an hour, Teak—and not one minute sooner," she added grimly.

Teak knew better than to push any further, so she only muttered, "Well, what can I do till then?"

Birdie King answered her sharply. "I don't care what you do, as long as you leave me alone and don't say one more word about that wallet."

Teak started to leave, but on the other hand, she didn't want to leave her mother's room, lest she forget or change her mind. So she climbed back up on the bed and curled up quietly to read the red leather-covered Bible, which Birdie always kept by her bed.

Teak liked this book especially because it had "funny papers" in the back. These were line drawings of ancient Egyptians, embalmed mummies, and curly-bearded Assyrians driving chariots. There were Cleopatra's Needles, obelisks which she had seen for herself in Rome and in Paris, and there were many different alphabets. Soon she was absorbed in trying to decipher a page from a Coptic New Testament.

Her mother calmed down. She realized, not for the first time, that it was probably very hard to be an only child with no one to play with. Would it have been easier to have had two children? She looked out the window at the Acropolis and decided that it would have been impossible. She would have had to choose between being a wife and a mother. She had made her choice. She liked the life she was leading. It was a lot more interesting than keeping house, which would be dull indeed. So she kept her promise and took Teak back to the shop.

The wallet—*her* wallet—was still waiting in the window. The shopkeeper had to reach into the window display with a hook and get *that one*—no substitute would do!—and he rubbed it up and polished it with a cloth and tied it up in paper and string. It seemed to Teak one of the happiest moments in her life. She got to carry the package all the way back to the hotel. She even forgot to thank her mother, though she remembered later, but her mother could see the bliss of possession spread across Teak's face.

They came back just in time for luncheon at the hotel. Teak let her mother hold the package while she ran to wash her hands dutifully in the downstairs lavatory, a grand place of marble basins and gleaming faucets. Teak's father joined them, apologizing for being late. Her parents then began talking above her head, but mercifully she was excused early and allowed to carry the treasure up to her room. There she was able to unwrap it, to touch the black pebbled morocco leather, and to sniff deeply the good leathery smell. It was perfect, and it was all her own. It even had a hidden compartment in the back for paper money or secret messages. Teak ran and got the spy bag out of the wardrobe and dumped out all its contents, which were pretty grungy, onto the bedspread. It made a mess all right. The *calculus alba* almost fell on the floor but she popped it back into the bag. Next she sorted out all the loose change that had been rattling around and made little piles according to countries. Then she got a piece of paper and wrote down what she had. Though she knew that she had traveled to nineteen different countries already, she only had money left from five. So she wrote down:

> 1 English sixpence and 2 pence
> 25 French centimes
> 10 Austrian groschen
> 5 Italian lire
> 2 Greek drachmas

Now they all had a special place to go. She put two Danish trolley ticket stubs from Copenhagen into the secret compartment. Then she decided to write her own name in her best handwriting (which wasn't all that good) and put that in it as well. She didn't have any address, and she really hadn't listened at lunch to where her parents had decided they might go next, so she wrote:

Thaddea King

The World

The wallet now felt heavy and full. Teak felt rich, and she tried stuffing it into the pocket of the new cardigan, ripping it in the process because the wallet made it too lumpy. She was too rich! Then she took it out again and rearranged the coins in alphabetical order according to English, which put Austria in the first pocket, though the coins were marked "Osterreich," which began with an "O." Teak began to appreciate Dr. Azibov Sobelow's problems. All this took up most of the afternoon.

She now knew what it was to have one's heart's desire at the moment that one desired it, which is one of the secrets of happiness. Her dream had come true.

Her joy in the wallet lasted fully five days. She could now "see" her parents and the world about her again. She looked happy. She called the tadpole "Hermes." All went well until they went to an outdoor fair in a park. There Teak saw a toy that made colored sparks when you pushed its handle. If only, if only! Off she went running to her mother.

"Mother," she cried, "did you see that sparkly gadget? Could I get one, please, PLEASE?"

Birdie King turned about and stood stock still and looked at her with a strange expression. "Teak," she said.

"Yes, Mother?"

"Haven't you forgotten something?" Seeing her child's innocent expression, she repeated the question with more emphasis. "Haven't you *forgotten* something?"

In all fairness, she didn't rub it in. Teak knew very well what she meant. She even wondered briefly if her mother and Mercy Muchmore were in cahoots. She begged no more. Becoming a slave to a dumb old sparkly gadget probably wasn't all that great an idea. Instead, she ran off to watch a juggler who was juggling carrots and cabbages and potatoes and making a crowd double up with laughter at what he was telling them.

When they got back to the hotel, she discovered that Hermes had grown two tiny hind legs, and there were stumps sticking out for front ones. He was most likely going to be a real frog any minute now! He could hop all over Jessie's lap and make her scream. Teak almost missed the twins and wondered if they were going to school in America and getting to see Grandma King.

She stood out on the balcony again and looked at the temples on the Acropolis and down on the people milling about under the orange trees, and she wondered where they all came from and where they were going. She wondered if she would ever come back to Athens.

16

At the Gates of Mystery

JUST AS SUDDENLY AS TEAK had left Lonesome and Dr. Azibov Sobelow and the Clackclock Stones, she found herself back there. She was again climbing with Lonesome up the path to the two great pillars of the Gates of Mystery through which you could see the Peak of Pook. It was as if no time had intervened at all. That was most peculiar, but there it was. The dimensions of time and space were not the same in Beejumstan as in her everyday world. In Beejumstan, unlike in Teak's hotel rooms, you seemed to have all the space necessary for whatever you were doing, but sometimes when Teak was awake in Greece she felt that she was carrying that very same space within herself. Time seemed to stretch and shrink in the same way.

"Oh, Lonesome," Teak called out to the rabbit, who was hopping along ahead of her, "Will you please tell me how Gezeebius goes to another Bubble?"

"Well," Lonesome slowed down and matched his pace to hers. "It's a bit tricky to explain. You see it's something you have to be adept at doing."

"What's 'adept' mean?" Teak was always running into new words.

"It means to be *very* good at doing something you are good at anyway," explained Lonesome. "And Gezeebius is very good at going in and out of other Bubbles. "You have to understand something hard to understand. Reality isn't just what you *think* it is. There are many different kinds, and people who live in only one kind don't understand the Bubble business at all. You see, if you're living inside a Bubble, you don't even know that it *is* a Bubble because you can't see that from the inside. Just like a fish doesn't understand that there is anything different from water. A fish doesn't even know how to be thirsty. But when a fish gets pulled out of the water it is very much surprised. Look at it this way—when you are in Rome or in Greece you think you are not here, and when you are here you forget that you are in Greece, right?"

"I suppose so," admitted Teak.

"But really, you see, you are in both places at once. The same is true when you are dreaming, right? You just hadn't thought of that. Now you have. Goodness! There are so many things that we do that we don't know we are doing! It happens all the time. Reality is what's *really* going on while you think something else is. There *is* another Bubble and it's hidden inside the Bubble of your world, but most people can't see it! Gezeebius, however, is different. He is wiser than the rest of us Beejums. He does know about more than one Bubble and can go off into another Bubble whenever it's important that he should. He can step into a past time and make it present, or he can step into what you would call the future and make it seem past. That's why he is an adept. He has reached the center of things, and by reaching the center he can go anywhere to fix a muddle, if you know what I mean. It's simple for him, but not for the rest of us, of course."

"Can Figg Newton do that?" asked Teak.

"Not yet, I shouldn't imagine, but he's probably practicing up on it. The only other Beejum I know of who could is St. Ninnius, but he's moved through to another Bubble for good, and we haven't seen him for centuries. I expect that there are some few like that where you come from. You could ask around."

Teak thought about whom she could ask as a gentle breeze riffled Lonesome's ears and lifted her hair. It was the South Wind, and she was sure that Figg Newton and Azibov Sobelow would say it was symbolic and important, but they weren't around at that moment. The upstarts were singing and flying in circles around them, their pretty wings flashing in the light. The purple heather was waving and the bluebells were almost ringing as the breeze caught and shook them. It was perfect Beejum weather.

Then Teak remembered that she had a message for Lonesome. "Lonesome," she said, trying to catch up with the rabbit who was bounding once again, "I found out about the portfolio. You really don't need one at all!"

"I don't? What does it mean?"

"Portfolio means to carry papers, but an ambassador without papers to a particular country can go everywhere. It means you can be sent anywhere."

"Well, that *is* a relief! I was worried that I wasn't properly equipped. Thank you so much, Teak, for remembering to inquire. That was most kind of you."

"It was nothing really. I like doing that sort of stuff. I think words are interesting."

"I *love* words," exclaimed Lonesome. "They always make me think of eggs."

"They do?"

"Yup. Eggs have feathers."

"They do?"

"Of course they do. What happens when the egg hatches?"

"A baby chick comes out."

"Doesn't it have feathers?"

"Sure it does, but what does that have to do with words?"

"What comes out of words? What are words for?"

Teak pondered while scratching her leg. "Meanings?"

"Exactly," said Lonesome looking pleased. "'Hair today and gone tomorrow' is awfully different from 'Hare today and gone tomorrow.'" Teak was a good speller but she hesitated—the words sounded alike to her. But Lonesome gave the clue away. "Very different, since it depends on whether you are balding or whether you are a rabbit. You see, there can be miles and miles between what I say and what you hear. Suppose your father looked out the window at the pouring rain on a grey gloopy morning and remarked, 'What an awful day.' What would you think then?"

"Oh, I know what I'd think!" laughed Teak. "I'd think he was cross and in a bad mood."

"I thought you'd say that," said Lonesome. "Cross at whom?"

"Me, most likely."

"Exactly. But chances are he wouldn't even be thinking about you at all—just the weather."

Teak lowered her head and then looked up carefully, taking this in.

"This is one of the main reasons people in your Bubble get hurt and angry with each other. They mix up the meanings. The problem is that each person gives his own meaning to what he hears. So he ends up hearing himself rather than the other person. And that causes all *kinds* of complications. Then, when you add in all the different languages—why, it's a wonder that you can buy a grapefruit when it's a *pamplemousse*."

"Stop!" panted Teak, climbing another rocky place. "You're making my head ache again."

"I'm sorry. Have you seen the Beejum flag?"

"You mean the one with the duck on it?"

"Yes, that one. Did you read the Beejum motto under the egg that's under the duck?"

"No, I couldn't understand it."

"It says *Eggsies exeunt egi*—eggs come out of me. There's Latin, Piglatin, and Ducklatin. The motto is in Ducklatin, which is what we prefer in Beejumstan. Be that as it may, it is a very profound motto because out of every egg comes another duck and yet another egg, and on and on. Which do you think came first, the duck or the egg?"

Teak laughed. "I bet the egg came out of a duck that wasn't a duck yet."

"Well, that's as good an answer as I've ever heard. Not bad, not bad at all."

They had reached the Gates of Mystery. Here Lonesome made some remarkable leaps from rock to rock, landing on top of the pillar on the left. It was something that only a rabbit could do, so Teak had to stay below. She gazed up at what seemed to be hieroglyphs carved into the two gigantic stone columns.

"What do those say, Lonesome?" called Teak, leaning back to look up.

"Those words were carved here way before the Dynasty of Chickabiddys," answered Lonesome, "and nobody could read what they said for centuries and centuries. Then Dr. Syzygy, the great archaeologist at Apesnose University, worked on them for many years. Finally, through a fortuitous fluke, he was able to decode them."

"What is a fortuitous fluke? Oh, Lonesome, sometimes I do wish you used simpler words!"

Lonesome drew himself up on top of the pillar and rebuked Teak severely. "It is part of my ambassadorial duties, me girl, to use the best of words. Precision and beauty of expression are one of the glories of civilization. If you cannot express yourself concisely with your tongue, you will go back to grunting and punching like a Cantankerous Beejypuss. I must reproach you here, Teak. If you do not understand something, ask me or someone else, or better yet look it up for yourself in a dictionary." Lonesome was looking quite severe. If you have ever seen a rabbit frown, you will get the picture. He was as earnest as a rabbit can be.

"But I did ask, and I don't own a dictionary," Teak reminded him.

"So you did. Well, a fortuitous fluke is a serendipity, a happy circumstance, an unexpected and helpful surprise. In this instance, it was a very ancient soup can label written in three languages. Dr. Syzygy had been busy with an archaeological dig around here. He and a crew of Beejums dug and dug persistently without finding anything more than some petrified ice cream cones and hot dog wrappers, which turned to dust the minute they hit the air—much to his dismay, I might add, because he had been doing extensive research into the shape of the first hot dog. But just as he was about to give up all hope, one of the workers' spades hit something metal. It was a chest that was tightly sealed and it had two wheels."

"Did they open it right away?"

"Oh my, no! A holiday was declared. Grandstand seats were set up and even Boxaphat, who was the Pompity-pomp of Beejumstan in power at that time, attended. Everybody that could came. But Dr. Syzygy was afraid of noxious gases—that means poisonous ones—so he wore protective clothing and a gas mask. I will never forget that moment or how wise he was to take that precaution."

Lonesome sat down on the pillar now and warmed to the tale. "Yes, I can see it as if it were yesterday. Have you

ever opened an icebox that hasn't been opened in a month
and all the food in it has gone oogy?" Teak shook her
head. "No, of course, you wouldn't have. Well, this was a
kind of icebox, and it hadn't been opened in centuries.
Peeeeeyoooooooeeeee!" Lonesome held his nose with his paw
and pretended to faint away on top of the pillar. Teak had
to laugh.

"What happened then?"

"Well, naturally, it exploded with a great bang, and the
stink was so strong we all nearly passed out. Poor Boxaphat had to be revived with some of Mrs. Daisymouse's
lavender smelling salts. Fortunately, there was a stiff
breeze which carried it away, and as soon as the danger
was past, Dr. Syzygy bent down and looked in—and there
was the open soup can! It was a can of alphabet soup.
What a moment of triumph for the history of Beejumstan that was! The noodles, of course, were petrified by
then. But not only were all the letters of the alphabet still
in the can, the label was in three different languages all
saying the same thing. There was even a recipe, which
took dear old Syzygy over seven years to translate. Turned
out to be for crossword fondue. All of these artifacts are
still preserved in the Soup Council Museum to this day.
Anyway, it enabled our scholars to translate the meaning
of the hieroglyphics on the pillars, and then they were
able to reconstruct much of the culture of Beejumstan
between the reign of Hippopotaymus the Semi-mythical
(who was mostly beebize) and the Dynasty of Chickabiddys: Chickabiddy the First, the Second, and Third. After
the rule of Timaeus of Taunton, under which the country

groaned." Here Lonesome paused, looking skyward and counting the rulers by the toes of his paws. For all the world, he looked like a schoolboy who had learned his history by heart.

"Then came, I think, Eggnog the Pimpled, followed by Tnoot the Good. Why was he so-called? Because he was a total abstainer. From what did he abstain? From killing his wife. Phew! I think I'm down to the twin lobsters, Humidor and Thermidor, and the late Boxaphat, and now," he concluded with a grin, "we have Rhubarb the Terrible." With that Lonesome collapsed with relief.

"Both Syzygy and Sobelow now believe that great festivals and fairy dances were carried on periodically among the Clackclocks—especially on the Octopuppy's Birthday, which is October 8, and is still celebrated in Beejumstan."

"Who was the Octopuppy?"

"Nobody knows, Teak, which is the point of the holiday. On the Octopuppy's Birthday, we celebrate all the heroic deeds done in the world that nobody ever heard of or paid attention to."

"That's nice," said Teak. It gave one hope.

"Well, obviously, the folk came up here for refreshments and the glorious view. That would explain the petrified ice cream cones, the hot dog wrappers, and a fondness for alphabet soup. The icebox itself proved to be a prototype of Cosmo's ice cream stand and is probably one of the oldest specimens in existence."

"So what does it say on the pillars?"

Lonesome leapt down bravely from the great height of the pillar and pointed up at the carvings. A translation into English was framed in a glass case at the side. Teak peered into it and studied it carefully. At first it made no sense at all. She read out LO & IFT but broke down with FPW EUO.... It was quite unpronounceable. Then she tried reading in a different direction.

L	O	&
I	F	T
F	P	W
E	U	O
C	T	T
O	T	O
N	I	G
S	N	E
I	G	T
S	T	H
T	W	E
S	O	R

"Life consists of putting two and two together?"

"Most profound, most profound. It is the philosophy of Beejumstan in a nutshell. Never were truer words written. You see, when you do that, you get a third—a baby aha! You get wiser. Then you put another pair of twos together and on and on. If you stop to think about it, that's the very basic way everything works. It's yoking opposites. Like a big Y."

Lonesome leaned over and drew a big Y in the dirt and then he drew one upside down.

Y   ⅄

"You mean like those symbols Dr. Sobelow was talking about?"

"Correct!" Lonesome made a long face trying to look like Miss Tnurk, the goatlady teacher at the Beejum school.

Teak decided to think about all this later or they might never get to Mount Pook. But she couldn't resist asking about the message on the other pillar.

Again, with a stupendous leap, Lonesome was up on the other pillar and bending upside down to examine it. "This one, Dr. Syzygy thought at first was the price list for the refreshments, but then it turned out to be another great truth. Let me see—" But Teak decoded it for him, reading from the glass frame.

N	R	G
E	E	A
V	I	S
E	S	A
R	N	F
F	O	R
O	S	E
R	U	E
G	C	K
E	H	I
T	T	P
T	H	P
H	I	E
E	N	R

"Never forget there is no such thing as a free kipper," read Teak.

"That's right." Lonesome agreed. "There isn't. It is one of the most dishonest and cruel deceptions to try to persuade anyone anywhere that anything comes for free. It doesn't. You even have to pay back for your life by living it. After all, isn't that the least you can do in return for such a gift! Why, you could get a whole civilization off track if everybody only accepted everything for free! The next thing they'd be saying is that the world owed them a living instead of their owing the world the gift of themselves. Dear me, I hope nothing like that ever happens where you come from. There would be scads of unhappy people. My goodness, it would be tantamount to going to a dinner party and having everybody including the butcher, the baker, the candlestick maker, the cooks, and the waiters, and the guests, and all the vegetables, the dumplings and stews, and puddings and pies *all* sit down with bibs around their necks expecting to be served supper! There wouldn't *be* any supper at all, don't you see?"

"I s'pose not," giggled Teak, thinking of a pudding with a bib around its neck. She hoped somebody in her world would think of saying the same thing, and oddly enough somebody did.

"Give and take, give and take," preached the rabbit, waving his paws up and down like a seesaw. "It takes two to come out even. Then everything makes sense as well as nonsense... Well, I do believe we'd best be getting on our way. Gezeebius is bound to be waiting." So saying, Lonesome jumped down and immediately resumed his bouncy climbing. And he taught Teak two Beejum songs that went like this:

> *Three ducks sat under a nonion tree*
> *and they were as happy as happy could be*
> *WHY?*
> *'cos one was an onh and one was an anh*
> *and one was a jolly rovoo, rovoo*
> *'cos one was an onh and one was an anh*
> *and one was a jolly rovoooo!*

and:

> *Once round a fairy fruitcake*
> *Twice round a fairy fruitcake*
> *Thrice round a fairy fruitcake*
> *to seeee the other side.*

And when they came to a perfect place for echoes, he did give a yodel or two. Then together Teak and the rabbit whooped up a storm.

17

Lost and Found

TEAK WAS STILL MAKING funny yodely noises in her sleep and woke herself up. This time she was on a small bed in a small bedroom in a small hotel on the island of Prinkipo, just off the coast of Turkey in the sea of Marmara. In fact she could hear the waters lapping just below her window and a donkey braying out back. There were lights flickering and floating on the ceiling. It was the sunlight reflecting off the water below. Teak tried to think of what it might mean.

Then she jumped out of bed and began to get dressed for breakfast. She wondered if there were any Turkish Blaskells. Perhaps they had them and didn't even know it. Prinkipo, as it was called at that time, was so small an island that no motor cars were allowed on it. If you went anywhere, you went on a donkey. Teak saw men ride by who looked twice the size of the donkeys carrying them. The donkeys had sweet and patient eyes. They made her think of Mimosa, Lissabelle Ann's donkey that had carried Figg Newton up Criss-Cross Hill.

Birdie King was enchanted with the island. She said that it lay like a small jewel on blue velvet. Out one window you could see the coast of Asia Minor and out the other side you could see the coast of Europe. Prinkipo and the other little islands near it were covered with umbrella pines, which all leaned in the direction of the wind. There was such a beautiful piney smell to the air, and the colors of warm tan, dark green, and brilliant blue mingled with the fragrance. The small hotel was bright white and it had a square marble terrace that overlooked the sea.

The hotel was not far from the dock where the ferryboat to Istanbul picked up passengers. Teak would walk down in the morning with her parents to see her father off for a day's business in the city of Istanbul, and she and her mother would go down again in the late afternoon to meet him upon his return. Thaddeus King Jr. was involved, it seemed, in the transition of Turkey from its Asiatic to its European identity. Thanks to Atatürk, their new leader, the Turks were in the process of giving up the Arabic alphabet and taking up the Roman alphabet, so this was a time when you could see both the old and new customs. Teak's mother explained that you read Arabic from right to left.

"Why don't we read from left to right and then right to left on the next line. That would save a lot of time, don't you think?" pondered Teak.

"Well, the Phoenicians way back had the same idea," Birdie explained. "That's why some of the letters got stuck in opposite directions when things settled down."

"Ha! Then maybe I was once a Phoenician and that's how come I write my L's backwards sometimes," Teak grinned, happy for any excuse.

Istanbul was the new name given to the city of Constantinople. It was a most beautiful, ancient, and exotic city. Teak's father was explaining this to her one morning as they stood on the dock waiting for the ferry. In his way, he tried to help Teak get an education as she went. One of her fondest memories of him was a time he had read aloud to her and she had seen the great care with which he used his forefinger to turn the page. It was as if he loved the book.

Teak's parents were taking her with them for a change, and she listened to the complicated history her father was unfolding to her. There seemed to have been a lot to do with conquests and trade and Crusades. But it was much too much for her to remember, and after they boarded the ferry she half listened and half looked at the other passengers on the boat. Most of the men were swarthy and had very bushy black mustaches. Some of them were dressed in long striped shirts like the Egyptians and others wore business suits that didn't fit very well and didn't have neckties. The women wore dresses, but there were still quite a few dressed all in black from head to toe. Their heads and faces were veiled, and all you could see were their eyes going peekaboo. Birdie King whispered to Teak that they were Muslims, and that the men wearing those red hats that looked like upside-down flowerpots with black tassels on them were men who had made the pilgrimage to Mecca. The hats were called fezzes. The children and babies all had great big black eyes. One boy, who looked to be about Teak's age, stood and stared at Teak the whole trip and only smiled at the very end. He had a very nice smile, thought Teak. It lit up his dark face and showed that his teeth were very white. He had lost his two bottom baby teeth. There Teak was ahead of him; hers had grown back in quite a while ago. She smiled back at the boy.

Teak stood on the deck with her head through the rails and watched the flying fish leap out of the water, skim the surface, and dive back under again. She had had no idea fish could fly. What did they see when they came out of the water into the air? The water was a very dark green, though it looked bright blue in the distance. As they approached the harbor of Istanbul, Teak's mother pointed out the great domes and minarets of the huge mosques, the beautiful places of worship for Muslims. They and the city stood bathed in a golden autumn haze. The air hung like gauze, catching the light and rendering the city mysterious. Teak was impressed.

Then they passed a large smooth grey rock that stood out of the water. Teak was told that that was where the Turks used to put stray dogs and leave them to die. This upset her and she hoped it wasn't true.

When they disembarked, they took a taxi to the Great Bazaar. Istanbul struck Teak as one of the noisiest cities she'd ever been in. Street peddlers were hawking their wares, which they carried in boxes hung on chains around their necks. Beggar children ran barefoot after the car begging for coppers, whining and pleading *Baksheesh, baksheesh!* Motorcars careened around corners, as in Athens, blaring *ahooogah, ahoooogah!* and people had to jump for safety. The horns were those rubber ones on the outside of the car that the driver squeezed with his hand. It seemed to Teak that the Turks were twice as alive as other people. Everywhere they were gesticulating and waving their arms and hands about something. She noticed that there were bead curtains instead of doors in front of some of the shops and old men sat on stools fingering circles of fat amber-colored prayer beads while they talked with one another. Other men were smoking what her father said were hookah pipes—heavy ornamented jars of water on the ground connected by a long tube to the tobacco to be smoked. Very complicated. When her mother smoked, she put a cigarette in a tortoiseshell holder and closed her eyes when she puffed. Teak didn't like the smell of cigarettes much; she wasn't going to smoke, she decided, when she grew up.

They got out of the taxi and entered the Grand Bazaar. This was a covered labyrinth of shops that wound around and branched off in all directions. Entering it was like stepping into nighttime out of the day. Electric lightbulbs were strung along the alleyways, and all the shops were brightly lit from within. Inside the Bazaar Teak stood at a corner, watching a man hammering on a brass tray while her mother and father had an argument. Her father was in a hurry for an appointment, and her mother wanted to window-shop, and who was to take Teak? She hated it when her parents disagreed, so she slipped around the corner and began looking in first one window and then another. Presently her father gave a smart wave in the distance, assuming that Teak would go with her mother, while her mother mistook the wave as hailing Teak to follow him. Relieved, Birdie strode on. Neither parent was used to keeping an eye on a child. There had always been Nanny or Hanka or someone else.

Unconcerned, Teak turned down another arcade full of glittering windows. There were so many shops! One was full of wooden boxes with fancy designs on them and copper pitchers with long straight handles. They came in five different sizes. She wished she could give them all to Figg Newton for his laboratory. In another shop, people were sitting at tiny tables drinking coffee out of tiny cups with no handles. It smelled of coffee and roses. Then there was a woodworker's shop, across the way a store with every conceivable kind of clay jar and pot and large covered copper jugs, and this was next to a shop full of baskets, ropes, and beautiful brushes and brooms. As her nose led her on, twisting and turning, she passed a confectionery store where a man was pouring dough onto a large marble table. He rolled the dough as thin as paper and then sprinkled it with sticky chopped dates and raisins and syrup. Then he folded it, and refolded it, and refolded it, again and again. On a tray were samples of the finished product—"Baklava," he said, when he saw her looking. Then came a leather shop, which had a powerful wild smell. There were bags and pouches and hassocks and swordsheaths and belts and reins and saddles. In the jewelry shop windows were gold and silver filigree work, brooches, and pins and precious and semiprecious stones. Bracelets shaped like cuffs lay beside heavy necklaces weighted down with dangling coins.

In a trance Teak wandered further and further. She still felt secure that her mother was somewhere behind her, just the way Nanny never let her out of her sight. She tried to read the signs and prices, but many were still in Arabic by preference. Only when she came to the end of this arcade and found that it did not open onto the wide main corridor with the lights running on and on did she realize that she wasn't where she thought she was. When she tried to retrace her steps, neither mother nor father was anywhere to be seen, and she wasn't sure which way she had come. There were cross alleys she hadn't noticed before. Slowly it dawned on her that she might be lost— lost in a place where she couldn't speak one word of the language around her!

She started to run, trying to retrace her steps by the contents of shop windows, but she made a wrong turn and then another. There were crowds of men and women ambling and shuffling in both directions, but no one paid her any attention whatsoever. A clammy sense of panic began to rise in her chest. She stopped running and tried to remember what Nanny always told her. "Find a police-man," she had said, "if you ever get lost." But there wasn't a soul about who remotely looked like a policeman.

In front of her was a carpet shop with the most beauti-fully designed rugs hanging outside and framing the door. Inside she could see others heaped up on tables or rolled up underneath them. As she put out a finger to touch one at the door, she heard a man's soft voice come out of the dark interior of the shop. He spoke in English. "My daughter, do you know how many years it took to make that carpet?"

"No, sir," answered Teak, peering into the store. Inside, on a straight narrow wooden chair, sat a very old man with a short white beard. He wore a long woolen robe and had what to Teak looked like a white woolen bowl on his head. His hands were elegant and strong, and he wore a gold ring with a ruby on the little finger of his left hand.

"It took twelve years, three months, two weeks, and five days. In every square inch there can be a thousand knots, each knot tied in by hand. And some of that work was done by children not much older than you, because this is a very old carpet. They were boys when they began the work and young men when it was finished."

The man's words were precisely spoken and comforting. Teak was beginning to think that there was something very special about old people. They certainly were more interesting than most other people, and probably they were wiser as well. There was a mysterious power and dignity about this man, quite unlike any other person Teak had ever known. She couldn't tell if it came from the piercing yet kindly expression in his eyes or the comforting depth of his voice. He radiated strength and wisdom. Teak liked this man right off, trusted him. Strangely, she felt safe.

"This carpet," the old man continued, "is most precious because of that." He spoke English fluently, almost as if he had lived in England.

"How do they know what colors to put in?" asked Teak, peering closely at one spot of carpet.

The man rose and came to the door, smiling. "Ah, they must follow the directions of the designer. He has the whole plan, and he calls out and tells each one what to do next. It is very much like life, don't you agree? Imagine a little fly walking on the spot where your finger is pointing. Here it would seem all blue to him. Right? But suddenly it becomes red, then gold, then red again. That fly would be quite perplexed, quite confused, wouldn't he, and none of it would make any sense to him. What could he do, do you suppose, that would help him?"

Teak frowned.

"What is the insect called?" hinted the carpet seller.

"Fly. He could fly up and see the whole thing."

"That's right. He could see how beautiful and how necessary each of the colors was to the whole pattern. So the rug-makers have to be very patient and trusting, even when they don't like a color, even when they don't understand the commands of the designer. In the end, much that seems puzzling at first comes to make very good sense later on. Is that not so?"

"Are all of these made by hand?"

"Every one, my child. It would be impossible to count the hundreds of thousands of hours of labor, patience, and devotion hidden in my shop alone. This is why we say our carpets are alive, and when we kneel and pray upon them, they carry our prayers to Allah, to God, the Great One." Then he showed Teak a number of smaller rugs that each had a point designed in them. "Do you see these points? The point in the carpet is always set toward the holy city of Mecca, sacred to Islam, which is our religion."

"In Arabia?" Now Teak remembered what her father had told her while waiting for the ferry. And that made her remember that she was very lost.

But the man went on. "See here—a mistake! In every work of art, every Muslim makes at least one mistake." He smiled at Teak's amazement.

"On purpose? But why?"

"Because, my daughter, only Allah, only God, can make something of absolute perfection. We need to remember that to be human is to be imperfect."

"You mean, its all *right* to make mistakes?"

"Of course, of course!" laughed the old man. "How else can we learn? Only it is not a small piece of wisdom not to make the same mistake twice. It is wise to realize that to persist in a mistake is to make another one! What you learn from a mistake is its redemption. But—" and here he paused to look intently at Teak, "one must not forget about the learning or one is lost all over again."

At the word *lost,* Teak remembered her situation and the predicament she was in. She looked up at the old man and said, "Please, sir, I think I have made a mistake, *a very big one.*"

"I know that, my daughter, I know. You are lost. But you will be found. You see, we believe that Allah has a plan. Someday in the future you will remember this day.

It is as if, like the fly, you just moved from green to red, but it will be green again in a little while. For now, perhaps, you have learned a little lesson about trust from these carpets. Perhaps even, when you see a beautiful carpet like this again, you will walk upon it with greater reverence for so much hard work. Nature makes things beautiful without effort, but we must strive for that ability. And, my child," and the man put a firm hand on Teak's head, "perhaps you will remember an old friend. He will certainly remember you."

Then the old man leaned over and touched Teak's forehead with his thumb. "And, now, we will go and find your mother, who is looking for you. Give me your hand. For a little while, you must follow my directions."

Teak willingly put her hand in the hand of the carpet seller and felt it firmly grasped. The old man asked the potter next door to keep an eye on his shop. Then he stopped at a stand and bought two sweetmeats, one for Teak and one for himself. He popped one into Teak's mouth himself. It tasted deliciously of honey and roses. A Turkish Delight.

As they made their way the length of the arcade, people stopped to look at the odd pair. The white-bearded and dignified old man in his woolen robe and the young girl in her short flowered dress and little boots. Some people smiled and bowed to the carpet seller, putting their hands over their hearts, and saying, *"Salaam aleikum,"* which means "Peace be with you." It seemed that people felt he was someone important, even though he just sold carpets.

"Who *are* you?" asked Teak.

The old man smiled. "My name is Sheikh Mustafah. I am a Sufi. But in our belief, even a sheikh must have a trade and live in the world humbly as befits him. We like to remain hidden. What is your name, daughter?"

"My name's Thaddea King, but everyone calls me Teak."

"It sounds like you are royalty," he teased.

"Nope," grinned Teak. "I'm American." And Sheikh Mustafah laughed. "My family comes from Boston." She almost said she came from a teapot. "We are just living over here."

"And where is your home?"

"Everywhere. We live in hotels. Lots of them."

Mustafah stopped and turned to look at Teak. "Then the whole wide world will become your home! Isn't that splendid! We have something in common."

Together they came out of the Grand Bazaar and into the bright daylight. The traffic was going every which way—cars, trams, wagons, donkeys. There was dust and confusion. Teak saw a crowd standing around a man with a dancing bear. The bear had a muzzle and was standing on its hind legs and turning in circles. The keeper looked like a Bunnywidget, only bigger. He had the same kind of trousaloons. But the bear was dusty and sad looking.

They crossed a street and came to a cobbled courtyard. "Tell me, Teak, is it hard for you to say good-bye?" The question was so unexpected that Teak could feel tears pricking behind her eyes. Already she had been thinking of having to part from this wonderful strong friend—a man who had been so kind and protective to her.

Mustafah must have had an intuition. He looked at his watch and then motioned for Teak to sit down on a bench in the courtyard. "I want to share one last thing with you, my child. Something I had to learn as a very young boy. I, too, traveled a great deal in the world. First it was to find my Teacher and then it was to teach myself. I found that I was afraid to love people because I would only have to say good-bye again, usually forever in this life. And then I discovered a very great secret—"

"What is it?"

"For every good-bye there is another hello. As you grow older, perhaps you will discover, as I did, that in a strange way you are saying hello and greeting the same one you said good-bye to. It will be a different face and a different body, but the light in the eyes of everyone is the same light. It is the light of the Great One. We are all one Spirit, one Heart, you know, but it is just delightful to see how many disguises and masks the Great One can wear. When you understand this here," and he pressed his hand over Teak's heart, "it can ease the pain of some of those painful good-byes. Can you understand this at all?"

Teak looked into Mustafah's eyes, trying to memorize that light that shone out of them. She nodded her head briefly and clung to Mustafah's hand tighter and tighter, because that moment was coming all too soon.

Before long, they reached the Blue Mosque, and on the sidewalk in front of the garden beside it stood her mother with a Turkish policeman in a proper policeman's uniform. When Birdie saw Teak, she became more excited than Teak had ever seen her. She was beside herself with both relief and fury, which is the way mothers are apt to feel under such circumstances. But before she could shake Teak to pieces with love and anger, Sheikh Mustafah lightly touched her arm. "Please, Mrs. King, not this time. I believe your daughter has already learned a very great lesson today."

Amazed, Birdie King gave a big sigh of resignation and she reached for her purse. She was somewhat confused by the apparent dignity and authority with which the old man held himself, and yet she did not want to seem unappreciative. Anticipating her dilemma, he bowed with a kind of understanding. "Meeting your young daughter Teak has been a reward in itself, my lady."

All this time, he had continued to hold Teak's hand tightly. Now he let it go and looked straight down at her. There was a rare and meaningful twinkle in his eye. Teak knew that she would never forget it.

"Maybe we shall meet again, my daughter. Who knows. *Inshallah!*" And he touched the cheek of the girl playfully. Then he put his hand on his heart, bowed briefly to both of them, and strode off through the small crowd that had gathered around them.

Birdie King seemed subdued. The policeman had been very impressed by something, and he had spoken to her, saying something in French.

"What did he just say, Mother?" asked Teak.

"He said that you are a very fortunate girl and blessed to have met such a great man. He is known as one of the greatest sheikhs of Turkey, and he is a very wise Sufi Teacher."

Neither mother nor daughter could figure out how he had known where to find Birdie King. He just did.

Teak asked if they could look inside the mosque. There was still time. Everyone had to take off their shoes. There were paper slippers for foreigners, but none small enough for Teak, so she shuffled in a pair of big ones all through the cool dim beauty of the ancient space. Her mother tried to show her things, but to tell the truth Teak had stopped noticing. She was too busy trying not to forget the wonderful expression in Mustafah's eyes.

18

Gezeebius

TEAK AND LONESOME reached the foot of the Peak of Pook and the most difficult and challenging part of the climb. They came to a small wooden hut in which a rope and some climbing picks were stashed. Carefully Lonesome tied the rope around his waist and after a given length, he tied it around Teak's waist.

"What's that for?" asked Teak a little uncertainly.

"That's in case one of us slips or falls," said Lonesome cheerfully. "It's just a precaution." And he went on securing the knot tightly. "It reminds me of a time when Gezeebius posed me a dreadful question. It was before he made me a guide to the Peak of Pook."

"What was the question?" asked Teak.

"I think it would be too hard for you to answer at your age. I certainly had a hard time of it. He said to me, 'Supposing that you were holding onto the hand of your Master with one paw and the hand of your student with the other, and you *had* to let go of one or the other. Which would you choose?" Lonesome shuddered at the memory, which meant considerable flopping and trembling of ears.

Teak thought about it and shuddered as well as she considered the options. She would be trusting her Teacher to take care of her, yet her student would be trusting her... "I wouldn't want to answer that one," she said thoughtfully. "At least, not yet."

The climb turned out to be fun. You had to hang on for dear life with hands and feet, like a fly walking up a wall. In very rough places Lonesome had the advantage of being able to leap from rock to rock. When he got to a safe place, he would twist the rope around a rock to secure it and then pull Teak up. Nobody slipped, though it got tricky when they reached some snow and icy bits.

"Don't look down," advised Lonesome. Then he joked, "You can see why Gezeebius is lucky to have his cloud! But first he had to come the hard way many times to make it safer for the rest of us."

The climb got easier as they neared the top, and just at the lip of the summit Teak almost got overconfident. Then she looked down and saw how high and steep the peak really was. Her head swam and she felt dizzy.

"Look up!" warned Lonesome. "You're almost there." So Teak steadied herself. She reached the top and lay half on the ground with her legs dangling over the precipice. Lonesome did not assist her but let her claw her way to safety all by herself. "You made it!" said Lonesome proudly. "I just knew you would. Well done!"

Teak stood up and brushed herself off. Then she looked around. The summit was tucked in a little hollow of crags like the center in a crown of rocks. In a pleasant clearing was one very old bunkle tree with a bench all around its trunk. The view was breathtaking. Far and wide the snow-tipped mountains encircled the Peak of Pook. The sky was a piercing blue.

There was a medium-sized cave with a nice carpet on the floor, and a laundry line stretched from it to another rock. On it flapped one of Gezeebius's robes and two of his attendant Noodlenip's bright red-footed leggities. At the back of the clearing, tethered firmly by an anchor and a long rope, was the *Cloud of Unknowing*. It was swaying gently this way and that in the breeze. Gezeebius was nowhere to be seen, nor was Noodlenip for that matter.

Just as Lonesome was pointing out that you could see the ocean way off in the distance between two of the mountains, a large brown owl flew over them and settled on a ledge above the cave.

"*Pax vobiscum* and *caveat emptor*, whoo, whoo, whoo!" hooted the owl in a precise baritone voice that somehow managed to sound like it was winking at you.

"Oh, hello, Whitsworth," said Lonesome. "What language are you studying now?"

"Latin," winked the owl. "Hick, hike, hock. Whooyus, whooyus, whooyus!" He recited this with considerable pride and finished by expelling a pellet with a fine zing. It ricocheted off several rocks and fell to the ground. "*Ex pluribus unum*," he added with satisfaction. "Three in one shot ain't bad. Where was I? Whooyus, whooyus—"

"My name is Teak," said the girl, thinking Whitsworth had asked her the question, which he hadn't really.

Whitsworth cocked his head, ruffled his considerable feathers, blinked eight times in rapid succession, and tried to focus on Teak. "It looks like a boy. Upon my word, it *is* a boy! I just learned the Latin for boy yesterday." He held up a wing. "No, no, don't tell me! It'll come to me in a second...POOER! That's it!" he shouted and gave a jump that almost cost him his balance on the ledge. "P U E R," he spelled, *"puer aeternus.* That was in the text on page sixty-six." Then the owl stuck his beak closer to Teak, who was still in her lederhosen; Whitsworth shook his head and blinked his large yellow eyes again. "On the other hand, you might be a girl...hmmm...then you would be a...a...*puella,* that's it! So which are you?" Teak admitted that she was a *puella.*

It all sounded Greek to Teak, but just as she was feeling more and more confused, Lonesome whispered to her behind his fluffy paw. "Pay no attention. He's just showing off. Gezeebius is training him to be a translator of ancient scrolls and texts. He is already fluent in half a dozen languages, including Chinese."

"Ah chu," pronounced Whitsworth solemnly, having very good hearing.

"God bless you," said Teak politely. *"Gesundheit!"*

Whitsworth frowned and shook his head at the girl. Maybe he hadn't studied German yet. He blinked his great yellow eyes with embarrassment.

"Would you like me to count to ten in Hungarian?"

But before Teak could answer the question, a tall figure in a white woolen robe came around a boulder, accompanied by a host of animals, including a familiar donkey.

Behind the animals came Noodlenip, cap and all, carrying what looked like a baby hedgehog. It was adorable. "Ooooh!" Teak sighed, wanting to hold it.

Gezeebius stopped and looked at Teak without saying anything, but there was a twinkle of mischief in his eye as he waited for Teak to take him all in.

What did Teak see? She saw first the great mane of white hair and the full white beard which fell like a waterfall down the front of Gezeebius all the way to his feet. In fact there was a little loop at the bottom which enabled him to straighten the beard with one of his big toes. Very convenient. His white woolen robe had a rope around the waist, and attached to this cincture was a thong of leather, which held a gold key, a silver key, what looked like a fountain pen, a magnifying glass, and a Swiss army knife. Out of a pocket across his chest stuck a compass, a carpenter's square, and a neatly folded handkerchief embroidered in blue with the initials WOM. His feet were protected by sandals, and in his right hand he was holding a tall staff studded with nails of different metals. And on that hand was a gold ring inlaid with a familiar glowing ruby.

All of this Teak took in with sharp eyes. She really was getting very good at noticing. She saved the face of Gezeebius for last, perhaps because she felt so overawed by his presence. Finally she took a deep breath and raised her eyes to meet those of the Wise Old Man of Beejumstan. Then she found herself gazing into the warm, friendly and mischievously twinkling eyes of her friend—have you guessed it?—Sheikh Mustafah of Istanbul!

Gezeebius spoke. "I told you, my daughter, that we might meet again sooner than you thought."

With a shout of joy, Teak ran to him and was embraced by Gezeebius in a great-grandfatherly hug. Any animal with a tail to wag was wagging it. It was an absolutely splendid moment. Lonesome was moved to wipe his whiskers, which he only did on very special occasions.

"But—but—" started Teak, "how—?"

"Do you think that you are the only one who lives in two worlds, my daughter? The only question is, are you living in my world or am I living in yours? I am teasing you, Teak, but I am also very serious. This question of different worlds or different Bubbles is not all that hard to understand. It depends on how you look at and think about the world and the people around you, for only you can make sense of what you encounter outside yourself and what you feel inside. You could say that you play a big part in making the Bubble you live in. Do you remember when you wanted that black leather wallet so badly in Athens that you didn't pay attention to anything else?"

Teak blushed, embarrassed that Gezeebius knew about her Gimmie Attack, then slowly nodded her head.

"And do you remember when you rescued Lonesome and the children from the evil witches?"

Teak was quick to nod this time.

"And what were you thinking about in each case?"

Teak chewed her lip for a while, then answered, "I guess that when I wanted the wallet I was thinking only about me, and when I rescued Lonesome and the children I was thinking mostly about them."

"Yes, that's it," said Gezeebius, "and both of those Teaks are you. And this is true for everyone else as well. Teak, all human beings are alike in what they are given inside—every single one has a Big You and a Little Me. And every single one expresses these in a different way."

Teak was chewing her lip again. After a little while she asked, "You mean we are all alike only different."

"Exactly. Just as all people have faces with two eyes, a nose, a mouth, and a chin, but no two people look alike. Everybody is unique and the same in *being* unique. And that's true on the inside as well. Everybody is the same in having been given life and a Big You and a Little Me in the first place."

"What do you mean by a Big You and a Little Me?"

Gezeebius pulled a piece of parchment out of a pocket in his robe and, using the compass and fountain pen on his belt, drew a wheel with many spokes. "Show me," he said, "where you can be in the wheel and see all the spokes at once."

Teak pondered a moment. Then she pointed to the center of the wheel.

"That's right. But supposing you were shut up in your own little Bubble like this"—and now he drew a small circle just touching the inside of the big circle at the end of one of the spokes, and in it he put a T for Teak—"and you were all alone on the end of just one of the spokes? What would you do?"

"I guess I'd go round and round in circles like the merry-go-round in Paris!" Teak laughed.

"Well, that's it. The Big You sits in the middle watching the Little Me go around and around. And the Little Me gets so involved in the everyday world that it forgets the bigger world and the Big You in the middle. But the Big You never forgets the Little Me. It's the Big You that lives in both Bubbles at once." And Gezeebius pointed to the center of the big circle where all the spokes met.

"But, Gezeebius, why is it called the Big You and not the Big Me?"

"That, Teak, is a mystery that you will have to discover for yourself. You will have to ask that question many times. You might even have to shout, 'Hey, Big You, who are you really? Who am I?' But I can give you a helpful hint—any time you think the Big You is a Big Me, you will be in Big Trouble. But whenever you are aware of the Big You, you will know that you are not all alone. What do you see when you look at the Big You at the center of the big circle?"

Teak looked again at the drawing. "It's the one place where all of the Little Me's come together. And there are a lot of Little Me's but only one Big You."

"AHA!" said Gezeebius, and smiled. Teak beamed back.

"Now, come and meet Mimosa and some of our other good friends. I see you have already met Whitsworth!" Gezeebius laid his fine hand on the neck of the donkey and introduced her as Mimosa, Figg Newton's friend.

The animals, who had each come up to the Peak of Pook on the *Cloud of Unknowing*, now crowded around Teak so that she could pet them. Noodlenip held out the baby hedgehog, and Teak touched its little pink tummy and saw its tiny sleepy eyes close above its wee pointy nose. He was introduced as Montague. Little did Teak know that she was rubbing the tummy of the next Pompompity of Beejumstan!

Whitsworth flew around them. *"Vidisti fratrem, vidisti dominum tuum!"* he intoned, attempting to say something appropriate to the occasion, meaning "Behold your brother, behold your lord."

"Enough, Whitsworth!" laughed Gezeebius. "Go and review your Brythonic numbers and leave us in peace!"

Instead of feeling rebuked, Whitsworth was delighted. Now he flew around them chanting, *"Yan, tan, tethera, pethera, pimp! pethera-bumpit, figgit!"* This was followed by another zinger of a pellet that knocked a clothespin off the laundry line.

"Nice shot," praised Gezeebius. Whitsworth, now exhausted, flew back to his branch and began to preen his beautiful brown feathers. Teak noticed that he could twirl his head around like a bottletop. It was a wonder that it didn't come off.

Mimosa, the donkey, came closer to Gezeebius and leaned against him. He scratched her softly behind her furry ears. And as he did so, Teak remembered what Dr. Azibov Sobelow had advised her to do when she met Gezeebius. So Teak asked him if this might be a good time for a Beejum story.

"Hmmmmm," pondered Gezeebius, "it might be at that. What would you like to hear a story about?"

Teak looked at Mimosa and Mimosa looked at Teak. "Do you have one about donkeys?" she asked.

"Hmmmmm, I just might do." So Gezeebius walked slowly and thoughtfully over to the bench under the bunkle tree and sat down, stroking his beard, and looking off into the distance. The animals followed and settled themselves expectantly in a half circle in front of him. Lonesome stretched out off to one side. Everyone looked gratefully at Teak for asking such a good question. Teak sat down close to Gezeebius's knee, and Mimosa folded herself next to her so Teak could put her arm over the donkey's shoulder. It would be a story for them all.

"Hmmmmmmmmm," said Gezeebius a third time. "I might have one about donkeys at that." And so he began, "Once upon a time—"

"Excuse me, sir," piped up Teak, "but why is it that all the best stories start with 'Once upon a time'?"

"Well, Teak, that is a very interesting question, to which there is an interesting answer. 'Once upon a time' is a secret signal to you that the story to follow has a hidden truth that is true for *all* time, because the only real time that is once and always with us is *now.*"

"*Illud tempus!*" chortled Whitsworth, back to his Latin again. "I know what that means. It means 'that time, that special and always time.'"

"Aha!" whispered Teak to herself.

"And it also means," continued Gezeebius, ignoring Whitsworth for the moment, though he was secretly pleased, "that the story has an outside and an inside. The outside part tells about the particular characters, the plot, and the setting or time and place. The who, what, where, and when of it, so to speak. But the inside carries the message and meaning hidden within the story, and that usually deals with *why* you are bothering to tell the story in the first place. It's the inside of the story that speaks to the inside of you and of everybody. It tells a story about what could happen in your own inner kingdom, the kingdom within you."

"Temenos!" hooted the owl joyously. "That's Greek! It means '*that* place, that secret, special place.'" Whitsworth was so stuck up, but you couldn't help liking him. He tried so hard to be helpful and informative.

"Thank you, Whitsworth," Gezeebius said graciously. "Your scholarship is coming in very handy, as always." And to Teak, "Can you understand a little bit what I am trying to say?"

"I think so," said Teak. "You mean that the story part is for the Little Me, but the meaning part is important to the Big You. They're supposed to work on different levels." Teak was beginning to get the idea of it, after hearing it over and over again in different ways. "It's like the parables and fairy tales and myths that Grandma King reads to me."

"Aha!" smiled Lonesome, very pleased with his pupil.

"Aha!" smiled Gezeebius, very pleased with Lonesome.

"AHA!" shouted Teak, very pleased with herself.

"Ahasuerus!" cried Whitsworth, but he couldn't remember who that was or where he'd read about him, so he didn't pursue the matter, and rolled his big yellow eyes skyward again.

Everybody laughed and thumped tails.

At that moment a familiar face appeared at the edge of the summit, and then all of Mr. Rathbone climbed up. He looked radiantly happy.

"I hope you don't mind my joining you. I just celebrated my Aberduffy Day and I'm on my way to another Bubble, but I did want to see Teak one more time and to say hello to everybody."

Teak ran over to him and pulled him by both arms to join the circle. "*Now* can you tell me what Aberduffy Day is—please, please!"

Mr. Rathbone, a much younger and more vigorous Mr. Rathbone, looked over to Gezeebius for permission. Gezeebius nodded.

"Well, Teak, when you go back to your parents they will tell you that old Mr. Rathbone died. They may say it was about time, because I was very old, and they may bother to comfort your grandma, whom I admired and loved dearly as a friend," he added, chuckling. "Now you won't have to ask where I went to! I'm here and on my way most gratefully."

"Can you come back to Beejumstan?" asked Teak.

"As far as I know," he replied.

Teak certainly hoped so. "Well, that's good," Teak announced, and she sat down close to Gezeebius with a sense of relief.

Whitsworth had to have the last word. "*Aber, aber, aber* ...hmm, that means 'river' in Gaelic. *Duffy, duff, dubh...*

means 'dark.' Seems Beejums don't die in darkness, they celebrate Aberduffy Day! Why not?"

Teak had a quick thought. "I guess if we all have to die, it must be as natural as getting born. We might as well celebrate. Why not?"

"And now with your permission," said Gezeebius, "perhaps we can resume the Tale of the Three Donkeys."

"Why not!" chorused all the Beejums, happy as happy could be.

19

The Tale of the Three Donkeys

"Once upon a time, Teak, there were three donkeys who lived in the same stable, and this stable was in the countryside, a fair distance from the nearest big city. Every day, together or separately, the donkeys trotted out to market with heavy baskets at their sides, and every evening they munched their hay back in their stalls and compared notes about the day's events.

"The first donkey was by far the strongest and the handsomest, and he always had the best tales to tell. It seemed he always carried the heaviest load or the best of the produce. He was, if the truth were known, the most conceited donkey that there was anywhere about. And when his companions teased him about this, he simply put his nose up in the air, and closed his eyes with a long-suffering expression, and told his two friends how incapable they were of understanding him, because if they did, they would realize that he was really the *humblest* donkey in the world!

"Now, the second donkey was just as big as the first one and was a very presentable donkey indeed. But he was shy and suffered from a very poor opinion of himself. He always felt inadequate and stupid. The stories that he would tell invariably dwelt on his mistakes or his clumsiness—how he had stumbled and how his baskets had fallen off and spilled or how the other donkeys at the market mocked him. Secretly, he thought he was the worst donkey in the world, and apparently so did his master, who beat him daily with a stick and insulted him as a matter of course.

"The third donkey was, in truth, the smallest of the three, but she was certainly the most realistic. She knew she was a good, solid, and dependable beast of burden, and when she came home at the end of the day there was little for her to brag about and still less to be ashamed of. She did the best she could with what she had at the moment it was most needed. She didn't tell many stories about herself, because she knew that sometimes she was good and sometimes bad, sometimes smart and sometimes stupid, and that was the way of it. She got along very nicely with the other two, because she always listened to them with interest, if not curiosity, and in this manner she profited from their experience as well as her own.

"One morning, an important man was going to ride to the city and needed to hire a donkey. So he came to the stable to make inquiries of the owner. Naturally the owner came into the stable and chose the first donkey. He was always the first chosen! So the man got on the donkey and began riding toward the city, and as he went down the road the news of his coming spread. People began to gather, and to point, and to shout, and to clap their hands. Soon they were waving palm fronds, calling him king, and throwing the fronds under the donkey's feet.

"The first donkey was delighted to be recognized as a king. Finally! It was about time! And he thought how splendid it would be to wear a golden crown and be the first King of All Donkeys. He completely forgot about the rider on his back, as he pricked up his ears smartly, pranced a little this way and that, and switched the tassel on his tail in what he thought to be a regal manner. He bowed his head graciously to the applause of the crowds, attempting withal to appear modest. However, when a young man, who had climbed up a tree just to see him better, waved and called for his attention, he just could not resist responding to such an effort to admire him. Thus it came about that he raised his head to acknowledge his admirer and, in so doing, stepped into a hole, fell, and broke his leg! His rider, who had almost been thrown off, dismounted, and decided—since he had gone only a third of the way to the city—to retrace his steps and return to the stable to hire another donkey. As he walked back, a wagon came to pick up the first donkey, and eventually he was carted back to his stable in considerable disgrace.

"When the man spoke to the owner of the donkeys, he went straightaway into the stable and chose the second donkey. But the second donkey, having heard the roar of the crowd, suspected the importance of this rider and immediately decided that he was unworthy to carry such a personage. Besides, his own coat was too mangy and his tail all ratty, so people would only make fun of his ugliness. None of which was true.

"When the owner came to get the second donkey, he braced himself on all four feet and absolutely refused to budge. And we all know how stubborn even a small donkey can be! And all the while this donkey was thinking bitterly to himself that if this man were truly a king, he should have hired a white horse! What on earth could he, a miserable donkey, do for a king! Why should anyone choose him to ride upon? So, the owner cursed the second one roundly and beat him soundly and called him the stupidest of all donkeys. And, indeed, at that moment, so he was.

"Finally, the third donkey was brought out, and she sturdily and sensibly carried the man, without further to-do, to where he wanted to go, which was the big city of Jerusalem. She did the best she could with what she had at the time that it was needed. And she thought no more about it, since it was another day's work, although she had to admit there was a lot of attention given to the gentle rider on her back.

"And strange as this may seem, that donkey ride has gone down in history, and that very donkey has been mentioned in a book that has sold more copies than any other in the world! That donkey has been painted over and over again carrying one of the greatest Masters of your world, Teak. It is quite true he could have ridden to the city on a fine white horse, but he didn't. He chose a humble donkey who was willing to serve."

When Gezeebius finished telling his story, Mimosa was very pleased, as you might imagine, and she thanked him by putting her head on his lap.

Then Noodlenip said it was time for refreshments, and off he sped to make preparations. Gezeebius invited Teak to visit his quarters in the cave. It was very simply furnished. A bed, a chair, a wardrobe. The most beautiful thing was the rich Turkish carpet on the floor (which was not surprising). There was a table, which, like Figg Newton's, had a candle on it, and behind it stood a large luminous crystal. The cave was very peaceful, and it looked out on one of the most beautiful views there could be.

Teak knew that this cave on the Peak of Pook must be Gezeebius's Quiet Place. And she grew very pensive.

"What are you thinking, Teak?" asked Gezeebius.

"I wish I had a place like this," answered Teak.

"But you have it already!" laughed Gezeebius.

"I do?"

"But, of course, all of this"—and Gezeebius swept his arm around—"all of this is within you. It is happening in you, just as you are happening in me. With every encounter, we enter each other. When you grow up, my dear, perhaps you can remind others that every single human being has a sanctuary in the heart—a safe and holy place. And everyone can decorate it any way they like. It is your own Quiet Place where you can invite your Divine Guest to visit, your Big You."

"Are you my Big You, Gezeebius?" asked Teak.

Gezeebius smiled. "No, dear, I am only chosen to remind you and others that you already have a Big You.

It's so easy to forget when you are born into another Bubble. The Great One lives in you as *you*, which is what all the true Teachers tell us. But every Big You needs a good donkey. What kind of donkey are you, Teak?"

Teak squirmed. She didn't know how to answer. Finally, she admitted, "I think I've felt like all three of those donkeys."

Gezeebius nodded his head and smiled. "So have I."

"Did the donkeys have any names?" asked Teak.

"Indeed they did. But it's a funny thing. They all had the same name—it was Little—"

"Me," interrupted Teak. And she, too, put her head on Gezeebius's lap and he stroked her hair fondly and she felt blessed.

20

Earth, Water, Fire, Air

TEAK WAS WOKEN very suddenly at four o'clock in the morning. The whole island of Prinkipo was shaking and shuddering. Teak's bed was rattling, things were toppling off her bureau, wind was banging the shutters, and she could hear frightened voices calling each other in the hotel corridors. Outside it sounded like the world was coming apart.

She sat up abruptly in bed and screamed, "Mother! Oh, Mother! What's happening?"

The door burst open. Her father stood there in his pajamas and dressing gown. With one big swoop, he picked up his daughter in his arms, grabbed a blanket, and carried her out the door to the stairs. "It's an earthquake—a bad one!" There was urgency in his voice.

Again there came a strong shock. The whole building creaked, sagged, and shook. Plaster was falling on top of them as they went down the hall. Some few guests held candles, and she saw her mother helping an old lady whose eyes were wide with alarm. People were moaning, screaming, shoving, and shouting at others not to push as they tried to get down the stairs and out into the open. There was no electricity, and it was difficult to find the way in the darkness.

Once they got outside, the air was warm, wet, and windy, and the few candles became useless. Teak could see villagers running and could hear them shouting up the hill from the jetty. Some had lanterns. Teak's father handed her over to her mother, who took her hand and told her to cover her head with the blanket. Then they made their way, following the villagers toward a knoll with umbrella pine trees. They could hear the cracking of buildings and the high-pitched screams of babies.

Teak's mother was out of breath. "Let's stop here," she puffed. So they sat down at the foot of a tall pine and waited for Teak's father to find them. In the east, the faint light of dawn was stretching over the choppy sea. The aftershocks continued, and Teak's mother held her close. Teak thought ruefully that it took an earthquake for her parents to hug her. It felt so good, sitting there snuggled next to Mother. She didn't care if it was raining and blowing. Now she felt safe.

After an hour or more, Teak's father discovered them and led them back to the hotel. The road had deep cracks in it. He told them that several people had been killed in the quake, and that it would be days before they would know the extent of the damage.

They were not allowed to go up to their rooms until the building was inspected, so they sat out on the marble terrace, where a makeshift breakfast was served—bread, cheese, and olives. The manager was dressed, but all the hotel guests were still in their nightclothes, feeling a bit self-conscious but laughing now and exchanging tales of their experiences. There were no other children staying at the hotel so Teak was fussed over and made much of by the other guests. As usual, she was the token child.

A few days later, Thaddeus King decided to move the family from Turkey. The breakdown of telephone service and electricity made it difficult for him to conduct business, so shortly they sailed on a ship to Egypt and settled in the Shepheard's Hotel in Cairo.

This was Teak's second visit to Cairo. She had already been there when she was five years old. Now she was eight. The ceiling in her room was much, much higher than in other places, and her bed had a pole at the back from which hung a huge white mosquito net. When she climbed onto the bed, the netting was draped all over it and hung to the floor. It was like sleeping in a cloud.

In Egypt, it became clear that Teak was becoming a problem to her parents. Not that she was being naughty; it was just that they couldn't take care of her and also get their work done. Besides, she really needed more school lessons. Certainly she could read well, and she was learning geography and snatches of history as she went from place to place, and she was grasping the basics of several different languages and could count money. But her parents realized that none of this was structured enough. Something would have to be done.

Teak's father made inquiries at the British embassy, and that was how a young lady arrived early one morning to take up her duties.

Her name was Miss Ursula Tinkham.

Miss Tinkham was very English. She was young and pretty, with merry blue eyes, rosy pink cheeks, and bobbed, frizzy, golden hair—hair so fine it glinted like spun gold. She had a tip-tilted little nose and held it in the air when she walked or rather swiggled across a room. She was enthusiastic, and her favorite expressions were "I say!" and "Gosh!" She was wellborn, intelligent, and she could type. Everybody loved her on the spot, except perhaps Birdie King, for the good reason that both Teak and her father were so frightfully keen about Miss Tinkham that she felt a bit left out.

Teak just loved Miss Tinkham. It was her first experience of a young, pretty, and vivacious grown-up. Everything about her was astonishing, and Teak idolized her, envied her, and for the first time got the impression that there was something positive about being feminine. Whatever she taught Teak, Teak learned quickly, and she learned a lot. She looked forward to Miss Tinkham's arrival at the hotel every morning and became downright possessive and jealous whenever she was summoned away to take dictation from her father or mother in their room.

Best of all, Miss Tinkham took Teak on outings. They went to see the mummies and the golden treasures of the Cairo Museum. They walked through its cocoa-colored caverns and looked up at the huge silent faces of the statues of pharaohs and gods and goddesses. She would let

Teak hold her hand, and together they would gaze upward, and she would whisper, "Gosh!" Soon Teak was also whispering, "Gosh."

Miss Tinkham would take her to the zoo, and they would look down into the monkey city—a pit filled with miniature houses that red-bottomed monkeys would run into and then bob up, peering out of windows and doors. And Miss Tinkham would laugh and smile at the monkeys' antics and cry out, "I say! Did you see that one?" And she always gave a few *baksheesh* to the miserable beggar children whose eyes and faces were covered with tsetse flies. Teak's parents never did.

At night in bed, Teak would put herself to sleep doing her multiplication tables and imagining Miss Tinkham's delight when she could rattle off her eights and her nines without a hitch. She could just see those blue eyes sparkle and the shake of her finespun hair, and hear her lilting voice saying, "Oh, I *say*, Teak, that was jolly well done!" Teak knew that there was nothing, nothing in the world that she would not do for Miss Ursula Tinkham. She would be the pattern for every princess or goddess in every book of fairy tales or mythology that Teak would read for years to come. "Ursula" became a magic name for Teak, and she would repeat it to herself slowly, feeling the syllables like sweet grapes in her mouth. And she was happy when her father had to leave again on a business trip, because she would have more time with Miss Tinkham herself.

Of course, they drove out to Gizeh to see the Great Pyramid. Teak was amazed that while the banks of the

Nile were all green and lined with palm trees, the pyramids were right at the edge of a desert of sand. It was very hot. Miss Tinkham showed her the Sphinx and told her the famous riddle: What goes on four legs in the morning, two at noon, and three in the evening? Teak knew the answer because she had overheard it in the bar at the corner of the hotel, the one that had a door made of a curtain of beads. "Man," she said, grinning happily.

Ursula was vastly impressed. "Gosh, Teak, you really do astound me!" she exclaimed. Then Teak didn't know whether she should confess the truth or say nothing. Seeing the admiration on her face, she decided to say nothing. She looked at her feet guiltily because she knew that Miss Tinkham thought she was being modest. Gezeebius would not have approved.

They took a ride on a camel, Teak tucked in front of Miss Tinkham. It had a strange rocking gait and though a man in a caftan was leading the beast, Teak felt very nervous. Horses had necks you could pat, but there was a whole empty space between her and the camel's head, which seemed to float independently this way and that.

Suddenly, almost without warning, the sky turned a mustardy yellow and on the horizon a wide ugly dark band of something was approaching. The Egyptians all began to shout that a sandstorm was coming! The ride came to a sudden end. The camel folded its legs and lay down so they could dismount. All the camels were then quickly tethered, and they turned their backs to the storm. The frightened animals spat and made horrible noises. The guide ran for a woolen blanket and ordered

Teak and Miss Tinkham to hide under it and turn their backs. The sand began hurtling against their legs. It stung badly, so badly that Teak began to cry out, "Ow! Ow!"

There was no other shelter, so the two of them sat down under the blanket and Miss Tinkham put her arms around Teak. How long it lasted, they would never remember. But it was an experience Teak would never forget. As scary as it all was, what she remembered best was the sweet urgent smell and silky warmth of Ursula Tinkham and her whispering, "I *say*, I'm so glad you're with me!"

They stayed in Cairo two months. Then one morning in the middle of a lesson on division, which was a cinch once you knew how to multiply, in came Birdie King holding one of those yellow cables in her hand. She read it aloud:

SAIL SS KALLIOPE ALEXANDRIA TO
PIRAEUS STOP MEET ME GRANDE
BRETAGNE ATHENS BRING BOTH TURKEYS
SEND DROMEDARY AND DRAGON GENEVA
LOVE ALL TKJR

Teak sat there stunned. It never had occurred to her that these golden days in Cairo would of necessity come to an end—that she would have to leave Miss Ursula Tinkham! Which probably meant that she would never in this life see her again! She didn't even listen to what her mother was laughing about.

"You know, Ursula, the concierge just told me that the Egyptian authorities called to make sure I understood that dromedaries could not be exported from Egypt without permission and due process! I had to tell them not to worry because the dromedary in question was just my tan leather suitcase which always humps in the middle when it's stuffed!"

And Miss Tinkham looked up and laughed too. "Oh, I say," she giggled, "what a scream!"

How Miss Tinkham, her Miss Ursula Tinkham, could sit there and laugh in the face of this awful news was beyond Teak. She fled to the bathroom, where she stood for a long time looking down out of the window at the trolley cars in the square, and the horse carriages, and the many Egyptians with their long caftans. The tears streamed and streamed down her face. This was the hardest of good-byes.

She remembered the wise advice of Sheikh Mustafah about how to deal with such separations, but she could not bring herself to take it—not yet. Not yet! She would never meet another young woman as perfect or as much fun as Miss Ursula Tinkham!

The *SS Kalliope* was a small steamer that carried cargo from Egypt to Greece and the islands in-between. It was not an ocean liner in any sense of the word. Standing on the dock, Birdie King and Teak looked with dismay at the rusty hull and crumbling paint of the very ugly ship. They both went up the small wooden gangplank with a sense of foreboding.

It was an exceedingly rough trip! No sooner had they set sail than the Mediterranean turned choppy, and soon thereafter the waves got bigger and bigger and angrier and angrier. They lunged and swashed with loud crashes against the side of the poor ship, as she shuddered on. There were very few passengers, and most of them were seasick Greeks and Egyptians. Teak and her mother, however, were both good sailors. After all, Birdie King told her, they should be, since they were both descended from several generations of sea captains who sailed out of Boston and Providence, all the way from New England to China in sailing ships half the size of this one.

Teak had plenty to notice during the trip. It was funny, for instance, to watch the soup in the soup plates slop slowly in one direction and then in another. At mealtimes, a wooden frame was raised around each table so that the tableware wouldn't fall off. The poor waiter staggered about like a clown in the circus carrying his tray. He was very talented and didn't drop a thing. Teak also found that if you timed it just right, you could go down the up stairs or up the down stairs, depending on which way the *Kalliope* was lurching. Sometimes the stairs just seemed to drop away from you, leaving you airborne. Shoes made a sticky sound as people made their way down the linoleum of the narrow gangways, and though Teak could not understand any of the languages people were jabbering at each other, she could hear a sense of adventure if not alarm in the voices.

She was not supposed to go out on deck, but a young Greek boy in his teens, sensing Teak's longing to see what it was like, took her out while her mother was drinking hot bouillon in the tiny lounge. The two had to hang on to each other and lean hard into the wind, which ripped through their hair and stung their faces with salty spray. The waves were a deep jade green, moiling and boiling and hissing and spitting alongside and often over the railing. Sometimes the prow of the ship would point almost straight up in the air and then come down into the water with a loud spank, and the spray would fall in long ropes all over the bow and the heavy loading machinery. It was cold, and in a few minutes, both were soaked to the skin and glad to climb back over the heavy door jamb to warmth and safety. But Teak loved all of it. It even felt familiar, as if she had done this many times before. She wasn't afraid of the sea. It was a whole lot better than an earthquake. Teak felt strongly that the earth was supposed to stay *put*.

She shared a stuffy little cabin with her mother, who trusted her to sleep in the upper berth. On the second night, she put Teak to bed and left her alone while she went up to the lounge again. Teak lay on the top bunk, rocking with the ship. Faint strips of light came through some slats in the door, and through it Teak could hear occasional voices grow louder and then softer as they passed the cabin. Everything around creaked and squeaked as the small ship shouldered and juddered its way through the rough sea toward Crete.

Teak couldn't sleep, and she lay there thinking strange thoughts. She wondered how deep the water was below the boat. She wondered who she really was. Where had

she come from? How did her Big You get into her Little
Me? How come that at odd moments like this she didn't
feel at all that she was a young girl, but more that she was
really an old man pretending to be a girl? Why not an old
woman? Why was it that when she was in Beejumstan she
could understand what Lonesome and Gezeebius were
talking about, but that when she was in this world she
had such difficulty applying the things that she knew
were wise and right? Could she have lived before? If so,
what might she have been? She stuck her small foot out of
the bed and looked at it sticking out of her pajama leg
and tried imagining it to be a great big foot. Had she
once been a sailor, maybe like one of those Argonauts in
the *Tanglewood Tales?* Had she ever fought a battle with a
sword or a javelin? Been a nun? Had she ever been a
farmer with a ferocious bull in his field or hunted foxes in
a red coat in England? Or been a Scottish chief? It was
really fun picking out what person you might have been.
Why, you could have been any number of things, maybe
lived in any number of places, hundreds or maybe thousands of years ago! Teak was still wide awake when her
mother came back, and Birdie chided her for not sleeping.
Pretty soon she rolled over and went to sleep, well pleased
with yet another secret to speculate about. One thing she
knew for certain: she was growing older. She would have
to sort out the things in the spy bag.

The next morning the sky had cleared, and the sea was
a bit calmer, although it was still a deep angry blue and
filled with whitecaps. Teak went on deck with her spy bag
and stood for a while smelling the salt freshness of the

air. Off in the distance the triangular shape of the island of Crete shimmered in the sunshine. It looked very brown and dry.

Then Teak walked to the stern of the ship where the blue and white striped flag of Greece snapped in the wind. She opened her spy bag and took out and opened the old cigarette case, releasing all the tattered Pumpernickels; with a small pang she let them flutter away into the white wake of the ship. The time had come. It would be dumb to go on with them when you knew that you were growing older. But the little white stone and the gimmie wallet remained.

Teak walked across to the other side of the deck, where she saw a tender making its way out to the *Kalliope*, which with long groaning noises was slowing down and stopping. The tender was loaded with some very strange-looking passengers. Very strange, indeed. They were all men, silent and swarthy, dressed alike in white and black horizontal stripes and wearing black skullcaps. Every single one of them looked sad. Teak tried waving at them, but not one waved back.

The tender drew up next to the *Kalliope*, and a gangplank was lowered with a loud rumbling. Teak poked her head through the railing of the deck. She could see water spouting through various holes out of the rusty side of the ship. Now the men in the tender were ordered to board the *Kalliope*, and as they began to file up the gangplank Teak saw that each man was chained to the next one by a heavy clanking chain around his ankle. She had never seen such a sight—it was dreadful!

Teak ran to find her mother and she came to watch as well. Someone told them that these were criminals and political prisoners, which meant that they hadn't agreed with the government. What a contrast they made with the blue sea and the free fresh wind!

Teak asked her mother about prisoners, and she answered very thoughtfully. "There are many different kinds of prisoners. Usually they are criminals who have to be locked up for breaking laws, murderers and robbers and the like." Then she added with a sigh, "But we can be imprisoned by ourselves."

"How?" asked Teak.

"Well, you can be imprisoned by your own opinion of yourself or of others." Teak thought of the children in the witches' cave. Her mother gave another sigh, "And you can be chained by hope and by your own desires."

"Why is that so terrible?" asked Teak.

"Because you're kept so busy wanting something you haven't got, you forget to enjoy and be grateful for what you already have. You feel trapped inside and unhappy. I think you must remember what your dear Grandpa King used to call 'an attack of the gimmies'—you know, give me this and give me that!" She smiled ruefully as she made the remark.

Teak had a flash of memory not only of her own Gimmie Attack but of something that had happened in Cairo. She saw her mother looking at her father who was looking at Miss Ursula Tinkham. Maybe Mother had been wishing that she were as young and captivating as Miss Tinkham. Teak now took her mother's hand and gave it a squeeze; her mother turned her face away from Teak but she squeezed back—hard.

The taxi trip from the harbor at Piraeus to Athens was uneventful this time, and for once Teak had fun in Athens shopping with her mother. They even went past the shop where she had suffered the Gimmie Attack, and she felt a bit older and wiser than before.

The first night in the hotel, after Teak had gone to bed, three strange things happened, one after the other. First, she heard men's deep voices. She got out of bed and went to the balcony and saw a wondrous sight. A procession of black-clad priests, all bearded and wearing black hats, were solemnly marching up the street. They carried flares, which lit up their faces. They were singing prayers in a talking way or talking them in a singing way. The solemn low voices rose and fell. Teak felt the awe of the occasion so strongly that she found tears in her eyes.

Back to bed.

A few hours later, a terrible commotion in the square below. The building opposite had caught fire. The flames were so high they lit up the tops of the orange trees and turned the lion with the shoe polish into a red beast. Firemen and bucket brigades added to the confusion, and Teak could see all the other hotel guests were out on their balconies as well. Finally the fire was put out. The air smelt bitter and smoky. Teak decided that you never knew from one moment to another what would happen next. All those poor people turned out of their homes! Everything gone! She shuddered at the realization.

Back to bed.

She couldn't sleep. She lay there listening to the gradual calming down outside. Voices fading away. The room filled with a silvery light, the very sound of silence.

And then the nightingale sang.

Teak slipped out of bed yet again. She stood on the balcony in her pajamas, barefoot, shivering a little, and saw the full moon soaring high above the white temples of the Acropolis. Out of all that turmoil, such a serenity, such a timeless promise of beauty. Teak could not find the words yet, but in her heart she heard Gezeebius speak:

"Never forget this, my child."

And she knew she never would.

21

The "Inhuman" Condition

TIME PASSED, as it has a way of doing. Teak continued to travel about, with and without her parents. She had been sent to different boarding schools for a term or two, in France, Germany, and Italy, and had begun to be fluent in several languages and to make new friends her own age. She could ride, ski, and swim well and was proving excellent at tennis. Despite the ribbing of classmates, she actually enjoyed her studies and treasured her textbooks. She could outspell all the other girls whatever the language for the simple reason that she had been born with a strong visual memory. But Teak's biggest problem only got worse—all those awful good-byes to people she had grown fond of! Actually, she tried not to like other people too much, so it wouldn't hurt so when she had to leave, but whether it was *auf wiedersehen, au revoir,* or *addio,* it still meant good-bye to a Heidi, a Patsy, or a Francesca.

As she continued to travel, Teak observed that each country seemed to have a flavor all its own. There was a

Swiss way of doing things, an Icelandic or Hungarian way of behaving, and it meant that wherever you went you had to fall in with that particular rhythm of life. In some countries you had to keep your hands on the table, in others they had to be on your lap. She discovered that just as in every nation there was a different language, different music, different food, so also there was a different Teak. It was most peculiar. Only in Beejumstan could she be her own flavor all the time. She really wondered what it would be like to be an American Teak (she had hardly lived there)—or would she feel different and peculiar in the States as well? It was weird not to grow up in one place where you felt you belonged. She wondered what it would feel like to be a tree with roots in one particular place. She knew that Uncle Amyas had a large house in New Hampshire, besides the one in Boston, and that when Justin and Jessie said "home," The Thistles was what they were referring to.

She really tried to imagine what the essence of such a home could be. Perhaps it was the familiarity of things and sounds, like a screen door banging in the summer or voices floating from one room to another or a well of warmth and coffee smell coming up the stairs as you went down to breakfast. Perhaps it was the way the curtains move in a breeze at the window, or the familiar way your feet feel on the stoop coming home from school, or the way a laundry line screeks when it moves, the way the walls brace themselves in a big wind, or the way birds chirrup at each other in the hushed sunlight of evening. Smells, surely, of baking bread, of leather schoolbags in the fall, new sneakers, white paste when you made your own valentines. Her cousins, especially Jessie, had described these in moments of homesickness. They told her that there were stores called five-and-tens, and that you could tell just by the colors in them what season it was— red for Valentine's Day; green for St. Patrick's; yellow and purple and pale pink and green for Easter; red, white, and blue for the Fourth of July; orange and black for Halloween; and finally red, green, and white for Christmas. It was nice to think of the passing of time as a dance of color and sound and taste and smell. Teak longed to see a real cowboy and wished she could meet a brave Indian with eagle feathers. She envied her cousins. She really did.

In these various schools Teak attended, she also learned some strange things about history. In each country you were taught a different view of it entirely. One country's hero was another one's villain. At times, you could hardly believe it was the same person they were talking about! It was very confusing; one didn't know who to believe. It was even worse when it came to nationalities! If you went with the negative impressions that people tried to give you, then the English were stodgy, the Welsh were thieves, the Scots dour and stingy; the Italians cowardly, the Germans cruel; the Swiss humorless, the Russians melancholy; the French provincial, the Spaniards proud; the Turks savage, the Chinese a menace; and the Americans tasteless, loud, and rude. On the other hand, other people would tell you about the wonderfully musical Welsh, the thrifty Scots, the romantic Italians, the intellectual French, the industrious and sensible

Swiss, the scientific and inventive Germans, the mystical Russians, the artistic Chinese; and they would praise the English sense of chivalry and tradition, and speak of the courage and passion of the Turks and the Spaniards. And the Americans—ah, they were so highly original, resourceful, and democratic!

And the different religions. What a mess that was! They were all supposed to be serving God, but if that was the case why didn't they work together? Why all the arguments and mistrust and even fighting and killing for heaven's sake? And just look at the Catholics and Protestants, who were supposed to be following the same path. She remembered how the study of religions had been Figg Newton's undoing, but things seemed so much more complicated in Italy or in France than in Beejumstan. Why did they all seem to believe that their way was the only way? If Gezeebius was right, the real only way was inside everybody and so it was the *same* only way! How silly grown-ups could be!

Teak herself had met people of all these nationalities and of many different religions, and it was a real puzzle to find out how these conclusions had been reached. She decided it was wisest to form your own opinion. People were just people when it came down to it.

One spring, just before her eleventh birthday, Teak was enrolled in a school near St. Gallen, in German-speaking Switzerland. She really liked it. Compared to the one in Italy, it was heaven. And she became quite a popular girl after an April Fool's Day prank. She and her roommate,

Trudi, a Swiss girl, talked one of the servants into unlocking the science lab's glass closet in which there was a real human skeleton. Together they sneaked it up to the faculty W. C., dressed it in a skirt and sweater with a scarf tied under its chin, and placed it on the toilet seat with a mushy letter from a boy in its boney fingers. To top it off they stuck a cigarette between its teeth. Then they all watched for the teachers' reactions. "Oh, excuse me!" one would exclaim and shut the door in a hurry. Then slowly, there would come a double-take. The best thing was that most of the teachers thought it was funny and didn't say anything, curious to see their colleagues react. Until the science teacher that is, who was definitely not amused.

Trudi and Teak also managed to delay classes by almost forty minutes one day by switching all the numbered keys of the students' numbered lockers where they kept their books and papers. That caused a huge pandemonium and brought the two girls some friendly congratulations. Several tests were even canceled.

Then on Good Friday, a few girls were taken to the cathedral in the city to hear a choral concert. It was a performance of Johannes Brahms's *Requiem*. Teak was the youngest to go, and she sat next to Frau Professor, the headmaster's wife. Teak had never been to a concert before. The music was so awesome, so profound, so moving and stirring that Teak's eyes filled with unexpected tears, and she was grateful when the old woman put her arm around her shoulder as if she understood. The music to Teak was like an opening into what she thought heaven might be like. That would be a Bubble even beyond

Beejumstan. No one had told her that there was a kind of music so different from that of the little orchestras playing on ocean liners and in hotel palm courts where the grown-ups danced fox-trots and tangos. Brahms came like a thundering revelation.

In the summer Teak's family met in Guildford, in England, for a holiday. Grandma King joined them, and one day Teak told her what she had been observing about the lack of understanding between people of different nationalities and religions. "Why are people like that?" she asked.

They had just finished tea and were sitting at a table looking out on a lovely English garden. Her grandmother began by saying that often we tend to see most clearly in other people the very things we do not like about ourselves. "You can learn a bit about who you are, Teak, by what you see in others. We all mirror each other. Your Grandpa King used to say that we should indeed love our enemies, as Jesus taught, for the good reason that they always help us to learn things about ourselves that we would never learn in any other way!" Here she rested on her cane and smiled ruefully. "Just remember it's not what happens to you in life, dear, it's what you *do* with it that counts—how you react to people and to situations. There you really do have a free choice. So when you are told bad things about other groups of people, you can choose to stick up for them. And when you personally dislike someone, it helps to ask yourself if that person reminds you at all of yourself."

Then she laughed and added, "I'll give you a good example. I can't stand people who give themselves airs and stick up their noses and think they are better than other people. I think they are snobs. But, between you and me, there are many times I catch myself being a snob because I was born a 'proper Bostonian.' You see, I was brought up to believe that Boston was the hub of the universe, and therefore automatically—without having to do a thing— that made me better than other people. Your grandfather used to poke fun at me. You see, he was Canadian by birth. He helped me to see that I was living a kind of myth. All nationalities live in their own myth. Each one thinks it is somehow superior to its neighbors. And what can that cause, Teak?"

Teak knew that answer right off. "Wars."

"That's right! Did it ever occur to you how lucky a child you are to have lived in so many different places?"

Teak, looking very dubious, shook her head vigorously.

"Well," Grandma King continued, "I've thought about it. When you grow up, you won't get caught seeing other people in just one way, because you will know better. You won't have learned this out of a book, mind you, but because you have lived together with so many different people in so many different places, you will be able to see what they have in common. Human beings all need the same basic things—food, water, shelter—but most of all they yearn to be loved and appreciated, and to know that they are not living in vain. Then they know that their life has a very special secret meaning in the eyes of God because everyone—although alike in being human—is unique. That makes you a Unique Teak!" And Grandma threw back her head and laughed at her own joke. Then she scrabbled her ringed fingers on Teak's sweater to tickle her, and finally gave her a hug.

"But what about if you like somebody so much, you wish you were them?" asked Teak awkwardly.

"The nice thing about that is that 'it takes one to know one.' So whatever you admire in another person is something that you can and need to express yourself. That's why there have been so many great teachers in the world. They all came to remind us of who we really are—figures like Buddha and Krishna and Moses and Jesus and Mohammed, just to name a few, and Socrates and Lao Tzu." Here Grandma looked up at a cloud trying hard not to leave anybody out.

"And Gezeebius?" ventured Teak.

"Who did you say?"

"Gezeebius. He's an old man I sort of met who told me about the Big You and the Little Me. I think I know about the Little Me part well enough, but I still wonder about the Big You."

Grandma King paused and looked at Teak. She had her stumped. "Well, dear, I'm glad you have met a wise teacher. I'm sure that if you ask him, you will begin to find out the answer. These are questions that can take lifetimes to answer. But that's enough philosophy. Let's go out and walk in the garden—there is nothing more lovely than an English garden! And to think that all these lovely colors just spring up out of this brown earth—how *do* they do it?"

"Maybe they don't ask any questions—they just do it," giggled Teak.

They stepped out of the hotel and walked on the gravel path between the cabbage roses, the hollyhocks and larkspur, the clematis and mignonette. Grandma King had her cane and walked slowly. "Come to think of it, your Grandpa King was my teacher. He was the dearest and wisest and kindest man I ever met." And she gazed off at the great green and heavy leaning branches of the beech trees and sighed softly. "I miss him, Teak, oh so much! But I have you and you remind me so much of him. You both have the same kind of mind. I hope I live long enough to find out what you will do with yours!" And she smiled. Then Grandma King pointed to a toad under the hedge and Teak stood for a moment looking at it before she got down on all fours under the bushes. It wasn't proper behavior for a young lady but she wasn't that grown-up yet.

In the winter term, back in Switzerland, Teak had some hard classes, especially math and German, which had curtailed any extra time for pranks. Now it was late January and not a picture-postcard day at all. Instead of snowing, it was raining and turning what snow there had been into dirty slush. It was so dark and overcast that the streetlamps were on, and the buses had lights on inside them. The streets were wet and glistening, and the air was damp and cold. The people hurrying by on the sidewalk were all carrying big black umbrellas, and their faces looked red and cross.

Teak and about twenty of her schoolmates were on a school outing. They had come to the old city of St. Gallen on a bus with steamed-up windows, which now smelt of wet wool, sausages, and grubby girls. The noise was fierce, what with the laughter, shouts, and insults. Teak heard nothing, because she was having a fight with her friend Trudi. It was a deep and hurting fight that had been going on since they got on the bus. Trudi sat stonily silent to her left, and Teak was looking out the window through a patch she had rubbed clear with her mitten. She was fighting back tears of rage.

Trudi summed things up by saying, in German of course, "And I'm not going to walk with you because you are a stupid girl. They all call you a baby, a baby. Your head sloshes with milk when you walk!"

"I don't care," Teak retorted. "You have only three peas in your skull instead of brains, and they rattle when you walk! Pfui!"

It was a bad day, all day. The class shuffled through the now empty white and gold Baroque interior of the cathedral, and they slipped around in paper slippers over the inlaid wood parquet floors of the famous ancient library. The guide lectured to them about how the Irish monk St. Gall had founded his monastery here over a thousand years ago, but Teak didn't listen. She normally would have loved the Egyptian mummy and the priceless illuminated manuscripts (one of which was reproduced in her mother's red Bible), but she neither looked nor saw them. She walked around in a black fog. In fact the teacher thought that Teak might be coming down with a cold, so he would come and push her along gently as she lagged behind the others.

By the time the bus returned the girls in a soggy mass, they all seemed tired and subdued, and Teak had decided she loathed the Swiss—all of them—because Trudi was Swiss. Trudi was a bully; a brat; she was mean, unfair, and stuck up. She was dumb, so who would want to bother having a friend like that! Boy, would she be glad to leave *this* school and say good-bye to dumb old Trudi. And all the other dumb kids for that matter.

She was still angry and hurt when she went to bed in her dorm. Gezeebius flashed through her mind as she was falling asleep, but she tried extra hard not to keep thinking about him.

22

Gumblegurk

TEAK FELT HERSELF being lifted roughly by the scruff of her neck and dropped summarily on top of Mount Pook right in front of the cave of Gezeebius. No amusing train ride on the 7:67 this time! She fell flat on her face in the dust and could only see the sandaled feet of the old wise man, the fringe of his white beard, the hem of his robe.

"Get up!" ordered Gezeebius.

Teak climbed to her feet obediently but she couldn't look up.

"Teak, look at me!" commanded Gezeebius. Teak sullenly looked up into the eyes of her teacher. They were stern, grave and yet understanding. "I am about to visit my friend Gumblegurk the lampmaker and I would like you to come with me, but I am going to be quite busy when I get there, so you may have to amuse yourself for a while. Do you wish to come?"

"Yes," muttered Teak. She looked around hopefully to see if Lonesome was anywhere about.

"Very well then, go over and help Noodlenip get the *Cloud* ready and look lively about it!"

The prospect of flying or sailing, whichever it was, on the *Cloud of Unknowing* was an exciting new adventure for Teak. She ran over to Noodlenip who was already putting provisions in a pile to be taken aboard.

Noodlenip smiled at her and asked her to go over and untie the long rope and anchor that were holding the *Cloud* moored to the mountain. "And don't let go of it, whatever you do!" he added.

Teak went and untied the heavy rope. She could feel the *Cloud* tugging away heavily. It felt like flying a very heavy blanket for a kite. "Pull her down slowly," said the Elbedridge, nodding his red cap because his arms were full. Teak pulled and hauled, and slowly the *Cloud* descended until it was only a few inches off the ground. Following instructions, she wound the last bit of rope around a big rock several times. Then she helped Noodlenip load the boxes of provisions in the bow. As she stepped in and out she tried to fathom the consistency of the material the ship was made of. It was soft and light, yet quite firm. You could poke a finger into it and make a hole, but then the hole would fill up again immediately. There was nothing on earth like it that Teak knew of.

Inside the ship were a rope ladder, a large hook for the anchor, a book of crossword puzzles, a bucket, the Beejum flag, and a lantern. There was a wheel to steer with, and a mast and a sail. Curled up in the middle of the ship and almost invisible was a large white cat.

"That's Pussywinkle," said Noodlenip, bending briefly to scratch behind the cat's ears. "She's the engine."

"She *is?*"

"Of course," laughed Noodlenip. "The *Cloud* runs on purr-power. When we get to the right altitude, you can pet her yourself. Then she purrs and we sail along beautifully. We only need the sail when she's out of sorts."

Noodlenip had just finished explaining this when Gezeebius appeared and boarded the ship. He sat at the prow after puffing himself a comfortable bench out of the cloud material. He motioned for Teak to come and sit beside him. Noodlenip weighed anchor, the *Cloud* began to rise, and Pussywinkle began to purr loudly without any prompting at all. The *Cloud* was turned in a westerly direction and began to float smoothly and gently over the countryside of Beejumstan. It was a majestic sight, beautiful beyond belief. Teak's spirits started to rise, and she began to forget about being either cross or ashamed. However, Gezeebius had not forgotten, but he sat there saying nothing, allowing Teak to drink in the experience of the moment.

Teak looked over the edge of the cloud ship and saw the whole country spread out below. There was the Wendward River stretched out like a silver thread, and in the distance the twin spires of St. Ninnius were gleaming. Apesnose University looked to be made of stone lace in this light, and the Beejum houses in the town were gently lurched against each other in friendly communion. Little streams of smoke were spiraling up, here and there, from the chimneypots of small houses dotting the countryside.

There seemed to be a luminous peace down below. It reminded Teak of some of those round paperweights made of glass that you can look into and see a magical colorful design.

"Gezeebius," she asked softly, "are we in a different Bubble?"

"Indeed we are," the old man replied. "Just look again." And as he spoke, the light shifted and the whole country turned to gold—all the houses, everything. Teak held her breath. All she could feel was the air gently pressing coolness into her face, and all she could hear was the steady purr-purring of the cat. This only lasted a few seconds; then Gezeebius broke the silence, and the country shifted back to being its normal self again.

"Teak," Gezeebius began, "you've been thinking a lot about people lately, haven't you?"

"Yes, I s'pose I have been," answered the girl.

"Would you mind if I shared a few thoughts with you as we sail along? It might pass the time, you know."

"No, I wouldn't mind."

"I didn't think you would," smiled Gezeebius. "Well now, let's talk about friends. How do you suppose one goes about making friends?"

"I don't know," said Teak sadly, "I don't seem to have any. Right at the moment that is."

"Friendship," said Gezeebius, "is like love on a seesaw. If one friend gets off, the other one goes down bang and gets hurt. To have a good time you both have to give and receive. By that I mean you have to give of your real self— not just to care, but to care *enough* to give and to forgive.

Usually forgiving is a matter of understanding *why* the other person is acting the way he or she is. This means respecting others as equals every bit as precious and unique as you are. Then both of you are on the seesaw. But when you treat another person as an object—a 'stupid thing'—you not only diminish your friend, but you diminish something in yourself. You lose as well."

"How come?"

"Because you prevent the other person from giving the gift of himself or herself—the something precious and real in the other. It is as if you slam the door in the other's heart and then get mad that no love comes out! So you blame the other for what you did yourself and naturally vice versa or is it versi visa?"

Teak tried to smile politely at the feeble joke, but she was beginning to squirm. There was a moment of silence. Pussywinkle had stopped purring, and the *Cloud of Unknowing* had floated to a stop. So Gezeebius suggested that Teak stroke the cat gently, which she was only too glad to do. "But, Gezeebius," burst out Teak, "how can you love somebody you don't even like?"

Gezeebius smiled at the question's directness. "That, my dear, is a question everybody would like the answer to! And there is an answer to it. This is why I thought you would enjoy meeting my friend Gumblegurk, because he can explain it far better than I can." With that Noodlenip announced that they were just about there and to hold on tight as they were beginning their descent.

The *Cloud of Unknowing* came to a rest about fifteen feet above a clearing near a small coppice of green larches.

There it rocked and swayed gently as Noodlenip dropped anchor with a plunk and then lowered the rope ladder. Teak climbed down first, followed by Gezeebius. Pussywinkle decided to stay on board the instant she saw Noodlenip opening a can of sardines.

Teak could see a long wooden barn with chimneys at either end. It had many small windows in a row, and in each of these stood a lantern. As they approached the house, it was evident that these lamps were being lit by someone inside because one by one their soft welcoming candlelights began to shine in the approaching dusk.

Gumblegurk came out himself. He was a roly-poly Bunnywidget and wore the traditional garb of his people: a homespun tunic over baggy trousaloons, cinctured with a woven striped belt that was tied jauntily over his plump tummy. On his grizzled head he wore a knitted cap that looked more like one of Uncle Amyas's ski socks than anything else. Gumblegurk had very bushy eyebrows and a most kindly pink face. Even before Gezeebius introduced them, he put his hands together and bowed deeply to his two visitors.

Teak had never been bowed to before in her whole life, but she decided the wisest thing to do was bow back, which she did. Gezeebius laughed his approval. "Well done, Teak, well done!"

Gumblegurk hurried back to the door of his workshop and shouted in some orders, which gave Teak a chance to ask Gezeebius why Gumblegurk had bowed that way.

"He was bowing to the Great One, Teak," explained Gezeebius.

"But I'm not the Great One, you are," she protested.

"Everyone is, my daughter," murmured Gezeebius. "Come along in now," he said and guided Teak toward the door. Teak turned and looked about her before entering. It was getting quite dark now, and the trees were hushing their leaves and waiting for the stars to begin shining, one by one.

Together they entered Gumblegurk's Lamp Shop. Teak stood amazed at the blaze of lights and the glowing warmth of the place. Gumblegurk looked lit up himself! He began clapping his hands, and young Bunnywidget apprentices hastened to light up one table of lamps after another in response. There seemed to be hundreds and hundreds of lamps, no two alike. There were old ships' lanterns made of brass and glass, and trainmen's signal lights; fussy lacy little boudoir lamps, sensible desk lamps, chandeliers of crystal drops, oil lamps like Aladdin's. Lamps made of coffee grinders, china vases, ginger jars, chamberpots, boa constrictors, cricket cages, and paper balloons! They came in every size, shape, color, and style imaginable. Some were beautiful and gave out a lovely glow; others were dirty and grimy and very dark indeed, as if they needed repair. Some were positively hideous and had fake waterfalls or fountains moving in them or tawdry-looking bellydancers; others were sweet and fancy and fit for a baby's nursery—a baby duckling made of yellow china with a blue bib. Never in all her life had Teak dreamt there could be that many lamps in one place.

Gumblegurk rubbed his hands and spoke briskly to Teak. "Which is it, lass, *one light or many?*"

Teak was stumped, but she knew it was a very big question.

"Ha! I've always wondered about that myself. Well, Gezeebius and I have some business to attend to. How would you like to look around? I tell you what! Why don't you pick out the lamp that you like the very best of all and the one you like the least. And when you find them, get one of my assistants to put them on this empty table here in this corner. Take all the time you want. There are plenty here to choose from, I do believe." Then he waved a friendly hand to Gezeebius, and the two went off and left her.

Teak set off slowly and systematically on her quest. The young apprentices kept quietly about their tasks of cleaning and polishing so Teak was able to concentrate entirely on what she had set out to do. After a full hour of wandering up and down she still had not been able to decide which of them she liked the best or least. All she knew for sure was that there were some that were more to her taste than others. Some really looked pretty awful, and she couldn't imagine Gumblegurk having anything at all to do with them.

Teak was torn between picking the most garish and the most ugly lamp. Finally, she selected a clumsy, dark, rusty black iron lantern. It reminded her dimly of Hanka. Hardly any light came through the crusted, dusty windows. It even had cobwebs on the handle, and it looked dreadfully neglected and in need of cleaning and repair. It looked even uglier when Teak herself placed it on the table Gumblegurk had indicated. She was too ashamed to call an apprentice for help.

The choice of a favorite lamp was even harder. There were so many that suited her fancy. Finally she selected one. It had a solid octagonal base of bright brass and two handles made of smiling brass dragon dogs. It gave out a lovely gracious light through a beautiful octagonal lampshade on which were most tastefully painted colorful flowers and green leaves. Teak knew right away that Grandma King would have loved it. She especially liked Chinese things, and Teak knew the lamp was Chinese because the handles looked just like King Ching. That lamp would look nice with the old leather-bound Chinese sea chest that her grandmother had told her about— one that would be hers someday. Her great-great-great-grandfather had brought it back all the way from China, she had told Teak, and it had the date 1799 hammered onto it in brass studs. Teak, of course, had never seen it, but she was positive this lamp would go well with it in her living room, if she ever grew up to have such a thing as a home. So shyly she asked an apprentice to carry it over to the table.

When Gumblegurk and Gezeebius returned, they knew full well that it had been a difficult choice for Teak. Such choices always are.

"Now then, love," Gumblegurk asked, "tell me why, precisely, you settled on these two lamps?"

So Teak explained the best she could, and then she added that there had been many, many others she could have and would have chosen in either category.

"They're sort of like people, aren't they," chuckled Gumblegurk. "Some you love, some you like, some you can tolerate, others you can't stand, and some you might loathe quite heartily. Am I right?"

Teak smiled sheepishly because that was just the way she felt at times—there were so many different kinds of people! "Yup," she agreed, hearing herself being corrected to say "yes."

"Well now, you don't have to be ashamed to admit it. Everybody feels that way, now and then, and that's perfectly natural. But there is something you can remember that can help you love people you don't even like."

"There is? I think that's impossible where I come from," Teak said quite emphatically.

"Well, it's impossible with lamps too if you only look at them from the outside," retorted Gumblegurk.

"It sure is!" agreed Teak.

"But that's not the only way to look at a lamp, is it?"

"Why?"

"Well, look at this one. It gives light, but it also has a shadow. Can you have a shadow without a light?"

"No."

"Are they always the same shape?"

"No, not always."

"Could you tell what the lamp looked like if you only saw its shadow?"

"Not really." Teak was thinking how her own shadow could be tall and skinny or short and squat.

"That's very important," said Gumblegurk solemnly.

"It is?"

"You'll see."

And while Teak was pondering the matter, Gumble-gurk leaned over and blew the cobwebs from the dirty old lantern. Then he lifted it up. "I bet you don't know who invented the first of these—it was someone in your world called King Alfred the Great. He made one with windows of horn and called it a 'lanthorn.' The funny thing is, he did it at just the same time that Figg Newton was working on the same idea." And Gumblegurk gave Teak a knowing wink.

Then he unlatched the squeaky little door in the old black lantern and opened it. "Look in there, lass, and tell me what you see."

Teak leaned over and looked in. Inside she saw a bright, clear golden flame.

"Can you see it?" And when Teak nodded, he added, "Look very, very carefully."

Teak looked very, very carefully.

"Can you remember what it looks like when you close your eyes?" Teak nodded again. "Well, close your eyes and really remember it."

While Teak's eyes were closed tight, Gumblegurk took the lampshade off the brass Chinese lamp, and when Teak opened her eyes there was another bright golden flame. Both were identical.

"Oh, my," thought Teak aloud, "that's peculiar." And she realized that even had the lamps been electric light bulbs, the idea would still be the same. Light was light.

Next the apprentices waved to the girl and they began opening or unshading more lamps, inviting Teak to peer into as many as she chose. Every single one shared the same light. It was as if each one had a little sun within it.

"You see, Teak," explained Gumblegurk, "there are two ways of looking: outside and inside. Usually all we are captivated by is the outside, and so we see all the differences—nationalities, color, beliefs, names, and personalities and on and on—and sometimes we are scared by the differences. As if it just wouldn't *do* to put that fireman's lamp together with that delicate French antique! Mercy no! But try finding your way in a hurry on a dark road with the antique!" Teak giggled.

"But if you know for a fact that you have such a light inside yourself, then you must know for a fact that the same light shines in everyone else. Because that light is a gift from the Great One in you and in all life. *It is the Big You* in all the Little Me's. I can make lots and lots of different lamps, but I could never make a flame!"

Teak burst in here. "That must be why it's called the Big You! It's because no Little Me could make it." The eyes of Gumblegurk and Gezeebius met above her head.

"That's it. I can't make a flame, I can only help it burn. That is why I bowed to you, Teak, and to my dear wise friend Gezeebius. I see the same light shining through both of you and everyone I meet, and though I may *like* this lamp's form better than that one, I am no longer deceived. I love the One Light shining through them all. And *that's* what I learned from working with lamps!" Gumblegurk ended with a flourish.

Gezeebius gave his friend a mischievous look. "You know, Gumblegurk, you have become quite enlightened!"

Teak was looking at the two lamps she had chosen. She wished that she might keep them both. She believed that with the right kind of stuff, she might clean up the dirty old black lantern. It probably just needed its windows washed. Gezeebius as usual knew what she was thinking. "You'll see them again, don't you worry. They belong to you in more ways than one."

Then Gumblegurk announced that his wife had some supper on the table and that she was looking forward to meeting Teak because all her own gossums were grown. So they all went on their way, leaving the apprentices to close up shop. Teak, who was the last out the door, took care to bow to the apprentice who was holding it. All the apprentices bowed back and waved as well. It seemed like a very nice custom.

As if to round out a perfect day, they went over to Gumblegurk's house, and there in the kitchen, besides Mrs. Gumblegurk, was dear Lonesome wearing a long white apron and a chef's hat! While Noodlenip was setting the table, the rabbit was busy concocting some *carrottes farcies en beurre* (which was what they called buttered carrots on hotel menus). Pussywinkle lay purring by the fire next to an almost empty saucer of cream.

23

The Incurable Teak

THE NEXT DAY, two nice things happened: Teak and Trudi were right again and back to their friendly selves after Trudi offered to share half her chocolate bar and Teak accepted gratefully; and when the mail came, wonder of wonders, there was a letter for Teak from her mother telling that during winter break there would be a family gathering in Zurich. The twins and their parents would be coming south from Germany, and there were plans for some fun afoot. Teak, who had not seen the twins for quite a while, experienced that familiar flip-flop of excitement and dismay at the prospect of this reunion.

Duly the school holiday arrived, and Teak was put on the train all by herself from St. Gallen to Zurich. This was another first. Besides the faithful Fiumerol, now laden with travel stickers, she carried a flowerpot with one orange nasturtium in it, which she had grown from a wrinkled seed the size of a large pea—a present for her mother. She was also carrying a paper bag with two cheese sandwiches and four purple plums. There were three elderly Swiss gentlemen in the compartment and they insisted that she sit by the window. Their conversation in *Schwitzerdütsch*, the local dialect, was punctuated by friendly guffaws and many *yaw-yaws* or *ney-neys*. When she became hungry, Teak was a bit embarrassed about manners, so she offered the men one of her sandwiches, suggesting each could take a large bite. The men smiled and were quite touched but they declined. Speaking High German, Teak then answered their questions, and it turned out that one of them knew the head of her school. After that, she felt comfortable about eating her lunch.

She was met by her parents at the station and taken to a fine hotel right on the lake. When they entered the lobby, there stood Jessie and Justin, only different. They were no longer cute and adorable; they had grown taller and looked awkward and skinny. Their hair was still as curly and carroty red, and both children were covered with freckles—to Teak they looked like baby giraffes. Teak, by contrast, had filled out on her way up. Her forelock still fell over her forehead like a pony but she was almost pretty with her fresh peach complexion and deep brown eyes. Jessie was a little older than Teak; she was poised just on the very brink of adolescence and looked downright gawky. Both twins had braces on their teeth.

Now that Teak was getting older, the Beejums were not always in her mind, and Alfred Hampson was hibernating in the Dragon, her green trunk, in storage. She was even beginning to think of Lonesome as something she only imagined.

Jessie was the first to spot Teak, and her face lit up with pleasure. Justin grinned his old grin and came forward, and they shook hands self-consciously. Fortunately the grown-ups took over; Aunt Bessie dominated the conversation with her warm and hearty voice. It didn't take long for everyone to relax, and soon the ice was broken and the three young Kings were off playing a game of cards and comparing notes. The twins described their home in New Hampshire in glowing terms. They both had bikes, rooms of their own, friends and birthday parties, fun at the country club, and on and on.

The very next day, two large cars were hired and the family was off to Lake Constance, or the *Bodensee,* as it is called in German. Uncle Amyas had a prosperous Swiss friend, a client, to visit who lived in Rorschach, and he had recommended a large hotel by the lake as a nice place for lunch. In the summer, this hotel was famous as a spa or health resort, but in the winter it only kept the restaurant and the ballroom open for special events.

The drive over was pleasant. It had snowed again and the countryside sparkled under a blue sky. They arrived in time for drinks before lunch and sat in the lounge by the windows overlooking the lake, watching the ducks paddle near the shore. Teak surprised everybody by telling them that her math teacher at school had said the Bodensee was so deep and wide that you could pack the entire population of the world into it like sardines. Uncle Amyas remarked that this was an example of Swiss education and that Teak might forget a lot she had learned but never a fact like this one! But he said this with a twinkle.

Uncle Amyas and his brother Thaddeus smoked cigars, Birdie and Bessie King sipped glasses of sherry, and the children had glasses of sparkly apple juice called *Süssmost*. A few other people sat in the lounge reading the daily newspapers, which were attached to long sticks like flags to keep them straight.

Lunch was delicious, especially the main course, which was *Gitzlirippli*. The children had fun with the name of the dish until they found out that it was baby goat ribs. By then it was too late to do anything about it. After dessert, while the grown-ups had fruit and cheese, the children asked to be excused and went off exploring.

They found an upright piano in the empty ballroom, and Jessie and Justin played a duet of "Chopsticks" about fifty times, until even they got bored. After that they went down the corridor going in and out of the powder room and the gents. Nobody else was in sight. At the end of the corridor to the left was a wide flight of red-carpeted stairs that led down to the empty spa.

The children tiptoed down slowly, holding on to the banister, and, with the help of the safety light, Justin, the boldest of the three, discovered the switches that soon flooded the entire basement of the hotel with light. The spa lay spread out as silent and hushed as a cemetery. A series of wonders stretched before them—shallow white porcelain pools, deeper pools surrounded by tiles, exercise equipment, a leather horse, rings to swing on, bars to climb up, punching bags, and way down at the end some mysterious wooden boxes shaped like pyramids. "Wow!" breathed Justin.

The three of them played and swung and whooped it up. It was like being in the biggest school playground ever. Nobody heard them or interfered. Jessie took off her socks and shoes and waded in one of the pools even though the water smelt funny. Justin hung upside down on the rings and showed off, and Teak, not to be outdone by any boy, flung herself astride the leather horse and practiced falling off and landing on her feet. After all, every Thursday afternoon at her school they marched down to the village gym to do much the same thing. The only really hard part there was that they had to run a certain distance barefoot in the snow!

Gradually the three worked their way down to the pyramidal boxes. There was an opening at the top of each and a door that pulled open. This revealed a chair inside. Obviously, you could sit in the box with your head sticking out, but what for? They took turns sitting in one. Teak got in last and the twins closed the door.

"Hey," exclaimed Justin, "there's a switch here. Let me see what happens. Just a sec—" Justin flipped the switch and a buzzing noise began accompanied by a rapid increase in heat inside the box.

Teak got really scared. "Let me out! Let me out of here! Quick!" The twins tried to open the door but it would not open. Aghast, they stood watching Teak turn redder and redder. Then they fled to get help.

Teak thus was left imprisoned in the torture box, which actually was a kind of sauna for people covered with wet toweling to sit in and sweat. Try as she could, she could not free herself and so there she sat, sweat streaming down her reddening face, looking over the vast arena of silent porcelain appliances!

It was probably only a matter of minutes, but it seemed like an eternity before the hotel attendants followed by the children's parents came flying down the stairs. Aunt Bessie was screaming, Birdie King was white, and the fathers were furious. A hotel attendant quickly turned off the switch, and with a powerful wrench got the door open. Teak toppled out so close to unconsciousness that she was summarily dropped into one of the pools— clothes and all—to cool her off.

Teak then was wrapped in towels while the hotel did its best to dry her clothing. A doctor was called. Uncle Amyas was forced to cancel his appointment. The only positive thing in Teak's opinion was that the twins took the brunt of the scolding as she was in no state to bear it. The outing ended in disaster.

In the end, since it would have taken hours to dry her clothing, Teak was wrapped in a heavy flannel dressing gown, miles too big, and then in several woolen blankets and carried to the car by an extremely distressed hotel manager.

Teak kept her eyes closed all the way back to Zurich. Under the circumstances, it seemed to be the most prudent thing to do.

After the spring term, Teak joined her parents in Belgium, where they stayed in yet another Grand Hotel, this time in Brussels. She sat with her parents in their bedroom while they discussed what to do with her next. Her father had to go to Morocco; her mother had a deadline for a book of short stories she had almost finished. Should Teak go to Grandma King in America? No, she was not strong enough to take care of a child. A summer camp in Switzerland? A family in France willing to take her? Should they try to hire a tutor or governess?

Teak protested every notion except the idea of visiting her grandmother. But it was out of the question. She was not old enough to cross the Atlantic on a liner all by herself. She began to feel more and more wretched and miserable. It was as if she was nobody's pet, just a lump of something to be disposed of. She was now thoroughly convinced that neither of her parents wanted her because she was such a bother. She wished heartily that she had never been born.

Nothing was decided and it was time for lunch. As they walked down the long grey-carpeted hall to the lift, her parents continued the discussion, leaving her to trail behind. She walked slowly, scuffing her shoes harder and harder until finally her mother turned around and scolded her.

"Stop it, Teak," she said irritably. "That's bad for the carpet and even worse for your shoes." Glumly Teak joined them in the lift.

When they got down, her father crossed the lobby and asked the concierge for his mail, and then, with a decisive look on his face, he steered his wife toward the dining room. Teak followed.

After they were seated at one of the best tables by the window, the waiter handed everyone a menu. While Teak was trying to decide between *escaloppe de veau* or *truite maison*, her parents opened their mail.

"Why, here's a letter from Megan MacGregor!" exclaimed her mother. "It's been forwarded from the office in London."

Teak's father ordered lunch for everybody without consulting anybody for a preference. He ordered the chicken, the *coq au vin*. Then he turned to his wife and asked, "Who is Megan MacGregor?"

"Oh, you remember! Megan is that nice woman I've told you about over and over. She's a writer. I met her in London at that publisher's luncheon. You remember—she's the one who adopted the little girl who had such a dreadful childhood, whose father disappeared and whose mother died when she was only ten, leaving her all alone and quite homeless. A refugee. I think they were Russian and the girl's name was Lara but they changed it to Rowan. Anyway, Megan is married to a Scotsman who went to school with Bessie's brother Seamus. They have a summer place in the Hebrides on the Isle of Skye. She's inviting us all to visit them there. And Rowan is now only a year younger than Teak. Thad, what do you think?"

As Teak sat poking listlessly at her chicken, she knew what her mother had in mind. They would ship her off to some godforsaken island in Scotland. It made her feel like throwing up. She refused to clean her plate. Then her father got angry and ordered her up to her room. And to think that years ago she had wanted to go to Skye!

The next few days, Teak sulked and protested and protested and sulked. Her mother looked at her carefully and decided to take her shopping. She had an idea to cheer up her daughter. They went to a department store and Birdie bought her a very flat-looking brassiere. When later her father was told she had acquired her first bra, he winked and said she must have grown her own brussels sprouts! Now her secret pleasure at being a bit grown up was spoiled by a flood of embarrassment. So she ran off and shut herself up in her room the next few days and played cards, rotating the various games of solitaire she knew. She kept scores of statistics and had a system of "A" and "B" victories. "A" victories were the ones in which she didn't cheat at all, and "B" victories were the ones resulting from taking an extra turn to see if the cards were entirely against her. Generally they were.

Her mother tried to get her to go out, and her father even gave her extra pocket money, but Teak felt that she was being bribed and refused it. The more they tried to humor her, the more unpleasant and difficult she became, making it even more likely that they would want to dispose of her elsewhere. "So what? Who cares? This is ridiculous!" were phrases she kept repeating to herself. It was not a happy time. In fact, it was awful.

And sure enough, another letter came from Megan MacGregor. It was exactly what Teak expected. Megan deplored the fact that her parents were too involved for a visit but was absolutely delighted that at least they could have a visit from Teak. It would be lovely to have another girl about the place. Nice for her husband, Alastair, and good company for Rowan. Teak's mother showed her the letter but Teak refused to read it. She really was acting like a spoiled brat and she knew it, which made it even worse. Mercy Muchmore would have called it a royal persnippety attack!

So she went back to her room and tried sulking over her stupid stamp collection. Her father had brought her some rare stamps from San Marino and Liechtenstein, but now even these gave her no pleasure. She was bored, bored, bored, and sick to death of traveling! She just wished to goodness that she had a home like Jessie and Justin, a bicycle, a room of her own to put her own stuff on the walls. She tried hard not to think of the Beejums and told herself that they were all imagination anyway. She decided that Beejumstan was just baby stuff to be forgotten and outgrown like Alfred Hampson and the Pumpernickels.

She even missed the gawky cousins. She thought they were a lot nicer than she remembered. Why couldn't she have had a twin or at least a brother? She was convinced already that Rowan MacGregor would be some soppy girl and no fun at all, and as for the Isle of Skye, they might just as well send her to Siberia. Still, the twins had been to Skye and liked it. But that was different. They were a family! By now Teak was close to tears of self-pity.

As she sat on the edge of the bed deploring her fate, her mother came in and informed Teak that she was taking her to a museum to do some research for her book. Teak didn't want to go, but a look in her mother's eye told her that this time there would be no way out of it.

A car with a chauffeur had been hired. Teak chose to sit up front beside the driver rather than sit in the back with her mother. She was interested in seeing the dials on the dashboard and in watching the driving. Cars had improved in the last five years. Now instead of putting your arm out the window to signal, there were little yellow arrows you could flick up on either side of the car. And you pressed the middle of the steering wheel to sound the horn.

Birdie King asked the chauffeur to circle through the heart of Brussels so they could see the famous square and the lovely old houses with their corbeled roofs, but Teak studiously ignored them and kept her head down, concentrating on the driver's foot switching from the clutch to the brake. She was not interested in sightseeing, which she now heartily detested. Once they were out of the city, she tried rolling the window up and down, to which her mother strenuously objected. She thus was able to spend far more time sneaking the window open a fraction of an inch while Birdie wasn't looking. She hated it, and she hated her mother nagging, and she hated herself most of all and the horrible mood she was in.

At last they reached the palatial grounds of the museum. As soon as they entered the huge building, Birdie King made a beeline for the exhibit on lepers in the Belgian Congo. Here were dozens of enlarged photographs of unfortunate victims stricken by the dreadful disease of leprosy. The pictures were sickening—people with no hands or feet, whose faces grimaced like lions; people bandaged; people crippled; people being attended by priests and nuns standing stiffly in front of low huts set up as medical stations.

While her mother bent over the cases taking notes on a small pad, Teak wandered around trying not to be sick. The real and dreadful suffering pictured in the victims' eyes only made her feel more guilty at her own health and good fortune. It reminded her of the starving Indian children that Hanka had reproached her with in Rome.

These pictures were as bad as pictures of World War I that Teak had seen a few days before in the basement of a ruined church in Ypres. Pictures of dead soldiers and houses in rubble. At least they had been dead, but the lepers ... Birdie King had thought that her daughter should know these things and that she might be as interested as she herself was in the torn regimental flags and medals, but Teak had been appalled. Fighting and killing was only something in make-believe. This was real! She had thought of Gumblegurk's lights and thought what a waste for people to kill each other when they all had the same light inside. It had been horrible and shocking, and now this!

Teak's mother was not totally insensitive to what her child was going through. She felt torn three ways as usual, wanting to be a decent mother, a good wife, and to finish her book as well. She knew that nothing in life had prepared her to cope with an almost twelve-year-old girl like this one. She fully intended to have her face some of the more drastic and unpleasant aspects of reality. It would only do Teak good in the long run. But when she saw the pallor of Teak's face and her dry swallowing, she decided it was best to cut short the lesson on leprosy and suggested they go outside.

They walked out into the fresh air and crossed over to a park, much to Teak's relief. There Birdie bought some sugared waffles at a stand and a cool lemonade. On the way back to the car, she decided to refrain from saying anything about the window, at the same time that Teak decided that it was dumb to fool with it.

That night her parents made the decision—whether Teak liked it or not—to ship her off to the MacGregors on Skye. She could travel up to Scotland from London by herself. They would leave immediately, taking the ferry over to England from Ostende. And that was that.

24

Sobkin the Supersensitive

TEAK THREW HERSELF into bed that night in Brussels in a state of despair. She tried to sleep, but she couldn't. All she wanted to do was fight someone or something. She punched her pillow with her fists, angered by helplessness, and helpless with anger. Lord, how she wanted to fight! To break out of the trap of these circumstances.

"Fight, is it? Fighting is what you want, eh? Heh, heh, heh!" cackled a voice softly, and when Teak looked up in the dimmed light there, between the sink and the window, stood Rudintruda.

"Go away!" said Teak petulantly, waving her hand at her. "Go away! I'm not afraid of you anymore."

"Oh, is that so?" Rudintruda retorted in a new and much more menacing voice. "You think you are done with us, do you? Well, we'll have to see about that and try to accommodate your young ladyship, you namby-pamby, weaky-teaky, lily-livered excuse for a girl who won't grow up! Well, you sound ready for the BIG stuff, eh?" Despite herself, Teak had to look at her suspiciously. She did sound different. "Yes, that's it. We must be ready for the BIG stuff!"

Rudintruda, as far as Teak had encountered her in Beejumstan, had always been a mediocre run-of-the-mill sort of witch of the fairy-tale variety. After all, she and Lonesome had dealt with her in the liberating of King Ching and the paralyzed children. She really was no longer afraid of her, or so Teak thought. Now, with a sinister soft screech, the witch began to whirl in front of her. She whirled and whirled, and as she whirled, a black cloud that enveloped her grew enormous. It began to fill the entire room. Red streaks of fire and mustardy yellow and green flashes shot out of it, and the inky blackness began to suck Teak and pull her down into the vacuum of a whirlpool. She tried holding on to the bedpost, but her fingers began to give way. She tried screaming but found no voice, and soon she was spinning down into it, followed by Rudintruda in a new form. She had turned into a beautiful woman with white skin, jet black hair, and scarlet lips. She had acquired a terrible powerful beauty. She looked just like a woman Teak had seen on a poster outside of a cinema theater—she was the very same one. Then Teak felt that she was spinning like a top in the palms of Rudintruda's hands.

Somehow Teak knew that she was dreaming, but she couldn't wake up.

"Aaah, my pretty," the witch hissed. "I have waited a long time for this. But there are friends of mine you must meet. They live a long way off. Toooo baaaad!" That was

the last Teak heard of her, because with a great whip of
her arm, she sent Teak flying through the darkness. Then
she came into a place of more light and saw that she was
arching over Beejumstan toward the limitless expanse of
the ocean.

Fortunately, she landed hard on a beach and not in the
water. Teak felt bruised and battered and out of breath.
The sun was glaring, the beach was empty and hot. There
was no one in sight and nothing but a huge pile of rocks
at the foot of some high, hard cliffs. There seemed to be
no escape, and Teak wondered if the tide would catch and
trap her. For the moment anyway, the sea looked calm,
bright and blue.

Teak sat down for a while and rubbed hot sand on her
painful bruises, not knowing what to expect next. It
wasn't too long before she heard a terrible unearthly
yowling—a high-pitched keening. "WOOOOOOOOE!"
it cried. "WOOOOOOE!" The woe seemed to be issuing out of a deep cleft in the cliffs further up the beach.

A loud clanking and clanging could now be heard
accompanying the howling. Horrified, Teak gaped at the
cleft, wondering what sort of adversary was about to
emerge. It sounded like a thousand trolley cars clanging
and clacking.

Slowly a monster emerged. How to describe it! It was
double the size of the largest dinosaur that had ever
existed. But it was not really a dinosaur. Teak knew at
once that she was confronting another dragon. It must be
a dragon. Yes, but weren't dragons given to breathing fire
and rattling their gleaming scales? Well, not this one! As

it approached her, trailing its long, long tail behind it, Teak saw that its entire body was made up of kitchen utensils—pots and pans, paddles and spatulas and egg-beaters, tin cans, brushes and mops of every size and description! All of these were waving, clanking, and clattering together in the most doleful domestic dirge. The poor dragon seemed to be blind. Instead of eyes, it had two faucets which streamed and dribbled tears down its long face and through the salad strainer that seemed to form its nose.

"Oh, WOE, WOE, WOE is me! Oh WOE, WOE, WOOE! Poor me! POOR MEEEE!" it wailed, and more water gushed in torrents out of the faucets. The dragon's body by now was half a block long! When Teak saw its misery, she ceased to be afraid and stood her ground. This dragon was old and pitiful.

"Stop it, stop it!" Teak shouted. "STOP!!" she bellowed. "Who are you anyway?"

"What was *that?*" screamed the dragon almost joyfully. "Is there somebody there?" Suspecting an audience, she quickly changed her tune to "Booooooo hooooooooh! BOOOOOO HOOOOOOH!" It was just the most piteous sound.

"It's me, Teak, and I asked you who or what you are!" she shouted, cupping her hands to make her voice carry better.

The dragon stopped and cocked one of its three ears, which were made of drain plungers. "Somebody wants to know my *name?* Is that possible? Do you hear that? Oh me, oh my, I can't believe it! Did you hear that?" At this the dragon painfully twisted herself around and seemed to be addressing her tail way down and back at the other end. The tail consisted of three kitchen mops tied together. The mops waved back and sang together in high screechy voices:

"*Is it true? Is it true? Somebody wants to talk to you?*"

"Hey," called Teak sharply, "I'm at the front, not way back there!"

The dragon slowly swayed her ponderous head back again and lowered it. She was waving all three of her ears. "Where are you?" came a tremulous voice.

"I'm here, silly old thing. I'm over here."

"I'm listening," sighed the dragon.

"Who are you?" repeated Teak.

"There you are, it's just what I said," answered the dragon weeping afresh. "Nobody knows, nobody cares! I'm nothing, and I live nowhere, and nobody loves me! AHWOOOO!" Now her howls positively ululated, echoing down the line of cliffs. "Nobody, nobody loves me! They call me Sobkin the Supersensitive! And you know, I had all the membership cards printed, and everything and everything, and I sent out invitations to a party, but nobody came, not a single soul joined the Club! AHWOOOOO!" she wept again, so hard that her whole body shook, making a tremendous racket.

"What club?" shouted Teak over the din, trying to make sense out of so much nonsense.

"The Poor-Little-Me-Club, of course! Oh, *do* tell me you've come to join! Do you hear that, Tail?" The dragon had again turned back to shout blindly down the beach.

"Someone's come to join at last! Oh, she must have, she must have!"

To which the mops screeched, *"Oh, pooh! Oh, pooh! Who would want to join with you?"*

"No, I haven't come to join the club," explained Teak patiently, and then seeing the terrible disappointment on Sobkin's face, she hastily added, "But maybe I can *deliver* you from a spell or something?" She really felt sorry for her.

At the sound of Teak's words, the dragon sat back on her haunches, totally nonplussed, and blew a long line of soap bubbles from its mouth.

"What's that?" she cried. "Why, that's impossible! Nobody, but nobody, delivers dragons. You're supposed to deliver princesses or the fair land *from* the dragons. Why, that's totally against the *rules!*...Isn't it?"

"Maybe it is," Teak conceded. "But aren't you the one that's in distress? It seems to me that you're far worse off than any stupid old princess. Just look at you!"

Sobkin was amazed by the audacity of the girl confronting her. She shook her old head this way and that in disbelief. Even the faucets let up for an instant. Then, drawing herself up with the dilapidated dignity of a dowager, she remembered her manners.

"And pray tell, who is my deliverer?"

"My name is Thaddea King," announced Teak with a bow, feeling a rush of new importance and strength. "But since I'm going to deliver you, you may call me Teak."

Instantly the dragon screeched back joyfully, "Tail, did you *hear?* Do you know what she said? She's royalty! And she said that I'm worse off than any stupid old princess!

And that she will deliver poor little me. Gosh, isn't that marvelous?"

At that the mops began screeching, *"Poor little you! Boo, hoo, hoo!"*

But Sobkin the Supersensitive paid no attention, for she leaped up and began to gallop and skip about, rattling and clattering all over the place. She stumbled into the ocean, crying "OOOPS!" and out again, looping herself about in coils, until finally she collapsed flat in front of Teak, turning her faucets upside down in a flirtatious manner that was quite engaging. Then the dragon confided, in what she thought was a whisper—but dragon whispers are louder than train whistles—"You know, Your Highness, you will never believe me when I tell you this, but the actual bona fide truth of the matter is that what I *actually* am is a stupid old prince. And you are the first person in umpty-ump years to discover this. Oh boy, oh boy, oh boy!"

Teak, thinking she was confused, reminded her, "Teak, not boy. I'm a girl."

"Oh, Teak," wept Sobkin, but now with joy and relief, "that's even better! Thank you for finding me."

"Why are you so sad?" asked Teak. "Why are you so supersensitive?"

"Must I tell you? Is that part of the deal?" The faucets were streaming again.

"I think you'd better," said Teak.

"But I can only whisper it to you. I wouldn't want Tail to hear."

"But Tail is part of *you!*" laughed Teak.

"That's impossible," retorted Sobkin sharply. "Even though I can't see, I know perfectly well that there is somebody else on this beach besides myself who talks back to me. But naturally I cannot confide in her."

Teak heaved a big sigh. "You certainly must be under a dreadful spell, Sobkin, but I have a hunch about this. Let me go down and investigate. You just *stay* right there and don't move."

"All right," agreed Sobkin, "but don't *say* anything!"

"I won't," Teak promised. Slowly she walked the length of the long dragon, reading the labels on the cans. They ran mostly to varieties of soups and vegetables, with a high percentage of string beans.

When at last she came to the dragon's tail, she looked at the three large mops and said, "This looks like the work of Idy Fix to me." Remembering that witches could change their shape, Teak suspected Idy might have made herself stringy, so she examined the strands very closely, and sure enough, hiding among the ugly straggles was Idy Fix herself. She was none too pleased to be discovered.

"Aha!" said Teak. "Just as I thought. But you sure have lost some weight!"

Idy was momentarily pleased at what she took to be a compliment. Without thinking, she said, "Thank you for noticing my charms. Smelly Stinka put me on a diet of worms." Then she remembered herself and quickly began hissing a spell.

> *Silly, sulky, stupid, dumb*
> *I'll enchant you till you're numb.*

That didn't work. She tried another.

Spilly, spelly, spoiled little brat
Back to baby when I've spat.

That set Teak off. She was no baby! All her frustration and anger of the last few days erupted, and she started throwing sand at Idy, and when the witch tried spitting only sand came out. Teak threw more and more sand at her, piles and piles of it, all the while yelling, "Come out of that tail, you miserable string bean of a witch!"

This was putting Idy in quite a fix herself, and finally she flew out with a scream, rubbing her eyes. Trailing a string of unrepeatable curses, she flew away on one of the mops, which was much too big for her to control properly, causing her to weave about in fits and starts. Finally she lost her balance and fell screeching far off into the sea.

"Aha!" repeated Teak, well pleased with her diagnosis. Then she walked back to the front end of the dragon.

"Well?" asked Sobkin, "what did you find?"

"Come with me," invited Teak, and she grasped the salad strainer firmly even though she had to stand on tiptoe to reach it. "Ow, ow, ouch!" squealed Sobkin, but she came along with alacrity. She was enormous. How awful, Teak thought to herself, to be as old and lonely as Sobkin.

It took quite a while and a lot of maneuvering for her to lead the front of Sobkin all the way to the back. It was a little like introducing a locomotive to its caboose. When they reached the two remaining mops at last, Teak pulled Sobkin's head down to where they were. "Sobkin," she said, "I would like to introduce you to your own tail."

"I've always been afraid of this," wailed Sobkin. "But, at least, it gave me someone—or something, I mean—to talk to. Are you *quite* sure?"

"Positive," affirmed Teak. "I saw Idy Fix myself. Your tail connects all the way up your back and neck to your head. Try wagging it."

"Oh no, I couldn't!" protested Sobkin, quite alarmed. "I might hurt its feelings. So often, it's hurt mine. Oh, Tail, Tail, how could you!" And the dragon wept afresh.

"That was part of the *spell*, Sobkin! That was Idy Fix all along, I tell you, and I've chased her away. Look here, I can't deliver you just like that—you have to do your part, you know. Fifty-fifty."

"Fifty-fifty?" Sobkin raised her head and thought about it. "I s'pose that's fair."

"All right then, you can begin by wagging your tail properly and not carrying on this way, fighting both ends of yourself. You have to make up your mind which end of you is boss."

"Oh, dear," sighed the dragon, issuing another cloud of soap bubbles that sailed off to sea.

"Go on, wag it!" commanded Teak. Sobkin wagged with great hesitation, but sure enough the mops swished this way and that. "Harder!" Sobkin wagged harder. The evidence was indisputable. She could actually feel the sand on the beach—it must indeed be her own tail.

"But—"

"From now on, Sobkin, you run your tail and your tail does not run you. Is that clear?"

"But, Tail was—"

"And stop calling it 'Tail'! Say 'my tail' this and 'my tail' that. It's not a person, it's just part of you, silly. Sobkin the Silly is what you are!" Teak laughed, and from the rakish angle of the faucets, she knew the dragon was pleased as well.

"All right," Sobkin agreed demurely.

"Good, then that's settled. Now what else can I do for you, while I'm here?"

The dragon gave another long, shuddering, bubbly sigh, and the faucets began streaming afresh. "Oh, you couldn't," she sobbed. "You wouldn't," she wept. "You shouldn't!"

"Shouldn't what?" asked Teak.

"Really deliver me. It's too big a favor!"

"How big?"

"You would have to fight a terrible fight. Only then could I be transformed and completely delivered. It's asking too much. I know it is, Teak."

"Fight whom? Fight what? I can fight anything. Look, feel my muscles!"

"SHHHHH!" warned Sobkin, and lowering her head she spoke in one of her earth-shattering whispers. "You will have to fight the Supreme Power of all this place, of all the world from here to there. You will have to fight Dark Shee." Sobkin shook and shuddered, making a horrible noise.

"Dark Shee?"

"Yes, Dark Shee. Of course, I have never seen her, but she has a terrible reputation. Not only is she selfish and moody, she's always blaming everyone and everything. I hear she's spoiled rotten and is constantly screaming, 'If *only*—if ONLY!' Never satisfied with anything, whining, complaining. And when this happens, the whole side of Beejumstan east of the mountains gets dark and foggy and cold and miserable."

Sobkin began to droop at the thought, slipping back into self-pity.

"Are you quite *sure* you can fight?" Sobkin sounded rather dubious. "You sound like such a *nice* girl."

"I don't know yet," answered Teak quite frankly, "but I'm sure ready to find out!"

"Are you all alone?" asked Sobkin anxiously.

Suddenly Teak realized that she was all alone. There was no Lonesome or Figg Newton or Gezeebius to help her. She remembered now that she had scorned and rejected them. They would be far away on the other side of the Klorox Mountains.

"Yes," she answered with a shiver of fear. "I'm all alone. Except for you," she added kindly. Now she reached out and patted her new friend.

"Well, now that you've got my back straightened out, maybe Tail—I mean my tail—and I can be of some assistance to you."

Now Sobkin reared herself up and swished her tail proudly this way and that. "Do you think you can climb up on my back?"

Teak backed off and considered the possibility. "I think so." So she tried at the front, but it was impossible. Then she ran down to where Sobkin tapered off to her tail, and from there she managed to scramble up the

ghastly assortment of rusty pots, greasy potholders, frying pans, rotten sponges, dustpans, moulting brushes,
until finally she reached the dragon's shoulders. And all
the while she could feel her great heart whirring and
rumbling inside her. It sounded just like the double-
decker buses in London.

Thus it was, without further ado, that Teak and the
great Sobkin the Supersensitive set off down the beach on
the desperate adventure to find the terrible Dark Shee.

25

Off to Skye

TEAK AND HER PARENTS left for England the very next day, crossing over by ferry from the continent and taking the train to London. They spent the next morning shopping at Harrods, buying their daughter the clothes she would need for Scotland. She had outgrown everything. Then Birdie King had to rush to see her agent, so Teak's father took her to the station between appointments. Everything happened in a rush, and they ended up eating a late sandwich for tea at King's Cross Station. Teak was to go all the way to Mallaig by herself and transfer there to the ferry for Armadale on Skye, where the MacGregors would meet her.

They sat at a little iron table surrounded by the hustle and bustle of travelers, porters, and the sound of whistles and bangs. Thaddeus King tried to make conversation with his daughter. "The Isle of Skye," he began, "is on the west coast of Scotland in the Inner Hebrides. It's supposed to have everything: mountains, sea, castles, sheep,

the lot, and most of the natives speak Gaelic. I've never
been there myself or met this friend of your mother's, but
I'm sure they will be good to you." He paused to look at
the dubious and forlorn expression of his child and
almost felt a twinge of sympathy. Then he hurriedly
looked at his watch, pushed back his chair, and said
abruptly that it was time to go.

They went together onto the empty grey platform, one
of many, all covered by a high framework of iron and
dirty glass. The locomotive was already steaming and
hissing; it was many times the size of the one for the train
to Beejumstan.

"Got your ticket? Passport? Money?"

Teak nodded. Her father then took out a five-pound
note and handed it to her. "Here's a little extra, but don't
spend it all at once. Remember, as good old Ben Franklin
said, 'A fool and his money are soon parted.'"

Thaddeus King climbed up onto the train with Teak
and walked down the side corridor looking for a compartment. He found an empty one, slid the door open
sideways, put Teak's battered old Fiumerol up on the
rack, and hung up her new mackintosh. "Alfred Hampson not with you these days?" he joked. Teak shook her
head. Alfred was packed away in the Dragon. "That's
good," said her father approvingly. "Well, chin up, Teak—
it's not the end of the world. See you in a couple of
months. Be sure to write your mother." With that, he
patted Teak on the shoulder, looked at his watch,
exclaimed at the late hour, and rushed away. Teak tried to
wave out the window, but all she saw was the back of her

father's black Chesterfield coat as he pushed his way through the stream of oncoming passengers.

She sat down by the window and watched them coming. She could tell the ones going on holiday from the ones that weren't, but none of them looked as appealing as the Beejums. Then she spent a little time inspecting the contents of her spy bag and discovered a chocolate bar her mother had tucked in. She still had the Greek wallet and found some shillings and pence and another five-pound note for emergencies. She hid the new bill in the secret compartment. Her address was still there: *Thaddea King, The World.* As she put the wallet back in the spy bag, she glimpsed the wee white stone, the *calculus alba.* She still had it.

The train took off, streaking through the oncoming sunset and the English countryside. Nobody came into her compartment but the conductor, who rocked on his feet as he clicked her ticket and told her that there was a dining car and that he would help her with her things when they got to Mallaig early the next morning. Teak listened to the train chanting *"Hunkachoo, hunkachoo, hunka-choo"* over and over, then curled up in a corner emotionally exhausted. She promptly fell asleep and wasn't even aware of the conductor covering her with a tartan wool blanket in the night.

When Teak woke up, she was surprised to find that she was not alone anymore. Sitting across the way was an amazing trio. The first was a huge stag with antlers, dressed in golfing plus-fours and an argyle checked sweater. He was busy reading *The Beejum Gazette.* Next to him was a cheerful otter in a kilt, and looking out the window, with his paws on the sill, was a fine brindle cairn terrier. He began wagging his tail when he saw that Teak was awake.

The stag was the first to speak. "Hello, Teak," he said in a very deep voice. "My name is Anghus MacMaybe, and my otter friend is Rory Dhu, and this is Snuffy MacDuff." Snuffy barked hello and wagged a merry tail.

Teak smiled.

"Our friend Gezeebius sent us to welcome you to Skye, and we will be popping in and out of your future there, so to speak. We come to you with an important message, because we know that you are about to engage in the fight of your life."

Now Teak remembered with a start that she still had to rescue Sobkin the Supersensitive and deliver her somehow from the awful spell of the witches. "What's the message?" Teak asked anxiously.

"You can't go to pieces. You've got Scottish blood!"

"I have?"

"Och, aye!" squeaked Rory Dhu. "Ye come from the line of the Kings of Albion, away way back when it was a quarter to August by the Clackclocks. It may but be a wee drap in your world, but a drap is all a Beejum needs to put fire in the soul." He shook his fine whiskers, stood up and hitched up his kilt, revealing the sporran he sported in front. "I am the Beastie of Clan Urquhart. Our motto is *Mean, speak, and do well!* And like you we travel *per mares, per terras!*" He pronounced Urquhart as Erc-ccchutt, as if he had a fishbone stuck in his throat.

Teak wished Whitsworth was around to translate, but Snuffy obliged. "That's by sea and by land. You certainly qualify. That's the hidden reason you're going to Skye, the Isle of the Mists."

"Do the Erchcahards come from Skye?" asked Teak, trying her best with such a strange name as Urquhart.

"Nay, lassie, they come from Cromarty, the Black Isle, on the other side. But ye'll be fightin' the good fight wearin' our colors. We're here to cheer ye on!"

"And to play a round of golf," added Anghus.

The train went into a short tunnel. When it shot out from dark to light, Teak found herself dressed in Highland battle gear and seated high on the back of the forward lumbering Sobkin. She was wearing the full regalia of a warrior, hunting tartan kilt and a leather jerkin, and she carried a blood-red targe, a round leather shield with knobs on it. She was once again a young Highland Chief of the Clan Urquhart. Taking a deep breath of the salty air and leaning bravely forward, Thaddea King solemnly vowed not to go to pieces.

26

The Fight!

ALL THE ELEMENTS now began to conspire against the girl
and the dragon. It grew darker. A wind rose, whipping up
the waves, and the tide began to narrow the beach, as
Teak had foreseen. She was high up on the dragon's back,
but fortunately, there was a dishdrainer for her to sit in,
which served for a saddle. Clouds were gathering; thunder
was rumbling. Teak's heart began to beat. She knew that
danger lay ahead. This was the BIG stuff that Rudintruda
had promised lay before her. Now she would find out
how brave she really was. She set her teeth and leaned into
the rising wind.

Sobkin the Supersensitive lumbered on, gathering
speed as she went, confident that Teak could serve as her
eyes. They passed clattering beyond the rocks, and even
though the waves were now crashing against her side,
Sobkin only stopped to catch her breath once. "Thank
you, Teak," she said simply. "Thanks ever so much for
delivering me. It is most kind of you. And, by the way, if

you look under the coffee grinder, between the frying pans on my right shoulder blade, you might find something useful."

Teak searched and, to her surprise, she found a jeweled sword hilt. She pulled on it hard, and out came a beautiful, gleaming sword. Marvel of marvels, it shed a bright light wherever it pointed, and all along the glistening blade she could read letters engraved, much resembling the Lindisfarne Gospels in the back of her mother's Bible:

*I BELONG TO SIR LOVALOT
PROTECTOR OF LOVALORE*

It was a magic sword! Every hero was supposed to have one and also his own steed. Teak patted Sobkin the Supersensitive gratefully. Somehow, she now felt well equipped.

They came to a huge portal in the rocks. It had a doorbell, the kind you pull on a rope to ring. Teak had to climb up on Sobkin's head, and Sobkin raised it slowly and carefully so that she could reach the rope and tug on it. As the bell clanged, the portal slid slowly aside, revealing a huge wide stone staircase that seemed to stretch upward for over a hundred years. Teak wondered if Sobkin could manage the climb, but the dragon reassured her. She had waited so long that time had ceased for her. She only asked Teak to guide her using the drain plunger that served as her middle ear.

Once Sobkin's mop tails had cleared the portal, it shut again with an ominous thud behind them. The climb took ages. Ahead of them was a strange glow. Finally, when Sobkin's front reached the top steps, Teak stood up and beheld a great cave all lined with glass. It reminded her of Figg Newton's "Looking Glass of Circumstance." Reflected light bouncing to and fro was what created the eerie, seemingly sourceless glow. In the middle of the cave stood an enormous outcropping of reddish rock. Teak sensed it was a place where blood had been spilled. She gripped the sword harder and felt for the wide leather belt holding her kilt. Then she reached for the red targe now strapped to her back. Holding this in her left hand and the sword in her right, she was ready. She lowered her head, gritted her teeth, and took several deep breaths.

Sobkin proceeded to encircle the central rock completely with her body so that the salad strainer of her nose met the two mop tails, which tickled a bit. Fortunately the seawater had washed most of the dust out of them, so she didn't sneeze. Teak stepped off her shoulder onto the red rock. There in the middle lay another sword. It too was red and had a glittery edge. Teak leaned over to read the inscription:

I BELONG TO BLAYMALOT
ENTHRALLER OF LOVALORE

Teak didn't know what "enthraller" meant. She reached to turn the sword over.

"Don't touch!" came a threatening voice, and from a hole in the red rock sprang Dark Shee herself, who picked up the sword and held it pointed straight at Teak.

Teak swiftly raised the sword of Sir Lovalot and pointed it straight at Dark Shee. The brave girl could see that her antagonist was just about her own height and weight. This was a relief, but there was something ominous about her. Dark Shee wore black tights covered by a dark jerkin, and there was a dreadful black hood over her face with two slits for eyes. And she had a black targe dotted with brass knobs in the shape of a serpent with a split red tongue and a gruesome eye. She looked dour and foreboding.

The fight was on! Teak summoned her courage and advanced thrusting her sword at Dark Shee, only to have it met by the thrust of her opponent's. Both fighters slashed and thwacked and dodged and feinted. And a very strange sequence began—the angrier Teak got, the more furious Dark Shee became. Everything Teak did was precisely matched by Dark Shee. The harder the one slashed, the harder the other. When Teak stopped to catch her breath, so did her opponent. When Teak wiped the sweat from her brow, so did Dark Shee.

Teak stopped. So did her copycat. Then Teak thought of Gezeebius and Grandma King; both of them had said something—but what? Dark Shee was panting as hard as Teak was. It had to do with enemies. It had to do with the Big You and the Little Me and the light... The glass-mirrored walls shed an eerie shifting glow which always placed the light at Teak's back so that her opponent was always in her shadow, making her most difficult to see clearly. Teak looked again very carefully and saw Dark Shee had no shadow! Was it possible she had no light?...

The mimicry of her opponent infuriated Teak and reminded her of the times Justin had teased her by echoing everything she said. Teak yelled, "Fraidy Cat!"

"Fraidy Cat!" retorted Dark Shee.

"Stupid idiot!"

"Stupid idiot!"

"No one loves you!"

"No one loves you!"

"You're all alone!"

"You're all alone!"

"STOP IT!" screamed Teak.

"STOP IT!" screamed Dark Shee.

They both stopped. Then Teak decided to see how far the mimicry would go. "You are stronger than I am!" she shouted.

And Dark Shee echoed right back, "You're stronger than I am!"

Hah! thought Teak. Something fishy is going on.

"Would you rather wrestle?" asked both girls at the same time.

"Sure," they echoed each other. So Teak and Dark Shee dropped their swords and hurtled at each other, rolling all over the red rock, wrestling and punching and grunting and growling. But neither was stronger than the other. At last Teak held Dark Shee in such a way that she could pull off her mask. And when she succeeded, the first thing she saw was a nose just like her own with a freckle on it. "You've got Phineas!" exclaimed Teak.

"Well, you get to have him all summer," said Dark Shee. "That's only fair." They looked at each other. Teak scrunched up her nose, and so did Shee. They were identical. They were twins!

"What are we fighting for?" asked Teak.

"I don't know, it was *your idea*," retorted Dark Shee.

At this Sobkin the Supersensitive raised her head just a little higher. Of course she had been listening anxiously all along. Then Teak remembered. "I came to deliver Sobkin the Supersensitive."

Teak's twin took a look at Sobkin. "Phew!" she said. "What a mess she is! Idy Fix and Rudintruda put a spell on her. It's all their fault. I only hold her in thralldom."

"Stop blaming the witches; you could have released her ages ago!"

"No I couldn't! I had to wait for you, stupid," and Shee was lifting her fists and putting a scowl on her face all over again. "The witches have me in thrall as well. They laughed at me and said that you would never have the guts to come and confront me."

"Don't call me stupid!" Teak's fists were also raised again. "I'm here. Now what! I think you're dumb. No, I think we're both stupid. We could be friends instead and go do interesting stuff together like sisters do. Going on with a fight that doesn't make sense is the dumbest thing of all. It's probably what Idy Fix is counting on. Pah!"

Dark Shee didn't look like any old Supreme Power anymore. She stood silent, waiting, hopeful and sheepish at the same time. Teak reached out her hand, and, in the same motion and with the same reluctant grace, her twin held out hers. "Okay," said both and they grinned identical grins. "*Pax*. At least for now."

At that moment, two wondrous things occurred. Sobkin the Supersensitive just went poof! and, wonder of wonders, out stepped the young Sir Lovalot. Teak was just about to pick up her sword when she saw him. He looked nice. Teak realized that she really didn't know any boys besides Justin. This young man was not much older, but he was handsome as princes go. There was something very special about him, and suddenly she felt shy. She couldn't help it.

"Gosh, Teak, how can I ever thank you! You were smashing!" he said. "I hate to leave now."

"Oh, don't go!" cried Teak.

Lovalot took her hand and raised it to his lips just like a real knight in a storybook. "I promise you we will find each other again when the right time has come."

Teak stood tall and tried to be brave in a whole new way, but there were tears in her eyes now. They looked deeply into each other's eyes, trying to remember this moment forever. Teak knew somehow that she would recognize him no matter how many years it would take to find him in her world. Sir Lovalot then took his sword back from Teak and held it high and flashing and swore to be faithful to the fair Lady of Lovalore. "Thanks again, Teak, for delivering me. I don't think Sobkin could have lasted much longer. All those cans were getting rusty!" Then he grinned and tilted his head just as Sobkin once had done, blew a kiss in Teak's direction, winked at her, and vanished!

It all happened so rapidly—how could he leave so quickly? How long would long be before she would look into those eyes and remember him or he remember her? Could this be a promise of real love to come? Could it? Could it?

At that very moment lights behind the mirrored walls came on, and Teak saw all her Beejum friends rejoicing. What she had not realized was that all those dull mirrors were one-way glass and that behind them encircling the arena were all her Beejum friends—Lonesome, dressed from head to foot in knight's armor and carrying a spear (just in case), Mercy Muchmore with a big basket of Blaskells, Figg Newton and Lisabelle Ann, Dr. Azibov Sobelow and Dr. Syzygy, Gumblegurk and Noodlenip, and even the great Gezeebius himself with Mimosa, the donkey. Cosmo the Lion, General Principles and Popova, Mrs. Daisymouse, and as many Beejums as Teak had met were all hidden there behind those inner cliffs of glass. They had seen Teak but she hadn't been able to see them.

The Beejums had been all in suspense, praying that Teak would remember all the things she had learned in Beejumstan, and it had been all that they could do to keep from revealing themselves to the brave but lonely girl. Now Lonesome was removing his helmet and trying to subdue his whirling ears and twitching whiskers. Azibov Sobelow was looking for a hanky in his H pocket, but it wasn't there becaause his wife had filed it in L for "linen hanky." Figg Newton had been fighting the temptation to put a pair of long-distance spectacles on his nose so that he could see better. Mercy Muchmore and Gezeebius were the only ones serene and confident that in the end Teak would prevail.

Unable to wait any longer, with a great bound and a clatter of armor, Lonesome leapt down, using his spear as a vaulting pole, and greeted Teak as the new Lady Lovalore of Beejumstan.

Then they all streamed down the stairs and out onto the beach for a picnic under the moon and the stars, and there was a great celebration. Gumblegurk had spread lanterns all about and built a grand bonfire on the sand, and Noodlenip was passing out paper plates and cups. Mercy Muchmore had provided hot dogs, Ob Long crackers, marshmallows, and alphabet soup—and her very best Blaskells. There was muddleberry and persnippety tea, and a huge salad for the vegetarians. Cosmo the Lion had brought his ice cream stand filled to the brim with all the flavors, and Mimosa was giving the Beejum gossums free rides. The Elbedridges and Bunnywidgets began to dance under the stars to the jigs and reels of the grasshopper band, and later Teak saw Figg Newton galloping his wife about in a polka. Tonight they all wore the national Beejum costume, so it was impossible to tell them apart. Ibn ben Nibl and Ali Krakotoa were teaching Whitsworth how to count in Arabic: *"Wahed, ethnien, thalatha . . ."*

Then Tucket and Whortle appeared with apologies for being late. They had to work through the last, the 7:77 train. They appeared arm in arm, the best of friends, and as soon as they reached the bonfire, they called out for everybody's attention. They had big news! Their respective son and daughter had just announced that they intended to marry on Criss-Cross Hill on

Mumbledumpkin Downs, despite their fathers' years of disapproval—true love was stronger than family opinion. So Tucket and Whortle's ruse had worked, and now they could drop all pretenses and resume their friendship in public. This was a cause for more toasts and general merriment all around, as you can well imagine.

Lonesome reappeared. He had discarded his armor and now was wearing a kilt in the Urquhart dress tartan. He had on a black velvet jacket with a fluffy white jabot at his neck, argyle socks with red flashes below the knees, and a *skean dhu*, the wee dagger tucked in. Never had he looked more splendid. He came up to Teak and winked at her. "Well, me lass, if this isn't a grand *whutterick-fuffing*, I don't know what is!"

"What's a *whutterick-fuffing*?" Teak always had to know about words.

"Well, that's a Scottish word, and it might come in handy. It means a 'gathering of weasels.' The Scots like to have a word like that just *in case* they see more than two weasels at once. Since that doesn't happen very often, and it really is such a special word, we Beejums have borrowed it to describe an old-fashioned bash like this one."

Teak looked at Lonesome, her beloved guide. Then she drew him to her and lifted his droopy ear. "I want to tell you a secret, Lonesome. I have discovered your true name."

"You have?" Lonesome looked startled.

"Yes, I have. And it's not Lonesome." She looked at the rabbit ever so fondly. "It's not Lonesome, it's Lovesome." And for once the Beejum rabbit was speechless.

Just then Anghus, Rory Dhu, and Snuffy MacDuff appeared. Lonesome was about to introduce them, when the three congratulated Teak on the fine and fair fight. All three wore dress kilts in their respective tartans.

"Och away, Lonesome, we've already met!" offered Anghus. "She knows we're here to help if she needs us at all." Rory Dhu, the otter, was untangling a set of bagpipes almost bigger than he was. Then he started to play "The Road to the Isles."

Looking at the three, Teak took heart about her future. And when they all assured her that the Isle of Skye looked *exactly* like Beejumstan right down to the Klorox Mountains, she felt even better. It would be interesting to have the outside and the inside of her match for a change.

Teak smiled at her new friends and then excused herself to go look for Dark Shee. After a thorough search, it seemed that like Sir Lovalot she had disappeared.

Finally, in distress, Teak went to Gezeebius, who was standing quietly looking out at the dancing silvery path the moon was making on the water.

"Gezeebius," Teak asked anxiously, "what's happened to Dark Shee?"

Then Gezeebius put his hands on either side of Teak's head and turned her wondering face up to his own, and he spoke:

"Teak, my dear, this may be hard for you to accept. You will never find Dark Shee again the way you did this day, nor will you ever be without her. She is truly part of you and will need your friendship all of your life. You see, every time that you fight her you redeem her. It is good, very good, that you know her name and that you share a freckle with her!" And Gezeebius gave Teak's nose a friendly tweak.

"I am part of you, too, and so is Lonesome, and so are all the others. You do not have to deny or reject us— please never do that again! We simply live in you. We want to live in your Bubble. We like to live in you every bit as much as you like to live in Beejumstan. All we ask, as you grow up, is that you do not forget us or the Beejum that you always have within you called Teak. I promise we will never leave you if you never leave us. And I promise that if you share us with others, we will share you with them. This I solemnly swear."

All the Beejums were now standing in a great circle around Gezeebius and Teak. They had their arms over each other's shoulders. Together they all leaned backwards a little and shouted a huge prolonged YUM (it sounded like Y-AAA-HM), and then they leaned into the circle and shouted "yum-yum-yum-yum-yum-yum-yum-yum!" as fast as they could. They did this three times.

"YUM! yum-yum-yum-yum-yum-yum-yum-yum!"

"YUM! yum-yum-yum-yum-yum-yum-yum-yum!"

"HUGS TO THE LEFT AND HUGS TO THE RIGHT!" At the end, they all gave each other hugs. The last thing Teak saw was the great stag, Anghus Mac-Maybe, leaning over carefully to hug the little otter, Rory Dhu. And Whitsworth was explaining that *yum-yum* was probably the Tibetan origin of *yummy* which was, in his humble opinion, what life was s'posed to be.

Teak opened her eyes. The three Beejums were gone, and the conductor was pulling down her suitcase. The train had arrived in Mallaig. Seagulls were screaming in Gullic all over the place, and in the early light of dawn Teak could see the fishing boats rocking at the wharf. The ferry was steaming in and the three MacGregors were standing by the deckrail and waving to her. They had crossed over just to meet her and welcome her. She could see Rowan waving shyly over the deckrail. The Isle of Skye hung suspended in a beautiful bluish mist off in the distance, and it *did* look just like Beejumstan!

A piper was playing and a band of scouts took up the refrain of "The Road to the Isles":

> *Oh, the far Cuillins are putting love on me*
> *As step I with my cromag to the isles!*

Teak ran up the gangplank to the rest of her life.

Cauda*

Gezeebius was right. It was true. All those Beejums lived safely inside the Bubble that was Teak. They would be there even when she would grow up and be an old lady of tseventy-tseven. She could share them with her own gossums and theirs in turn—if she chose.

And she chose.

*The Tail, the End (translation from the Latin by Whitsworth).

Acknowledgments

Thanks most especially and tenderly to my dear, departed husband Walter Alfred Andersen (Sir Lovalot) for making the writing of this book possible.

To my own Beejums: Timothy, Abby, Elisabeth, and Jennifer; and their Beejums: Christopher, Emily, Benjamin, and Lissie; James and Emery; Jessie and Cameron; Morgan and Rowan; and my great-grandchildren: Ann and Thomas.

To my brother, Fridrik Orcutt; Douglass Howell; and my godchildren: Paget Scott-McCarthy and Teak Ackmann, whose name I borrowed.

To Nicky Hearon-Brown, without whose tireless help on all levels I could not have succeeded; to Christopher Bamford, Will Marsh (special thanks!), and Richard Smoley, friends and editors; to Paul Cohen; to Alan King and my daughter Beth, whose daily help and kindness enable me where and when I am unable physically to cope. To Jessie King for typing a manuscript and for computer lessons; and to Jennifer Brown, "resident lovey."

Untold gratitude to Leslie B. Durst, who manifested the *calculus alba* in more ways than one!

To Andrew Harvey, who recognized the healing potential of Beejumstan and spontaneously dedicated himself to helping this book find its readers.

And to Walter Beebe, Terry Goodson, Isabeth Hardy, Olivia Hoblitzelle, Judy Powell, Edith Spenser, John and Ann Stokes, and Edith Wallace for their kind and thoughtful help.

To Jason Brown, Vee Guthrie, Theodosia Greene, Heather Hogan, Ian Kellas, Louise Macy, and Pat Winston for artistic help.

To David Collins, David Dressler, Linda Dressler, Penny Harris, Paul Kemp, and John Van Sorosin for their contributions and encouragement in the early days.

Thanks also to Bets Albright, Brewster Beach, Lydia Belanger, Carroll Bishop, Deborah M. Conner, Mike Dickman, Joel Elkes, George and Nancy Foote, Sally Hopkins, Jim Mauri, Claire Mielke, Thomas Moore, Glynis Oliver, Helen Pellathy, Kenneth Phillips, Mary Lou Rude, Daryl Sharp, Maury Stiefel, Rod and Sue Welles, Gregory and Lillian Whitehead, and Edward C. Whitmont for turning up in Beejumstan and lighting the way.

And especially to anyone this old lady might have omitted through a *lapsus mentis.* Eighty years is a long stretch.

ABOUT THE AUTHOR

Alice O. Howell was born in 1922 in Cambridge, Massachusetts, and, in many ways, her life curiously resembled that of Teak. In *The Dove in the Stone*, she writes:

"When I was little, almost five years old, my life changed drastically. I sailed from New York with my parents on a huge  liner to Europe. From then on for many years I learned a lot about waiting and separation. I sat on a great number of trunks and suitcases and hatboxes in cavernous, cold and grey railway stations, waiting for my parents to buy tickets in London or Istanbul, in Lausanne or Rome or other cities. It could be late at night or very early in the morning, and I would sit there waiting, trying to read the peeling steamship and hotel labels and hugging my stuffed terrier with the fraying ears.

"These stations were iron and glass caves, under the domes of which blue-smocked porters would push and pull bales and luggage on wagons, shouting strange imprecations to each other in incomprehensible languages. The air was always dim and filled with the dust and incense of coal. It felt like living in a dirty glass. People looked more like wraiths, their voices losing resonance in a mysterious way. A sepulchral fear would come over me. Off again, from the unknown to the unknown. Sometimes, my father would disappear, sometimes my mother, and sometimes both, leaving me to board the Orient Express with the nurse or governess of the period. We lived and often slept on trains.

"By the time I was twelve, my father's work had led us to over thirty-six countries, and I had also learned a great deal about exile. Painful partings from parents, from childhood friends, and from places cherished. But hidden in the pain was also a gift, one 'invented' by my mother, for on realizing my growing distress and anxiety, she hit upon the idea of an imaginary land where every night we might all meet together, no matter how distant we were from one another. Needless to say, as a child alone in hotels without radio or television in those days, the charm and over-whelming power of this suggestion was immediately apparent.

"It would be thirty years before I would hear of the Buddhist meditation on the Land of Pure Bliss and even longer before I would grasp what Carl Gustav Jung meant when he spoke of archetypes as primordial images in the collective unconscious. But I do know it comes instinctively and naturally to a child to be in touch with this numinosity. In no time at all, the imaginary land was patently 'real' to me, and populated with archetypal charac-ters, magical animals, and all the phantasmagoria that my uncon-scious, and that of my parents, allowed to emerge, nurtured surely by Bible readings, fairy tales, and myths as they came my way.

"There had been two surprising elements in the emergence of this inner landscape. The first was that, even though I shared the names and characters with my mother and even occasionally with my father, when I climbed into bed and closed my eyes and boarded the little train which would carry me there, when I got to Beejumstan itself, I never did meet my parents there, nor did I even miss them. I had found my archetypal mentors, a psycho-pomp rabbit, Lonesome, a Wise Old Man called Gezeebius, and a Fairy Godmother called Mercy Muchmore."

As the years passed, more and more Beejums revealed them-selves, and Howell began sharing Beejumstan with her own four children and her ten grandchildren, her godchildren, and pupils, and thus it could be said that this story has taken a lifetime to emerge. She lives today with the happy memories of her beloved husband (Sir Lovalot), Walter Andersen, who found for her, in the Berkshires of New England, the rambling white clapboard house they called Rosecroft. Her dreams did come true. She has a kitchen with geraniums, her own bed, her own pillow, a cairn called Snuffy MacDuff, and a cat called Dooby. And here she

continues to write and to drink muddleberry tea (served with Ob Longs and Blaskells) when family and friends visit; and she looks forward eventually to celebrating her own Aberduffy Day. She can be reached usually on the 7:66 train to Poppalopolis. Just look for a plump white-haired old lady and a well-dressed rabbit with one flop ear.

Alice O. Howell's other books include *The Dove in the Stone: Finding the Sacred in the Commonplace* and *The Web in the Sea: Jung, Sophia, and the Geometry of the Soul.* She also edited, with a commentary, *How Like an Angel Came I Down: Conversations with Children on the Gospels,* by A. Bronson Alcott.